DADDY'S ORDERS

AN AGE GAP ROMANCE

K.C. CROWNE

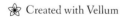

DESCRIPTION

I knew he wanted to punish me for my father's dealings…
I just never expected to enjoy it.

A dark past hardened me, scarred me,
Making it difficult to give a d*mn about relationships.

Then comes along Emily.
Fifteen years younger.
The innocent virgin and daughter of the man I despise.

She's twenty-three and drop dead *fu*king* gorgeous.
My trousers tighten the moment we meet.

I'm sure her and her conniving father plan to burn me
again. ***Wrong move.***
Now, I'll make it extra... ***hard***... for her.
Starting with a ticket to the Mile High Club.
Ending with her begging for mercy.

I've ordered her to stay with me on my private
island for one month.
And after all is said and done she'll have more
than just memories.
I have a special gift in store for Emily.

PROLOGUE

Have I gone mad?
My name is Emily Marone, and I'm caught in a dangerous web of desire and deceit.

A long tattooed finger slid inside my pussy.

Agonizing pleasure radiated from my clit to the rest of my body.

His lips, slightly rough, sucked my nipples firmly, sending both pleasure and pain through my body. A stark contrast to the softness I'd imagined my first time would feel like.

Here I was in an unnervingly precarious situation, sharing the intimate confines of a bedroom aboard a luxurious private jet, hurtling through the skies towards the secretive allure of a private island.

I asked him to take my virginity. The question was why?

This man was my father's nemesis, and now, here I was, a pawn in their longstanding feud.

This was more than a physical conquest; it was a psychological battle against my father, and ultimately me.

The sensation of his touch was new and frighteningly intense.

Waves of nervous excitement mixed with a deep-seated fear rippled through me.

I knew what was happening physically, but the emotional turmoil was harder to grasp. I was inexperienced, a virgin caught in a game far bigger than a fleeting encounter.

His thumb brushed tentatively over my clit as he probed gently.

He was older, perhaps around my father's age.

I had to promptly push that thought out of my mind because... well..eww.

Regardless, Logan was teaching me a lesson about age – that with maturity came experience.

"Fuck, you're wet; I need to taste you," he whispered.

He lowered himself until his face was right between my legs.

His tongue explored cautiously, clearly aware of my inexperience. My hands braced against the bed frame, my legs shaking not just with new sensations, but also with a deep fear of the unknown.

I ran my fingers through his hair, a futile attempt to find some control in this situation.

"Take me," I murmured.

He groaned like an animal ready to devour his prey.

He pulled his head back, and the loss of contact made me let out a desperate whimpering sound. His pause made me glance down. My innocence was evident in my reaction, a mix of confusion and curiosity.

His thumb continued to move slowly, almost reassuringly.

"Don't worry baby girl. I'm going to make you come.

You're going to come so hard you'll scream. This I promise you. And when we're done here, I'm going to take you to my island and have my way with you again and again."

I was silent, my mind racing. This wasn't just about me; it was a message to my father.

And based on how good he was at foreplay, he was probably right about the screaming part. I didn't trust myself to be quiet - and the fact we were smack dab situated on a plane with cabin crew - that would be a problem to say the least.

"I can't wait to drink your juices," he whispered, sliding two fingers into me this time, while his lips found another sensitive spot.

His fingers skillfully massaged my G-spot, triggering an intense reaction. Every part of me seemed to ignite with exhilarating pleasure.

Overwhelmed, I arched back, releasing a deep, primal moan as my body quivered. It was an overwhelming surge of ecstasy, the kind you hear about in books - but this time it was real. So freaking real.

He made a believer out of me.

As the waves of bliss subsided, so did my strength. Fortunately, Logan was there, supporting me and helping me move my body to the bed's edge as he planted his feet on the ground and stood up.

Staring up at him in this angle I was mesmerized by how large he was.

Then he undid his belt, lowering his pants and boxer briefs, revealing himself.

Holy fuck, he was impressively endowed, a fact that didn't escape me.

The sight caused a surge of anticipation.

"I'm ready to explode," he said.

He teased me as he rubbed his dick on my pussy, his voice low. "Tell me you want this."

"I want you" I breathed out.

He gently lifted my leg, guiding it around his hip.

"Tell me exactly what you want."

Despite my dazed state, I knew what he was asking. "I want you, to fuck me senseless with everything you've got."

CHAPTER 1

LOGAN

A Few Days Earlier

"Your daughter?" I asked. "Is this a fucking joke?"

"It's not. She's beautiful, intelligent. A perfect wife for a man in your position."

It was something else to see a man like Charles Marone sweat. Dressed in an immaculately tailored double-breasted suit, his fingers adorned with gold rings, everything about him projecting power and authority—not to mention his criminal inclinations—his appearance in my office should've been enough to put me on notice.

One small detail; he was on my shit list.

The man had come to make amends for the position he'd put me in, however, I never would've guessed that his *daughter* would be what he'd come to offer.

I sat back in my chair, putting my feet up onto the long, sleek sweep of my black desk.

Charles's dark eyes flashed for a moment. He was tall and well-built, with slicked-back jet black hair. I knew that he'd worked his way up from beginning as a low-level enforcer in the DiMato crime syndicate.

How many skulls this man had cracked over the years, I could only guess. His build suggested he'd had no trouble fulfilling his role as 'enforcer.' He was anything but low-level now—one of DiMato's made men, actually.

"I wouldn't joke about such things with you, Mr. Stone." I suppressed a chuckle at him addressing me so formally. He was really going out of his way to bow and scrape.

Fine with me. Like I said, the man was on my shit list.

"Let me show you," he said.

Charles offered me a small, nervous smile before reaching into his jacket's inner pocket and slipping out his phone. As he did, my eyes drifted around the three-sixty view of my office up on the fifty-fifth floor of the Broadmoor Building in Midtown Manhattan, the towers of the city rising up around me. The morning sky was dark with the thick rainclouds that had been hanging over the city for the last week. The weather was making me crave nothing more than a trip to my island estate.

After some swiping, he handed his phone over to me. As he leaned across my desk, Charles was near enough that I could make out the sheen of sweat on his brow. A few thick, dark hairs had fallen loose from his hairline and draped over his forehead. He looked as much of a mess as a man in his position could afford to look.

I leaned in, taking the phone from his hand, flicking one more skeptical glance in his direction before setting my eyes on the screen.

"As you can see," Charles said. "She's quite beautiful."

No fucking kidding about that.

The image on the screen was enough to make me sit up and forget about the groveling criminal across from me.

The shot was of a young woman in a skintight cocktail dress of shimmering gold, posing with a drink in her hand on the dock of a fancy boat out at sea, a party going on around her, the sun setting over the water in pinks and purples. She had long, black hair with a bit of a wave to it, and prominent, sharp cheekbones that would give any of the thousands of wanna-be models that stalked the streets of New York a surge of envy.

Her nose was slim and straight, her lips were full and luscious. And her body a perfect hourglass, the dress clinging to her ripe curves. Her skin was the same gentle olive tone as her father's.

There was one very distinct quality about her that caught my eye.

A quality that remarkably shifted my attention away from her body - as fuckable as it was.

The smile.

The kind of smile that could make heads turn. A smile that could stop me dead in my tracks, even in the streets of Manhattan.

Holy.

Shiiit.

A man in my position didn't find it hard to come across total knockouts, and perfect tens weren't exactly in short supply in New York. This woman, however, was on another level. It took all the restraint I had to stay cool and calm, to not let her beauty affect me on the outside the way it did on the inside.

"She's really something, isn't she?" he asked as I handed the phone back to him. "And she's not all looks. Emily is brilliant—receiving a top-tier education by the best private tutors the city has to offer. She speaks three languages and is fully trained in the kind of etiquette that a man like yourself would expect." He glanced away, rubbing the back of his neck with his hand. "We'd, ah, always imagined that she would end up with a man like you. Maybe not under these kinds of circumstances, but all the same..."

I chuckled. "You mean you never imagined offering her to a business associate in hopes that he'd call it good for the millions you owe him?"

Charles's eyes flashed as I reminded him of what was at stake.

"You screwed me, Chuck," I said, leaning back in my chair and clasping my hands together. "You sold all of this money laundering bullshit to me as the easiest plan in the world, something that would make us both millions and connect me with some of the most powerful underground figures in the city. Instead, I'm out nearly ten million and you're here hoping I take your daughter in place of your debt. This isn't the goddam Medieval Times."

Charles cleared his throat nervously. "Surely, Mr. Stone, ten million can't be that much of an issue for someone like yourself. I know that Stone Holdings is worth bill—"

"You think the money is the point?" I asked, cutting Charles off in a way that few men likely ever had. "Because it's not. The *point* is that you went behind my back with one of my subordinates. And now you're here offering your own damn daughter like she's some kind of thoroughbred in hopes to make up for the damage you've caused me."

Charles said nothing.

Good.

It meant that he knew there was no sense in trying to argue his way out of his position.

"I'm not interested in marriage," I said. "My company demands far too much of my time. But even if I were in the market to be married, you think that I'd want an unwilling wife? You think I'd let such a potential source of disloyalty so close to me?"

"No, no," he said. "You don't understand. Emily is gentle, obedient. As I said, she's been trained for this sort of arrangement all her life. Marriage in our world is looked upon like the royal unions of times past. Women are offered to cement alliances, to build ties between families."

I snorted, shaking my head. The whole notion disgusted me. I made a silent curse to Byers, the C-level prick who'd gotten me into bed with the Mafia in the first place. He'd been fired, but even that seemed too good of a fate for him.

"I don't want your daughter," I said. "I want the fucking money."

My right hand clenched into a fist atop my desk.

"I don't have it," Charles said. "I'm sorry, Mr. Stone, but you can't get blood from a..." he trailed off, a sheepish smile forming on his lips as he held back the pun on my name that he no doubt had in mind.

"Then I'll go to your boss," I said. "Tell him that one of his made men is on the verge of making a powerful enemy."

He stiffened his posture, a thought occurring to him that appeared to instill a bit of confidence.

"I already spoke to him," Charles replied. "He was the one who approved this offer. In fact, he seemed most keen on it."

"Of course he was," I said, my voice tinged with frustration. "He doesn't have to pay a dime. You ask me, he ought to be cutting me a check personally for the entire amount I'm owed. Hell, maybe throw in a little extra for the trouble you've caused me."

"That's not going to happen," he said. "This is the solution the boss and I agreed upon."

"Then maybe I'll just go to him personally to sort all of this out," I said.

Charles's expression hardened for the first time since our meeting.

"That would be a bad idea. Trust me—it'd cause more problems than you're ready to handle."

I narrowed my eyes. "I don't like being threatened."

"Then don't poke around in matters that are out of your depth. Sorry to put it so bluntly, but that's just how it is."

I shook my head in annoyance. "I'm not afraid of you or your boss for that matter. You don't get where I am without knowing how to handle yourself, Chuck."

Charles's unease was palpable, etched clearly on his face – a telltale sign I had come to identify all too well.

Years at the helm of a billion-dollar empire had honed my instincts: this man was wrestling with news he dreaded to disclose, a storm brewing behind his guarded eyes.

"What is it?" I asked. "All of it, right now."

"There's... a slight caveat on the deal."

"And?"

"I offered her as your wife, and I stand by that. However, once she's in your possession, I'm afraid that you're going to have to give her some time."

I set aside my disgust at Charles referring to his own daughter as a possession and challenged his words.

"What the hell does that even mean?"

Charles glanced away again, as if trying to determine how to begin.

"As I've said, my Emily has been training for this kind of arrangement her entire life."

His choice of words annoyed me. Most parents wanted

a marriage for their daughters; Charles wanted an "arrangement."

"If we go through with this, she's yours. But that means you're going to need to ease her into the actual nuptials. She's still very young, you see. Very young and, ah, *innocent*."

I perked up—internally, at least. Didn't take a master of picking up on subtext to understand what he meant by "innocent."

She's a virgin. I said to myself.

He went on. "So, before the actual marriage, you'll need to refrain and go easy with her, not to put too fine of a point on it."

"Don't sleep with her until the marriage."

"That's what I'm saying."

"So, you want to give her to me, but I am to keep my hands off."

"That's right. Once you're married, that's a different story. But until then..."

He trailed off. My mind went to work on the situation and soon it became obvious that there was an alternate explanation for why he didn't want me to touch Emily.

He was going to betray me.

Then, once he had his daughter back, 'innocence' intact, he'd pawn her off to whatever other powerful man he had in mind.

The thing about scum like Charles was that underhanded scheming came naturally. What he'd done to me would almost certainly not be a one-off thing.

I needed to have the upper hand against him and his daughter might actually be the way to get it.

I considered the matter a bit more, wanting Charles to

stand there and sweat a little longer. When I was ready, I stood and offered my hand.

"You have a deal."

A big, almost dopey grin spread across Charles's face. His huge hand shot out toward me, and we shook.

"So happy to hear this, Mr. Stone," he said. "You're going to be so thrilled that you took a chance on my daughter."

"We'll see." We let go of one another's hands. "I trust that you'll be in touch with next steps."

"That's right. I need to tell Emily."

I stepped around my desk, putting my hand on Charles's shoulder and leading him out of my office.

"Good. And make no mistake—despite the unorthodox nature of this deal, I expect it to be carried out in a business-like manner."

"I promise you that is exactly how it will be done."

We reached the door and I opened it, Charles and I saying our goodbyes as he stepped out onto the bustling floor of the C-level of my offices, disappearing among the throngs of personal assistants zipping through my office.

I was glad when he was gone. Men like him tended to put me ill at ease. Ever since taking the reins of my father's company, I'd built the enterprise up legally, above-board - at least that's how I made it seem to the rest of the world.

I stepped over to the nearest window, hands solemnly clasped behind me, and peered out over the sprawling cityscape. Rain tapped a haunting melody against the glass, each droplet a somber note, while distant lightning cast ominous flashes.

There was no doubt in my mind that the arrangement I had just agreed to promised more than met the eye.

The scent of betrayal hung in the air, a stab in the back when I least expected it.

In this dark game, it was better to be the betrayer than the betrayed.

Keep his daughter's innocence. The fuck I will.

I chuckled to myself as I considered the audacity of his proposal.

It was completely laughable. Emily was beautiful, no doubt about it, but I was going to use the situation to my advantage and have some fun in the process. I'd make Emily mine in every way and then she'd be no more use to her asshole of a father as a bargaining chip.

I'd get what I wanted, and ruin Charles in the process.

Didn't sound like a bad idea at all, really.

A smirk formed on my lips as the plan came together.

I couldn't wait to get started.

CHAPTER 2

EMILY

"Y ou need to be packed and moving ASA-fuckin'-P."

"What are you saying?"

I'd heard my father just fine, and the expression of irritation on his face made it clear that he knew I had.

"Don't make me repeat myself, Emily. You *know* how much it pisses me off when you do that."

"You're pissed off," I said. "What else is new?"

He shot me a hard look, sending the message loud and clear how he felt about my backtalk. Dad stood at the entrance to my bedroom, his hands on the doorframe as if he wanted to make sure there was no chance I could run by him and flee the situation.

Dad nodded to the big Louis Vuitton bag he'd hauled in and tossed onto my bed without warning only a few minutes ago. The bag fit in among the décor of my richly appointed bedroom, the space that had always felt like a gold-plated jail cell ever since I was a little girl.

"Pack that." He narrowed his eyes in thought after he issued the command, thinking better of it. "Actually, I don't want you screwing around."

With that, he stuck his head out of the bedroom and let out a sharp whistle, two members of our estate's staff dutifully appearing behind him. "Help her. She starts dawdling, you come tell me."

The staff members slipped past Dad and into my room. They made no eye contact with me as they entered—not out of rudeness, but because no member of the staff, especially the men, were *allowed* to do so. They hurried into my enormous walk-in closet and began right away going through my things.

"Stop!" I shouted.

The guards froze, expressions of worry on their faces as their eyes flicked from me to Dad. No doubt they were wondering which Marone to obey.

"I'm not going anywhere until you tell me *exactly* what's going on. You barge in here, telling me to pack for a trip where I'll be staying with some man I don't even know. And then you don't even give me a moment to process it before ordering the staff to start rooting through my underwear drawers!"

Dad opened his mouth to speak, closing it quickly and shaking his head.

"Leave us," he barked at the staff.

The staff members obeyed without a word, hurrying out of the room and shutting the door behind them. Once Dad and I were alone, he slipped one hand into his pants pocket and raised the other toward me, pointing.

"You're leaving. You're going to be staying with a man named Logan Stone on his private island."

"I'm *what*?"

"You heard me."

My first instinct was to ask just who the hell Logan Stone was. The longer the name stayed in my ears, however, the more I realized I knew exactly who he was. Marta, the head maid and pretty much my surrogate mother ever since my real mom died years ago, loved to disobey Dad's wishes, keeping me abreast on the happenings from the outside world. In addition to smuggling in movies and TV, she always made sure I had access to the latest gossip rags.

Logan Stone, if I remembered correctly, was some hotshot CEO in New York, one of the richest men in the world, if my information was correct. Supposedly, he was one of America's most eligible and desired bachelors, as well.

Still, I needed to play dumb. Dad did his best to make sure I was as isolated from the outside as much as possible. Admitting to knowing who Logan Stone was might tip him off. Lucky for me, Dad was never too hard to fool; thankfully, I got my brains from Mom.

"Who is Logan Stone?" I asked, putting my hands on my hips. "And why the hell am I supposed to go stay with him?"

Dad's eyes widened, his eyebrows arching. "First of all, don't you dare take that tone with me, understand?"

I formed my mouth into a hard line. Dad might've been easy to intellectually beat, but I didn't want to risk him putting his hands on me like he'd done so many times in the past.

"I understand."

Dad's expression cooled. "Good. Logan Stone is the CEO of Stone Holdings, one of the biggest investment firms in the world. He's a, ah, business partner—one that we owe quite a bit of money to, money that we don't have right now. So, in place of money, we're sending you."

I felt sick. Sure, I'd known since I was a girl that my destiny was to end up with some rich man that Dad had picked out for me without so much as a word of my own thoughts on the matter. All the expensive boarding schools and etiquette classes and language lessons I'd been subjected to over the years had never been about my own enjoyment, but instead to make me a prize, like some show pony.

Thankfully, Marta had balanced that education with one of her own. I thought about those old romance books she liked to slip under my bedroom doors, some of them set in Victorian times, featuring women being married off to men for strategic, rather than romantic, reasons.

"As if I were nothing more than a piece of property," I said. "Like some expensive piece of jewelry or one of your stupid cars."

Dad rolled his eyes. "Don't be so dramatic. That's always how you've been, you know? Major drama queen, just like your mother."

I *hated* when he talked about Mom like that.

He crossed his arms. "Anyway, this is what's happening, and I expect you to comply. Get it?"

In those moments I felt totally helpless, totally without power. I was an adult but never in my life had I been made to feel independent, like I was capable of making my own decisions.

"*Es muy estupido*," I growled under my breath in Spanish.

Dad scoffed. "I may not have taken the same fancy-ass private language lessons as you, kid, but I can interpret that one."

Without another word, he stuck his head out of the bedroom door and called out to the staff, ordering them to come back in. The pair obeyed, heading right into my closet once more.

"We need enough for a whole month," he said. "And she's going to an island, so make sure there's swimwear, sundresses, all that shit."

"Where's this island?" I asked. The more the men yanked my clothes out of the closet, going through my belongings without heed or concern for my privacy, the more helpless I felt. "If I'm going somewhere for a whole month, then I want to know where it is."

Dad snorted, as if amused by the way I was trying to demand something.

"It's somewhere in the Virgin Islands; that's all I know. The place is this guy's palace in the sea. You're flying there at noon to the nearest major airport, then taking a helicopter the rest of the way."

Tears formed in my eyes, one trickling out and darting down my cheek.

"What about Marta? Please..." More tears came, accompanied by a few weak sobs. "Please, can she come too?"

Dad rolled his eyes again. "No, Marta's not coming. And stop crying, you're a goddamn grown woman. Cut that shit out right now."

Something about being spoken to like that as the staff packed my belongings stirred something in me and I couldn't take it any longer. I tried never to talk back to Dad —too many hard lessons knowing what it got me. In that moment, however, I couldn't hold back.

"I hate this!" I yelled. "You can't do this to me! I'm not some... some damn show horse you can do with what you please!"

Dad's rage was instant and intense. His eyes flashed with pure anger as I spoke, and he cut across the long length of my room with surprising speed. One hand went to my upper arm, grabbing me hard enough to hurt. The other hand went up into the air, raised as if he were about to strike me.

Dad had only hit me twice. The first time was when I fought him about going to a normal high school; the other, when I demanded to go to college. I'd lost both of those arguments, of course, walking away each time with a red mark on my cheek. As Dad stood over me, I was certain that it would be the third occasion. My father didn't care for defiance, didn't care for me raising my voice to him.

To my surprise, he didn't hit me. Instead, he held his hand aloft for several moments, finally shoving me backward onto the bed. The staff did nothing, continuing their work, making a concerted effort not to notice what was happening. Dad paid them well to play dumb.

Dad shook his head, running his hand through his hair. "You're no good to me with a fucked-up face hours before he's going to see you."

Dad raised his finger toward me. "I'll tell you this much. This Logan guy, he's not going to take any shit from you. Bet you he'll knock you on your ass the first time you try. And... there's one more thing, too."

I moved slowly off the bed, my heart still racing from what had just happened. I plucked a few tissues from the box on my nightstand, dabbing my eyes and doing my best to work through the sadness and the fear.

"One more thing?" I asked.

Dad nodded. "That's right. While you're there, you're not to let him touch you."

"Touch me how?"

He snorted. "You might be naïve, but you know damn well what I mean. Logan Stone isn't to *touch* you, he's not to get between those virgin thighs of yours." A shudder of disgust ran through me at the way he spoke. Not wanting to incur his wrath again, I kept my mouth shut.

A tight expression of hard anger formed on his face. He stepped slowly, menacingly toward me.

"I mean it. You're only good to me pure, kid."

I felt sick to my stomach as more tears formed. I held them back and kept my mouth shut, not wanting to give Dad the satisfaction of knowing how his words affected me.

"One day I'll give you to your *true* husband. And when I do, you're going to be untouched for him, just like I've been training you to be."

I wasn't just scared and sick, I was *angry*.

"I won't marry anyone you choose for me. I'd rather die."

He snorted again. "You have no choice in the matter." The look in his eyes as he spoke was mad, menacing, evil. I was certain that he meant it.

"You've got forty-five minutes to finish packing. Either you help and have some say in what you take with you, or you let the staff do it. Either way, you're going—even if I have to drag you out by your hair."

Dad shot me one more hard look before turning and leaving, slamming shut the bedroom door behind him. The staff was still there, the pair of men quickly folding my clothes and putting them into my suitcase.

I stepped over to the big, arched window that looked out over the back sweep of the compound from my third floor bedroom, the garden neatly arranged below, the thick barrier of trees that surrounded the property beyond that.

I started to cry. I felt so damn helpless there wasn't anything else I could think to do. The staff ignored me, thankfully, either too professional or perhaps scared of Dad if they were to be perceived of butting in to say anything.

Rain pattered down on the windows. All I wanted was to throw them open and leap onto the soft grass below and keep running until I was long gone, until I was free. The notion filled me with excitement and fear all at once.

Before I could give the matter too much thought, a firm knock sounded at the door. Fear gripped me at the idea of my father returning.

"It's me, *niña*," said the voice from the other side. "Are you OK?"

Relief washed over me as I realized it was Marta. I hurried over to the door, wiping my eyes and turning the knob. Short, slender and strong-willed Marta Velazquez stood on the other side. Her hair was comprised of close, tight curls of dark red and her eyes looked at me from behind large, round glasses. It didn't take long for her to figure out what was going on, there was no sense in trying to pull the wool over her eyes. There never was.

"That *tirano* ," she snarled, stepping in and preparing to shut the door behind her. She quickly noticed the staff, however, and barked out orders for them to leave. They dutifully obeyed.

Once they were gone and we were alone, I let the tears flow.

"Oh, *pobre niña*." She wrapped her arms around me, my head falling onto her shoulder as I wept. "I could hear his voice from all the way downstairs. I'm so sorry this is happening to you."

She held me as I cried, so many tears coming from me in such a short time.

"I just don't know what to do. I feel so helpless." I raised my head, Marta quickly grabbing the tissues from my bedside table and handing them over to me.

"You know that's just how he wants you to feel, right?"

she asked. "That's how he works—he makes you feel small so he can feel big."

I blew my nose, and Marta led me over to the edge of the bed to sit.

"Let me do the packing," she said. "I can't believe he put a pair of men in charge of packing for a young woman."

She went to work, expressing her distaste as she pulled clothes out of the bag and set them aside before heading into the closet to find what she considered more suitable.

"I don't know what I'm going to do, Marta," I said, staring off into space. "Is this really happening?"

Marta sighed, pausing her search for a moment. "It's really happening. What your father has planned, exactly, I don't know. But I overheard him speaking yesterday with this Mr. Stone."

"Mr. Stone." I whispered the name. Other than what I had read in the tabloids, the man was a mystery for the time being. That would all change very soon.

"What do you know about this guy?" I asked Marta. "Is he some rich jerk who thinks he can have whatever he wants?"

"Mr. Stone... he is rich, I can say that much. I have *familia* in the city who work for him. He is wealthy as they come, more money than a hundred of your *padre*. And he is..." She trailed off, once more pausing her gathering of my belongings.

"What?" I rose slowly, turning toward her as I came over to help find clothes.

Marta smiled sightly. "He is... *muy guapo*. Hell, he's more than that, he's freaking hot as hell."

I gasped. "Marta!"

She shrugged, handing me a pair of jeans. "What can I

say? I'd show you a picture, but you know how your father is with staff having their phones during work."

"He's handsome?" I asked. "And what else? You said you have family who work for him? They must have said something about him at some point."

"They have. Mr. Stone is very ambitious. I mean, *very* ambitious. The company was willed to him by his father years ago when he passed. Back then, they were a small-time investment firm, still worth millions, but otherwise a very small fish in a very big pond. Mr. Stone, when he took over, brought the company to the next level, expanding out of New York, turning it into an international company worth *billions*."

"Wow." The idea of having something of my own like that was hard to wrap my head around. "He sounds... interesting."

"Other than that, he appears to be a good boss. He's tough but fair, always does things above board."

"He does? Then how did he get mixed up with someone like my father?"

Marta shrugged. "That's a good question, *niña*. Maybe you'll find out when you meet him."

The mention of what was to come in my very near future sent a fresh wave of anxiety running through me. Marta, sensing this, placed her hand on my shoulder.

"Calm yourself, *nina*," she said. "I know this is scary, but it doesn't have to be."

"It doesn't have to be? How do you mean?"

She shrugged. "Maybe this Mr. Stone will be kind, friendly even. Maybe he isn't like your father. Maybe this will be a good thing." She smiled. "Come on, how many Hallmark movies have I snuck in here for you where the young woman in a terrible situation meets a handsome stranger who sweeps her off her feet?"

The notion, despite being silly, managed to bring a small smile to my face.

"Those are movies, Marta. This is real life."

"Perhaps. But you never know, this man very well could turn out to be as evil as your father *or* he could turn out to be kind and loving. There's nothing wrong with having a little hope, is there?"

"Hope. I don't even know what to do with a word like that."

"You keep it close and don't let it fade. I have no doubt in my mind that one day, *niña*, things will turn around for you. Maybe not today, maybe not tomorrow,. but they will."

Marta cocked her head to the side as something else occurred to her.

"What is it?" I asked.

"You remember *Beauty and the Beast*?" she asked.

I smiled, the film having been one of my favorites since I was a little girl.

"Of course, I do."

"Your situation is not so different from Belle's, you know."

"You think this Mr. Stone guy will be like the beast?"

She chuckled. "Hard to say. Maybe he will be scary at first, only to reveal himself to be something different entirely. Either way, my advice stands—don't ever lose hope, *niña*."

A knock sounded, the door opening before I could say a word. The staff that had originally started packing my stuff was there.

"He didn't want you two in here alone," one of them

said. "He told us he wanted to make sure the job was getting done."

"Then do it, *idiotas*!" Marta shouted, waving her hand toward the men. "Get to it."

She turned to me as the flustered pair hurried back to work, taking my hands and holding them together.

"Hope. Don't lose it. It may be what gets you through what lies ahead."

As I watched the men return to packing my life away, I had the notion that it would take a lot more than just hope to see me through.

CHAPTER 3

EMILY

One little push. That was all it'd take to shove open the car door and just... jump out.

As I watched the streets of Manhattan through the car window, it was all I could think about. Well, that and the fact that I was actually in *Manhattan*. Dad never let me go there, even though the compound where I'd lived since forever was only a few miles away on Long Island. I'd been to Manhattan once, back when I was barely a teenager and Dad needed to take me to a specialist that didn't do house calls.

As we drove, my eyes went from the tops of the buildings—those gleaming skyscrapers that reached all the way up into the clouds—then down to the ground, to street level where thousands of people, from businessmen and women to shop workers to college kids and everything in between, made their way through the hustle and bustle.

I could've watched the view from the window for hours, mesmerized by the life and vitality of the city. Dad and I were in the back of one of his luxury cars, the driver hidden from us by an ink black partition.

As we drove, I found myself wondering over and over how easily I'd be able to jump out. Tuck and roll—that's how it was done in the movies I'd seen, anyway. I'd wait until the car pulled into a slow turn around a corner and then make my move. There were so many people out and about that once I hit the ground and got on my feet I could just melt into the crowd.

"Yeah... no, she's with me right now... no word yet from Stone about going back on the deal... as far as I can tell, he's still locked and loaded and ready to go. We're on our way now; the package should be in his hands within the hour."

I felt sick the way he spoke about me like I was an item, a bauble he could throw into the pot to sweeten the deal. Maybe I should've been used to it by then, but hearing those words from my own dad...

"Hey." Dad nodded sharply to me as he took the phone from his ear and slipped it into his jacket pocket. "You alive over there?"

"Does it make any difference to you?" I asked. "Seems like if I were dead I'd be one less problem for you to worry about."

He snorted, rolling his eyes and shaking his head. "I'm going to ignore the backtalk seeing as you're going to be out of my hair in the next hour anyway. But I need you alive and kicking for the deal."

"Well, I'm here talking to you, aren't I?"

Dad reached forward, plunging his fingers into the bowl of mixed nuts between us and greedily shoving them into his mouth. I was hungry, not having had a bite since earlier that morning. I reached for a few nuts of my own, but I didn't get far before Dad's hand shot out with surprising speed and grabbed my wrist.

"What do you think you're doing?" he asked. His hand

gripped me hard enough to hurt, but I was used to it. Instead of protesting, I did my best to ignore the pain.

"Having a snack."

"What're your calories at for the day?"

"Are you serious? You're really monitoring my intake on the day you get rid of me?"

"Of course, I am. Just because you're going to be some other guy's responsibility in an hour or so doesn't mean that I'm going to be slacking in my duties."

Dad had always been serious as hell about my diet. "No one wants a fat girl" is what he would say whenever he caught me eating.

"I barely touched my breakfast," I said. "And unless you want me to pass out from hunger before I see this man, you should let me have something."

He kept his eyes on mine, as if scanning for some sign that I was lying. When he was satisfied, he released his grip.

"Fine. Just don't pig out. If you eat too much salt it'll make you look bloated. We want you in your best form for the first impression. You only get one of those, you know."

He grinned, as if pleased with his own words. I took a few nuts from the dish and brought them slowly to my mouth.

We pulled in front of a tall skyscraper, the building steel and gleaming glass. Over the row of doors that led into the lobby was the word "Stone" in clear, bold letters. Dozens of people streamed in and out of the place.

"Is he here?" I asked.

Dad shook his head. "Nope. We're taking his personal helicopter to a private airfield north of the city. That's where he is."

The driver got out and opened the side door for us. Dad

stepped out first and I followed, onto the busy Midtown streets. The air was alive with the sort of energy only New York had. Once more, I found myself struck by the urge to run, to break free from Dad and this Stone guy and run as far away as I could from this nightmare of a life.

A smile formed on my face as I considered the idea, the daydream enough to make me forget, if only for a moment, that Dad had me by the arm, leading me toward an uncertain fate. I could run to the nearest coffeeshop and work as a barista. I'd make lattes and mochas for all the busy people in the city, goofing around with my coworkers as I earned my own money. Then, I'd go back to my cute, cozy, little apartment and work on my novel.

It was about as perfect a life as I could imagine.

"Come on." Dad jerked my arm hard, pulling me out of my daydream and back into the moment.

We stepped into the lobby, the space huge, sleek and modern. As we moved through, the driver carrying my bags right behind us, I found myself having a hard time wrapping my head around what I was seeing. There were so many people there, a massive company all built by one man. A tinge of anger ran through me at the idea of what someone could accomplish with freedom and ambition. I had the latter, but not the former.

Dad spoke to someone at the front desk. The employee nodded toward a security guard, who quickly came over and joined us the rest of the way toward a private elevator. We stepped inside, the elevator shooting us up into the sky. The back of the elevator was glass, and soon we had an amazing view of the city as we rose higher and higher. Despite my situation, I couldn't help but turn and watch, my hands on the glass and a smile on my face.

The elevator dinged and the doors opened onto the

roof, revealing a small, black helicopter at the far end. A pair of guards stood there awaiting us along with a third man, who I guessed to be the pilot. The guard in the elevator led us toward them, and it took all the restraint I had to not simply stand there and gawk at the view.

"This her?" the pilot asked. He wore dark aviators but I could feel his eyes move over my body in a way I didn't care for in the slightest.

"Sure is," Dad said. "Is he ready?"

The pilot nodded. "Just spoke to him. Plane is gassed up and ready to go as soon as we arrive."

My stomach tightened with tension, my head spinning at the idea of taking a private plane to a private island, flying thousands of miles from everything I'd ever known.

Luckily, or not so luckily, as the case might've been, Dad was there to make sure I stayed on task.

"Come on." He jerked my arm again, this time harder than usual.

We made our way over to the helicopter, the pilot helping the guard load my bags into the back after guiding us inside. Once more, I was scared and excited all at once. Never before had I been in a helicopter.

The pilot started the engine and we were soon up and on our way. I kept my gaze focused out the window, trying to ignore Dad next to me as the city grew smaller and smaller below. The view was amazing, like looking down at a living map. I could make out the shape of Manhattan, the island packed full of buildings, the huge rectangle of Central Park plopped right in the middle. It wasn't long before Brooklyn and Queens were visible in their entirety too, stretching all the way down Long Island.

We headed northwest toward New Jersey. The flight hardly took any time at all—it seemed like the instant we hit our peak we were already on the way back down, descending upon a tiny, private airfield.

We landed and the pilot helped me out, Dad not even bothering to ask how the flight agreed with me. I felt dizzy and disoriented once back on solid ground, still trying to wrap my head around how just a few minutes ago I'd been as high up in the sky as a bird in flight.

A sight off in the middle distance immediately took my mind away from that thought. I spotted a tall man in a white shirt and sunglasses leaning against a sleek, dark blue sports car. Not too far away sat a private jet.

"Is that him?" The words came out of my mouth in a whisper, barely audible over the whirring of the helicopter blades.

Dad smiled, waving in the direction of the man, who offered a slight, barely perceptible nod in response, his face impassive.

"That's him. Now, I'm going to tell you this, and I'm only going to say it once—you'd better be on your best goddamn behavior. God knows how much I've spent over the years shaping you into something presentable. If you embarrass me in front of Stone..." He trailed off, leaving me to imagine whatever threat he might have in mind.

We drew closer to the man, and I was able to make out more of him. The first thing I noticed was that he easily stood close to six and a half feet tall. He was dressed in a crisp, white button-up shirt, his sleeves rolled up and cuffed around thick, ropey forearms. Navy slacks and a pair of black loafers completed the look. Everything on his body appeared designed just for him and fit perfectly.

Not only was he tall, but he was also built, his shoulders broad and round, his chest massive, and his hands big enough to start me wondering what they might feel like on my bare skin. I found myself, to my surprise, growing more and more aroused, a tension forming between my legs that I hadn't felt in... God, I couldn't even remember the last time I'd felt such a way. One thing was for sure, he was sexier than any man I'd ever seen.

The man unfolded his arms. My eyes darted over his features, noting his square, strong jaw, cleft chin, slender nose, and thick, light brown hair with just enough salt and pepper to be interesting. I couldn't quite pinpoint his age, since it appeared he was prematurely greying. I guessed somewhere in his late thirties, a good amount older than myself.

"Mr. Stone!" Dad took on a strange, obsequious posture and tone, as if he were afraid of the man. As he stuck out his hand toward the stranger, I could sense the man's attention was all on me.

I was dressed simply, wearing a dark pink maxi dress and matching heels. The way the man's lips curled into a small smile at the sight of me made me think he was more than happy with what he was seeing, despite the modest nature of the dress.

"As you can see, Mr. Stone," Dad said, sweeping his hand in my direction. "Here she is, just as promised."

The man didn't say a word to Dad, instead stepping closer to me. He was so *big*—tall and muscular, everything about him imposing and more than a little intimidating. The man paused a few feet from me, taking one more look up and down my body.

It was strange. Normally, the idea of a man ogling me in that way would've offended, maybe even made me sick to my stomach. But with him, it was different. I *liked* the way he looked at me. In fact, I found myself wishing I'd worn something other than the modest dress I happened to have on.

"Mr. Stone," Dad said. "This is—"

He didn't get a chance to finish before the man reached forward and took my hand, which was raised in preparation for a shake.

"Pleasure to meet you." His voice was low and deep, commanding without trying. He turned my hand over and leaned forward, placing his lips onto the back of it. A shiver ran through me, the intensity of it making me a bit dizzy. "My name is Logan Stone."

He let my hand go, and I dumbly kept it in the air.

"Emily!" Dad said my name in a hiss. Out of the corner of my eye, I could make out the expression of tight anger on his face. "Don't just stand there—introduce yourself!"

I cleared my throat and composed myself.

"Emily Marone," I said. "A pleasure, Mr. Stone."

Logan nodded and offered a small smile before reaching toward the bag I carried.

"Allow me."

"No!"

By pure instinct, I wrapped my arms around the bag in a protective manner. Logan cocked his head to the side, seemingly confused by the suddenness and severity of my actions. Once more, Dad regarded me with an expression of annoyance and frustration.

"I mean, that's OK. A girl has to have her personal things, you know?"

I didn't want to tell him what was in the bag, and I most definitely didn't want Dad to find out. Inside were my personal effects, but most importantly, the bag contained a trio of journals that comprised the novel that I was in the process of writing—a romance that I'd been creating in secret for the last couple of years.

The novel was my hidden little dream, and there was no way on earth I could let Dad find out about it.

"Naturally." Logan's easy tone and calm confidence disarmed the awkwardness of the situation. "Anyway, shall we board?" He pivoted to the side, nodding toward the stairway that led up and into the plane.

"Please let me know if there are any problems," Dad said, coming over to Logan. He shot me another look, a clear reminder that his words were a warning that I needed to be on my best behavior.

"I certainly will," Logan said. "And I don't mean to rush, but we really ought to get moving. Can't park a private plane on the runway forever, you know."

"Of course," Dad said. "Thank you again, Mr. Stone, for taking this offer. I have no doubt you'll be more than pleased with your decision."

Logan turned his attention to me. "So far, I am. Emily, if you wouldn't mind coming with me..."

Without so much as a look back toward Dad, I stepped to Logan's side. Together, we ascended the stairs, Logan taking my arm and leading me up. We reached the top, Logan placing his hand on the small of my back as he led me through, his touch once more making me weak in the knees and tight between my legs.

"Wow."

The word tumbled out of my mouth before I could stop it, but it was my instant reaction to the sight of the interior of the private plane before me.

The interior was spacious, streamlined, and contemporary with bits of elegant flourishes here and there. The seats were plush and leather, the carpeting was beautiful, and there was even a bar set up. A small meeting area was at the far end, and near the entry door was a cozy little space with a TV that struck me as perfect for watching a movie or curling up with a book.

Down the length of the plane was a small hallway, the end of it leading to a bedroom. Something about the sight of the bed, coupled with being so near to Logan, brought to mind the sorts of things a man and a woman could get up to on a bed like that.

I remembered Dad's warning, how he'd stressed above all else that I couldn't do anything of the sort with Logan. Little did Dad know, his warning only put the idea more firmly into my head. Not to mention that there was clearly no love lost between him and Logan—this whole arrangement was a pretext for him screwing over Logan in some unknown way.

What if I were to lose my virginity to Logan? What if I were to give away my oh-so-precious purity in a way that was not only on my terms, but to a man my Dad clearly despised?

That would show him.

The door shut with a *thunk*, and I turned to see that Logan and I were finally alone.

He smiled.

"Wine?"

CHAPTER 4

LOGAN

Even from the pictures, I'd been able to tell that Emily was something special.

In person, she was even more striking, as beautiful as they came. No wonder her father treated her like gold—as if she were the most valuable thing he possessed.

Speaking of her father, I'd noticed something strange right away about the relationship between the two of them. There had been zero affection, no warmth, no indication that Emily was his flesh and blood. When she'd broken from his side and joined me, she hadn't uttered so much as a single "goodbye." It'd been as if she couldn't wait to flee from him, even into the company—or possession, in this case —of a stranger.

Perhaps that dynamic might make her more susceptible to my seduction. And there was no doubt that seducing this beauty was at the forefront of my mind. Emily's potential desire to get back at her father promised to make the whole process move much more smoothly.

"You alright?" I asked. Emily had been standing there stunned since I'd brought her onto the plane.

She shook her head and blinked hard, coming back into the moment.

"Huh? Oh, sorry. It's just... this is a really nice plane."

I chuckled to myself at how impressed she was. Cute, really. It was clear that not only had she never seen anything like it before, but that the rumors of her having rarely left her house were possibly true. As she looked around, it was impossible to not take notice of the inno- cent air about her, a charming guilelessness in spite of a face and body that seemed hand designed to inspire pure lust.

"Something to drink?" I asked, reiterating the question as I made my way over to the bar. "Feel free to turn me down, but I always like a little something before takeoff. Personally, I'll be having a little red wine, but you're more than welcome to white. Or a cocktail if that's what you're in the mood for."

I stepped over to the cocktail bar, glancing over my shoulder to see Emily nervously shift her weight from one foot to the other. God, she was sexy. Even in that simple dress it was impossible to not notice the curves of her hips, the way the fabric clung to her full, round breasts.

"I'm not sure."

I turned, crossing my arms and leaning back against the bar.

"Oh, you don't drink? That's fine, of course. I have non-alcoholic drinks, as well. Quite a few different ones, actually."

She pursed her lips and right away I could tell what was on her mind.

"It's not that I *don't* drink," she said. "It's more that..."

"You've *never* drank."

Her eyes flashed. "God, am I that easy to read?"

I smiled. "Maybe a little. But it's more that in my business, you live or die by being able to read people."

She offered a weak smile in return. "It's just that my dad, he... keeps me on a short leash. And he's very strict about my diet, including alcohol."

"Do me a favor," I said.

"What's that?"

"Take a look around the plane."

Though confused, she did as I asked, cocking her head here and there and glancing around.

"I don't get it. Is there something I'm supposed to be noticing?"

"Do you see your father anywhere?"

She chuckled, shaking her head as she realized what I was getting at.

"No. He's not here."

"That's right; he's not here. Now, you're something of a mystery to me, Emily, but I do know your age. You're twenty-two, more than old enough to have a drink. Now, is there something I can get for you?"

She turned her attention to the bar, licking her lips in anticipation. The sight made me wonder what other things she could do with that tongue and those lips.

"Well, I've always wanted to try wine. But I don't know where to begin."

I gave the matter a moment's thought. "How about something sweet? But not too sweet."

She smiled. "Sure. Sweet sounds like a good place to start."

"Sweet it is."

With that, I opened the mini-fridge and took out a half-sized bottle of Moscato. That in hand, I opened it, a *pop* sounding through the compartment. I poured a flute for

Emily, and a glass of Pinot Noir for myself. The process done, I walked over to her and handed Emily the flute. As I did, she slipped her bag off her shoulder.

"Can I take that?" I asked.

Her eyes flashed. "Um, no. That's fine. Thanks, but I'd prefer to keep this close."

I couldn't help but wonder about the bag's contents. It wasn't out of the ordinary for women to be protective over their purse. But this wasn't a purse, it was a mid-sized travel bag. Something special was inside, and I wasn't going to pretend that I didn't have a bit of curiosity about it.

"Sparkly," she said, her eyes on the bubbles, an eager smile on her face.

"We should toast to something."

"Such as?" she asked.

I smiled. "Well, since it's your first drink, I say you choose."

"How about this," she said. "We drink to... new friendships."

"I like that."

We tapped rims, then drank.

"How is it?" I asked.

She glanced away, considering the question.

"It's... good. Sparkly, tickles my nose. And it's sweet, but not too sweet."

"Glad you're enjoying."

Before either of us could say another word, the pilot came on the speaker.

"Mr. Stone, we're getting ready to take off in just a few moments, if you both wouldn't mind getting seated."

The speaker clicked off and I nodded to the nearest set of chairs.

"Shall we? Oh, and please take the window. The view over the city is something else."

She smiled at me before easing into the seat, her ass sticking out just a bit as she sat down. Everything about her seemed designed to appeal to the senses—from her figure to her scent, to the way she moved. Charles might've been as big of a prick as they came, but he'd trained his daughter well.

I sat down next to her, placing my glass of wine into the holder. We clicked our seatbelts closed, Emily turning to me with a broad smile. Considering her circumstances, it was interesting to see how excited she was. I'd have thought she'd have been a bit nervous at the prospect of being shipped off to live with some strange man, but that didn't seem to be the case at all.

The plane engines spun up, the sound filling the space as the pilot turned the plane toward the length of the runway. The engines grew louder and louder, a tinge of worry forming on Emily's features.

"Something wrong?"

"Is it supposed to be that loud?"

I couldn't help but laugh.

"Yes, everything's fine. Don't worry about it."

She smiled slightly but I could sense that the newness of the experience was getting to her. Emily took one more nervous sip of her wine before setting the flute into the holder. Her hands then moved to the arm rests, gripping them tightly, her eyes fixed forward as the plane moved faster and faster down the runway.

Her expression turned into a grimace of tension as the plane began to lift off. I couldn't stand it any longer, I needed to do something to comfort her. I placed my hand on hers, feeling the warm smoothness of her skin against my palm. She glanced over at me when she realized what I was doing. At first, she seemed uncertain about my touch. But it didn't take long before she turned her hand over underneath mine and weaved her fingers between my own, gripping my hand tightly.

I couldn't help but chuckle as I realized how strong her grip was. Emily may have been delicate in some ways, but she carried an inner toughness within her.

"I promise that we'll be fine," I said. "Nothing out of the ordinary is happening."

She nodded, her eyes still fixed forward.

"You want my advice? Look out of the window. Flying for the first time might be a little scary, but the view is worth it."

Emily nodded again before turning her attention to the window, looking out as we rose above the airfield. It didn't take long before Manhattan was before us, Long Island stretching all the way into the distance, the city surrounded by shimmering, blue water.

"That's something, isn't it?" I asked.

"It really is."

I craned my neck a bit to get a good look at her face. She watched the takeoff with a big smile that was almost child-like in its excitement.

It didn't take long before we were over the clouds, the sky a perfect blue above us. The pilot came back on the speaker and let us know that we would be at cruising altitude soon, and that the flight would take a little under five hours. It was the perfect amount of time to be alone with Emily to get to know her better.

As much as I wanted to keep touching her hand—to touch a hell of a lot more than just that, in fact—I moved it away. She turned in her seat, taking another sip of her Moscato as she looked me up and down.

"Something on your mind?" I asked.

"Just a personal question."

I chuckled. "Shoot."

"Well, I was wondering how old you are."

I grinned. "How old do you think?"

She didn't answer at first, instead letting her eyes linger on my face, as if really giving the question some serious thought.

"Well, you're older than me, that's for sure. Older than thirty, but not as old as my dad. I'd say... thirty-five?"

I chuckled. "Close. Thirty-eight."

It was impossible to ignore how attracted to Emily I was. But the more time I spent with her, the clearer it became that Emily wasn't exactly the most worldly of women.

And it was all because of her father. It made me sick to think about what he'd done to her, how he'd cut off his own flesh and blood from the world to ensure that she'd be a more attractive bargaining chip to some criminal lowlife. The thought made me more certain of his plan. All that work to preserve her innocence only for it to be stolen away by me, a man he hated.

"Where are we going?" she asked.

"My private island."

"I know *that*. But where is it, exactly?"

"You're familiar with the Virgin Islands?"

She narrowed her eyes in irritation. "Are you asking if I know where the Virgin Islands are?"

What came next, I most certainly hadn't been expecting. Emily let loose a torrent of Spanish, perfectly pronounced and accented. I didn't flinch as she spoke, letting her say her piece—whatever it might've been.

"You're going to have to translate that," I said. "Spanish isn't my forte. Though I did pick up on *estupido*."

"The Virgin Islands are in the eastern Caribbean," she said. "Just because I'm a little sheltered, doesn't mean I'm stupid."

I raised my palms. "Didn't mean to imply anything of the sort."

The anger faded from her face. "Sorry," she said. "It's just that I know how I might come off. I don't get out much, and it shows. It's kind of a sensitive subject." She let her shoulders slump forward. I could sense she regretted her little outburst. "Shouldn't have ripped into you like that."

I sat back, amused more than anything. "You speak Spanish?"

She shrugged and nodded. "Yes. A few other languages, too."

"Which ones?"

"Well, besides Spanish there's French, Italian, Mandarin, and a little bit of Russian. But not much."

I nodded slowly, impressed by what she'd just told me. "Wow."

She bought her dark eyes back up to mine. "I did receive just about the best private education money can buy. Dad was big on making sure that I'd be appealing to men for, well, other reasons than just my face and body."

Had to admit, my mind was already racing with possibilities. Her looks were what had initially caught my attention. But the longer I spoke to her, the more I began to realize that she was far more than just a pretty face. She was bright and sharp and, if her language skills were any indication, extremely well educated.

She sighed, shaking her head and taking a sip of her wine. "Anyway, the Virgin Islands. What about them?"

I chuckled at her attempt to get the conversation back on track. "Well, I own one of them, and have a private resort."

She blinked hard, and I could sense she was taking a moment to process what I'd just told her.

"How... you mean, it's like one of those beachfront hotels, but only for you?"

I chuckled. "Well, it's not a full-size resort. Just a good-sized house near the beach. It's nice. And, most importantly, it's quiet. When you spend most of your time living and working in New York, having a little piece of paradise all to yourself is just the thing."

"So, it's just you on this whole island?"

"Not quite. There are staff who live there and take care of it. And there's a security team."

"This... sounds like quite the place."

Without another word, she lifted her glass and took another sip before turning away from me and facing the window once more. As she watched the clouds roll by underneath, my mind began to race with possibilities for her.

Emily wasn't just a beautiful woman to use as a bargaining chip—she was an *asset*. It was perplexing to think about how her father didn't seem to understand how valuable someone like her could be, and not just as a way to buy favor with the highest bidder. A woman like her—sharp-minded and educated—would be more valuable than gold for a man in my position.

Right in the middle of my thinking, Emily turned in her seat to face me once again. She had a strange look on her face, as if there were something on her mind that she didn't quite know what to say.

Finally, she smiled a bit, lifting her eyes to mine.

"Yes?" I asked.

"There's something I'm wondering about."

"Let's hear it."

"Are you going to seduce me, or what?"

CHAPTER 5

LOGAN

I nearly spit out my wine at her words. It took all of the restraint I had to keep it in my mouth, to play it cool, to swallow then set my glass down slowly.

"Excuse me?" I asked. "Am I going to *what?*"

Make no mistake—I *wanted* to seduce her. A woman like her, innocent and inexperienced, would need a little finessing. I'd need to build her trust, to create tension and attraction. More than that, I was no stranger to the art of seduction, and was quite good at it. When I was a younger man, it was all about getting women into bed as quickly as possible. Now that I was older, the pursuit itself was almost as thrilling as the sex.

Almost.

She cleared her throat and squared her shoulders, as if prepping herself to continue.

"I asked if you're going to seduce me."

My mind might've been uncertain about what I was hearing, but my cock sure as hell wasn't. It stiffened to attention, eager to bury itself between the thighs of the gorgeous woman before me. I shifted in my seat.

"That certainly wasn't what I'd expected to hear out of your mouth, Emily."

Just like that, the confidence faded, her face turning a deep shade of red. She pursed her lips and tucked her hair behind her ear, glancing away. Every uncertain gesture she made managed to be more charming than the last. I sat back, draping my arm over the back of the seat.

"Well, that's what you want, right?"

"Of course, it is. It's what I wanted since the moment I laid eyes on you." No sense in being coy about it. Hiding how I felt had never been my style.

A small smile formed on her lips, as if she were pleased to hear what I'd just said. The smile faded quickly, however, as she attempted to put her serious face back on.

"Well, that's what I'm intended for. My dad told me in no uncertain terms that I'm *not* to sleep with you, that if I did there would be consequences. I'm supposed to spend time with you, tease you, make you interested and make you want me, but to never give myself to you completely."

The words came quickly out of her mouth, fueled by nervous energy. I said nothing, letting her go on.

"And truth be told, it was kind of a relief to hear that. Not that I'm not attracted to you—I most definitely am—but I was a little scared about the idea of sleeping with a man for the first time. When Dad told me I didn't have to go through with it, that part of the plan was to hold back, I was relieved."

That provided even more confirmation that Charles was planning on screwing me over in one way or another. I tucked that bit of information aside for later, not wanting to interrupt her very informative little spiel in process.

Fire flashed in her eyes. "But now that I'm here with you, I don't give a damn what my asshole dad says. I should be able to lose my virginity when I want, and to *who* I want to lose it to. It's not a freaking bargaining chip that he can—"

I decided it was time for the rant to end. I placed my finger onto her lips, stopping the flow of words. Her eyes went wide and I could tell right away that she wasn't used to anyone touching her like that.

"Now, I want to ask you a question, Emily. And before I take my finger away, I want you to really give the question some serious thought. Understand?"

She nodded, my finger pushing her lips up and down.

"My question is this: what do *you* want?"

I left my finger there for a few more seconds, giving her time for the question to linger in her mind. When I was satisfied, I slowly took my finger away.

"What do *you* want?" I repeated.

She took a deep breath, then shook her head. "I don't know. I mean, I think I do, but I'm not really sure."

Emily took another sip of her wine, then rose from her seat. I watched as she began to pace back and forth slowly. I watched her make her way down the length of the plane, my eyes locked onto her perfect ass as she moved.

"I may be naïve but I'm not stupid. And most importantly, I'm not some little pawn that my dad can do whatever he wants with. I'm a woman who can make my own decisions."

My cock was stiff, my blood pumping hard in my veins, and her energetic little outburst was only turning me on more. I unbuckled my seatbelt and rose, cutting the distance between us. Once I was close, I clamped my hands down hard onto her hips, holding her in place.

Then, I kissed her.

I moved in quickly, planting my lips on hers, feeling the soft, plushness of her mouth against mine, traces of sweetness from the Moscato still on her lips. Emily's body tensed stiff and straight as a spear, and I held my lips there for long enough to send the message.

When I moved my face back her eyes were wide, her lips parted slightly in surprise. I was so turned on that I could hardly think straight, but I kept my cool all the same.

"Now," I said, speaking slowly and calmly. "I'm going to ask you one... more... time... what is it that *you* want?"

She moved her eyes up and down my body. By this point I was so hard that there was no way to hide it from her. Emily's gaze lingered on my manhood for a long while. She licked her lips slowly, her eyes wide.

"I want you."

Good. But I wasn't done. I took hold of her upper arms and brought her against my body.

"It's not enough that you just *want* me," I said. "I need you in total. You have to give yourself to me, consent to me, submit to me. Are you willing to do that?"

She nodded without hesitation.

"Say it," I said.

"Yes. I want everything you just said."

Music to my ears. I placed my hand on her hip, turning Emily around as I nodded toward the bedroom at the far end of the plane.

"Go."

She did as I commanded, swaying her hips as she made her way to the room. I followed, my cock so stiff that I felt on the verge of exploding. She stepped over the threshold of the bedroom and I did the same, shutting the door behind us and flicking the privacy switch for the cockpit letting the pilot know not to contact me unless it was an emergency.

The bedroom wasn't enormous, but it was more than big enough for our purpose. There was a queen-sized bed, along with a dresser and small walk-in closet. A pair of large windows over the bed allowed for a stunning view of the clouds and sky.

There was only one view that I cared about—the impossibly stunning woman standing before me. Emily stood with her arms at her sides, her eyes wide. I could sense that she didn't have any idea where to begin.

I was happy to guide her.

I stepped over to her, putting my hands on Emily's hips and bringing her body against mine.

"I hate to ask this but are you really a virgin?"

She nodded. "Let's put it this way... that kiss you just planted on me? That was the first *anything* I've ever done with a man before."

It was almost too much to process, that possibly the most beautiful woman I'd ever seen in person had never been touched by a man before. All the same, virgins could be trouble; clingy and needy. Not to mention that there was the distinct possibility that Emily was lying—that she and her father were in on it together, playing some game to get the better of me.

Didn't matter. If she was lying about being a virgin, I'd know the moment I entered her. I was inclined to believe that she was. Either Emily truly had never been with a man before, or she was an excellent actress.

"I don't know where to start," she said. "You're going to have to show me."

"It would be my pleasure." I placed my fingertips on her breast, moving my hand down over her belly. The fabric of the dress was soft and fine, pleasant to the touch. "First of all, this is going to need to come off."

She nodded, preparing to reach around her.

"Allow me."

I moved her hands down to her sides. Once they were there, I reached around and undid the zipper of her dress, taking it down slowly.

"Turn around."

She did as I asked. The zipper open, I was afforded a wonderful look at the slender form of her upper back, her body toned and her olive skin flawless. I placed my hands on her, sweeping the top of the dress aside and moving my fingers underneath the straps. I peeled the dress down, Emily watching me over her shoulder, her profile like something out of a classical painting.

Once the dress was off down to her waist, I stepped back, sitting down in the chair on the other side of the bedroom.

"Now what?" she asked.

"Now you take it off the rest of the way."

Her upper back expanded as she took in a slow, deep breath. When she was ready, she placed her hands on her hips, moving them underneath the fabric of her dress.

"Slowly," I said. "And bend over forward as you do it."

Without a word, she complied. Emily bent over slowly, taking her dress down over her hips and ass. Her rear was perfect, filling out a pair of pink, lacy panties, the color closely matching her dress. I kept my eyes on her, letting my gaze savor each new bit of exposed flesh. Her legs were long and just thick enough, her thighs soft and inviting, her calves toned.

When the dress was at her ankles, she stepped forward and out of it, leaving it in a pile on the floor.

"Now turn, slowly."

I watched her as she did what I asked, giving me a full view of her body clad in nothing but her pink bra and panties. I was certain that she was about the finest specimen that I'd ever laid eyes on. Her breasts were full and round, her shoulders slender, her stomach flat and soft, her hips wide. I didn't think it was possible to become any harder, but the sight of her before me took my erection to another level.

"Do you want me to take off the rest?"

I rose slowly, shaking my head. "No. I want that privilege to be all mine."

I stepped over to Emily, placing my hands on the soft curves of her hips. She gasped at my touch, the way my hands moved along her curves. I traveled up to the narrow small of her back, stopping once I reached her bra strap. With a quick, deft motion, I opened the clasp. Her eyes widened as I did, and I could sense she was doing her best to wrap her head around the idea that a man was about to look upon her naked body for the first time.

I brought the straps slowly down her shoulders, lowering the bra and exposing her breasts.

They were about the most perfect pair that I'd ever seen in my life. Round and just the right size for a handful, her nipples dark pink. I took them into my hands, squeezing them gently, rubbing her nipples with my thumbs. She moaned softly, closing her eyes and enjoying the way I touched her.

"That feels really good."

I couldn't resist leaning in and taking one of her nipples into my mouth, licking and sucking and tasting the subtle saltiness of her skin. She moaned louder, running her hands through my hair and holding me in place.

"Wow," she sighed. "Wow. *Wow*."

I repeated the motions with the other nipple, focusing on her taste, the way she breathed as I introduced her to the world of sexual pleasure. When I was ready, I let her breast drop from my mouth before standing back up.

I stood tall over her, as I did with most people. She looked up at me with those big, dark eyes, as if nervously awaiting what I had in store for her.

I knew just the thing.

I placed my hand on the small of her back, guiding her over to the bed and sitting her down. She shook slightly, and I put my hand on her thigh to calm her down.

"You OK?" I asked.

She quickly nodded. "Yeah. Fine. Just... this is all so new to me."

I grinned, glancing down one more time at her perfect tits.

"Let me ask you this, have you ever done anything with yourself before?"

She cocked her head to the side, slightly confused at my question at first. Her eyes quickly flashed with realization.

"You mean like... touching myself?"

"That's exactly what I mean."

She shook her head. "I mean, there have been a couple of times when I'd been in the bath with the showerhead..."

Her face turned a deep shade of red as she looked away in a bashful manner. The combination of shyness and her utterly gorgeous body was irresistible.

"Does that mean you've never had an orgasm?"

Her eyes flashed at the mere mention of the subject and she tilted her head down.

"I don't know."

I placed my hand on her thigh, squeezing it gently. "That's where we're going to start, then. I'm going to make you come."

She nodded, her eyes still wide.

"Oh... OK."

"But tell me first, is that what you want?"

Another nod. "Yes." She said the word quietly.

"Not good enough."

"What?"

"When I ask you a question like that, you need to look me in the eyes and answer. So, when I ask you if you want me to make you come, you look up, look me in the eyes, and tell me that yes, you want me to make you come."

She took a deep breath before bringing her eyes up to mine.

"Please," she said. "I want it. I want you to make me come."

It was about the sexiest damn thing I'd ever heard in my life, and I wasn't about to waste one more second before making it happen. I moved my hand along her thigh, inching closer and closer to the waistband of her panties.

I slipped my fingers underneath the band of her panties and pulled them down along her thighs, down to her knees. Emily watched me with wide eyes.

As she kicked her panties off the rest of the way, I leaned in to kiss her once more. Emily melted into the kiss, my hand finding one of her irresistible breasts as I teased her nipple a bit more. As we kissed, I moved my other hand to her pussy.

Emily gasped as I touched her, as I dragged my fingertips over her lips and gently spread them open. She placed her hand onto my wrist and for a moment I thought she might stop me, pull my hand away.

But she didn't. Instead, she guided me right where she wanted, just above her opening. I pressed my fingertip down gently, making slow circles.

"Oh... Oh, my God." Emily spoke with her eyes closed, her entire focus on how I touched her, how I made her feel.

"You like the way I touch you?" I couldn't help but grin as I posed the question. The way she sighed, the way she moaned, made it more than obvious that she did.

She nodded, caressing my hand and making sure that I didn't move it anywhere. I continued with my slow circles, switching my index finger with my thumb and placing my finger at her opening.

"You're so damn wet," I said, the grin still on my face.

Instead of responding, she nodded and bit down on her bottom lip, her hips bucking against my hand. With a slow push, I entered her with my finger.

Emily was tight, very tight. She gasped as I pushed inside, and the deeper I moved, the more certain I became that she was indeed a virgin.

And I was going to give her the greatest night of her life.

CHAPTER 6

EMILY

His long tattooed finger slid inside my pussy.

Agonizing pleasure radiated from my clit to the rest of my body.

His lips, slightly rough, sucked my nipples firmly, sending both pleasure and pain through my body. A stark contrast to the softness I'd imagined my first time would feel like.

Here I was in an unnervingly precarious situation, sharing the intimate confines of a bedroom aboard a luxurious private jet, hurtling through the skies towards the secretive allure of a private island.

I asked him to take my virginity. The question was why?

This man was my father's nemesis, and now, here I was, a pawn in their longstanding feud.

This was more than a physical conquest; it was a psychological battle against my father, and ultimately me.

The sensation of his touch was new and frighteningly intense.

Waves of nervous excitement mixed with a deep-seated fear rippled through me.

I knew what was happening physically, but the emotional turmoil was harder to grasp. I was inexperienced, a virgin caught in a game far bigger than a fleeting encounter.

His thumb brushed tentatively over my clit as he probed gently.

He was older, perhaps around my father's age.

I had to promptly push that thought out of my mind because... well...eww.

Regardless, Logan was teaching me a lesson about age – that with maturity came experience.

"Fuck, you're wet; I need to taste you," he whispered.

He lowered himself until his face was right between my legs.

His tongue explored cautiously, clearly aware of my inexperience. My hands braced against the bed frame, my legs shaking not just with new sensations, but also with a deep fear of the unknown.

I ran my fingers through his hair, a futile attempt to find some control in this situation.

"Take me," I murmured.

He groaned like an animal ready to devour his prey.

He pulled his head back, and the loss of contact made me let out a desperate whimpering sound. His pause made me glance down. My innocence was evident in my reaction, a mix of confusion and curiosity.

His thumb continued to move slowly, almost reassuringly.

"Don't worry baby girl. I'm going to make you come. You're going to come so hard you'll scream. This I promise you. And when we're done here, I'm going to take you to my island and have my way with you again and again."

I was silent, my mind racing. This wasn't just about me; it was a message to my father.

And based on how good he was at foreplay, he was probably right about the screaming part. I didn't trust myself to be quiet - and the fact we were smack dab situated on a plane with cabin crew - that would be a problem to say the least.

"I can't wait to drink your juices," he whispered, sliding two fingers into me this time, while his lips found another sensitive spot.

His fingers skillfully massaged my G-spot, triggering an intense reaction. Every part of me seemed to ignite with exhilarating pleasure.

Overwhelmed, I arched back, releasing a deep, primal moan as my body quivered. It was an overwhelming surge of ecstasy, the kind you hear about in books - but this time it was real. So freaking real.

He made a believer out of me.

As the waves of bliss subsided, so did my strength. Fortunately, Logan was there, supporting me and helping me move my body to the bed's edge as he planted his feet on the ground and stood up.

Staring up at him in this angle I was mesmerized by how large he was.

Then he undid his belt, lowering his pants and boxer briefs, revealing himself.

Holy fuck, he was impressively endowed, a fact that didn't escape me.

The sight caused a surge of anticipation.

"I'm ready to explode," he said.

He teased me as he rubbed his dick on my pussy, his voice low. "Tell me you want this."

"I want you" I breathed out.

He gently lifted my leg, guiding it around his hip.

"Tell me exactly what you want."

Despite my dazed state, I knew what he was asking. "I want you, to fuck me senseless with everything you've got."

"You sure about this?" he asked with a grin.

"I think so. Is this... really going to fit?"

"It will. If that's what you want."

"It's what I want."

"Then touch it."

I quickly swallowed my nervousness and moved my hand closer to his manhood. My fingertips grazed the tip, his cock twitching a bit in a way that caused me to gasp in surprise. Next, I wrapped my fingers around him slowly, closing my eyes and taking in the sensation of how he felt in my hand.

Logan's cock was solid, hard as a brick. It was warm, too, his pulse throbbing inside. I had no idea what I was doing, my mind racing as I tried to recall scenes from the books Marta had smuggled me. My hand gripping him, I began pumping Logan's cock slowly.

He growled a bit, a guttural noise as sexy as anything I'd ever heard. More than that, it was encouragement that I was on the right track, that I was touching him in a way that he appreciated. I decided to go down, stroking him all the way to the base of his cock and teasing his balls. I cupped them, kneading them gently, knowing how sensitive they were.

Logan's hands fell onto my breasts again. It wasn't long before a clear drop of liquid formed on the head of his prick. A strange sensation came over me, and without thinking, I leaned forward and flicked my tongue over his tip, dabbing up the liquid. It was sweet and salty all at once.

Something about my mouth on his cock must've stirred an animal desire in Logan. A surge of energy ran through him, and once more he took hold of my hips. This time, he brought me back onto the bed with a forceful sweep, stepping out of his clothes as he loomed over me at the end of the bed. The sight of him standing like that, his cock at full glory, was enough to make me more turned on than I'd ever been in my life.

He prepared to move over top of me, a small smirk forming on his lips.

"Tell me what you want," he said.

"You." The word came from my mouth without a moment of hesitation. "I want you. Please."

That was all he needed to hear. With an agility that was surprising for a man of his size and build, Logan swooped in over top of me, gazing down with those striking ice blue eyes. I met his gaze, once more feeling like I was under some kind of spell.

"I'm going to ask you one last time. Are you sure this is what you want?" His tone was deep and serious. I could tell there was an element of play to his words. But it wasn't just that—he wanted to make sure I *wanted* what was happening, that I had all the opportunity to get out of it.

Although I appreciated it, I became more and more sure of how I felt and what I wanted with each passing moment.

"Yes, I'm sure," I said. "Please, don't make me wait a second longer."

To prove my point, I reached down and took hold of his cock, gripping and stroking it and guiding it down between my legs. By that point I was so turned on, so wet, that I was certain he'd have no trouble entering me.

"Protection," he said.

"We're good on that," I replied. "I've been on birth control for years, my dad made me."

A flash of anger formed on Logan's face at the mention

of my dad and the hold he had on my life. The expression quickly faded, however, replaced by a look of intense desire.

He reached down, his head grazing my lips and clit and sending a fresh wave of arousal through me. I squirmed at the pressure of his cock against me, my hips bucking. Logan kept moving forward, his head parting my lips and positioning itself at my opening.

One more hard push and I wouldn't be a virgin any longer. I was thrilled and scared and aroused all at once.

"You ready?" he asked.

I nodded. "So ready."

"Good. I'll go slow. Tell me if it hurts."

Logan did just that, pushing his hips forward and driving down into me. First his head moved inside, and then the many inches of his shaft. The feeling of him penetrating me was like nothing else. The sensation was like being split in half in the best way possible. There was a brief bite of pain, but it quickly receded and turned into a satisfying fullness.

Logan positioned his arms on both sides of my head, and I gripped them tightly, digging my nails into his thick biceps as he pushed deeper and deeper inside, my eyes locked onto his manhood as it vanished between my legs.

It didn't take long before he was fully buried. Thankfully, Logan held still for several moments, giving me ample time to get accustomed to his size. Pleasure throbbed outward, the intensity enough to make me squirm.

As he held himself over top of me, gazing down with those stunning blue eyes, a thought occurred to me.

I wasn't a virgin any longer.

"How do you feel?" he asked.

"I feel... so good."

He grinned.

I grew bolder, placing my hands on his slim hips and guiding him back up. He rose, his cock sliding out of me just a bit before he pushed back down. He entered me with more ease the second time, my walls stretched around him. I was so impossibly turned on, so wet.

He buried himself to the hilt again, then pulled back. My eyes stayed locked onto his prick, his length now glistening with my arousal. Logan plunged in with more force, enough to shake my breasts, the intensity of the pleasure stronger than it had been before. He repeated, penetrating slow and deep.

"Just like that," I said. "That's... that's so good."

Logan answered my words by leaning down and sealing my lips with a kiss. His tongue found mine, the twin sensations of his tongue in my mouth and his cock in my womanhood like nothing else. I angled my hips, wrapping my legs around his waist and pulling him closer. Logan lowered his body, pressing himself down upon me, overwhelming me in a manner that blocked out the entire world except for the two of us.

His pace was steady, pushing into me and pulling out in a constant, unrelenting way that lulled me into a perfect trance of pleasure. I opened my eyes, letting my gaze jump from his handsome face to the bulging muscles of his arms to the tense flexing and release of his upper body. His cock entered me with piston speed, the pleasure building and building and building until...

"Oh... OH!"

The orgasm had built until it was impossible to resist, the pleasure going off like a bomb and ripping through me. I shook and moaned and arched my back underneath him, my hands gripping the broad spread of his upper back, my nails digging into his skin as I came hard once more.

Logan released with me, the sensation of his cock pulsing inside me adding a different, yet just as lovely layer to the climax. He grunted hard, his expression tightening as he drained himself. Knowing he was shooting himself deeply into me at the same time as my own orgasm was enough to push the pleasure even higher.

He finished, his muscles relaxing, his cock staying inside of me as the last traces of the orgasm slowly faded. When we were both done, he carefully slid his cock out of me, the warm trickle of his seed dripping down my inner thigh, creating a tickling sensation.

Logan moved next to me, wrapping my body in his huge arm as he held me close and tight.

CHAPTER 7

LOGAN

What the hell just happened?

I laid on the bed for a time, Emily curled up next to me, her eyes closed and a small, pleased smile on her face. Hell, I was having a hard time not smiling like an idiot after what we'd just done.

There was no doubt in my mind that Emily had spoken the truth about her virginity.

I listened to the engines of the plane, letting the fact settle in my mind that my plan was coming to fruition. The next step could wait... for the moment I was simply pleased to have a gorgeous young woman lying naked in bed next to me.

It wasn't long before she opened her eyes, that sexy little smile still on her lips.

"Hey," she said, her voice soft.

"Hey."

With a slow, fluid movement, she sat up and stretched her willowy, olive-toned limbs. I couldn't do anything but stare at her perfect body as she did.

"That was something else."

"It most certainly was. How do you feel?"

Emily pursed her lips, giving the matter some serious consideration.

"I feel... different. I don't know; maybe I'm just being silly. But I don't feel like the same person I was half an hour ago."

"You're fully a woman now. You know how a man and a woman can truly connect."

"I do," she said, smiling at me.

And that was my cue to get up. I didn't want to deflower Emily then toss her aside. All the same, I didn't want to risk her growing attached to me. She needed to know that, while this was a meaningful occasion for her, I wasn't going to become her boyfriend. An entanglement such as that had no place in my life.

I took her arm and lifted it from my chest, sitting up. Emily sat up along with me, the smile fading into a wary expression, uncertain at what was happening.

"This has been lovely, Emily," I said. "However, we've got a long flight ahead of us and I have quite a bit of work to do while we're in the air."

More confusion took hold. I could sense that, while she hadn't been sure of what would happen after the sex, being unceremoniously dismissed wasn't one of the options.

"There's a bathroom just across the hall. There's a shower and even a bath if you'd like to relax. Go ahead and wash up. Take your time. I'll grab one of your bags from the cargo area. Which one has your clothes in it?"

She regarded me with a stunned look. Finally, after several seconds, she shook her head and came back to the moment.

"Uh, the one with pink trim."

With a nod, I stepped over to the closet and plucked out a towel, handing it over to her.

"Come on, I'll show you to the bathroom."

She got off the bed as if in a daze, joining my side without a word as we left the bedroom. There were two doors—one that led to a private office area where I could take calls and work in peace, the other leading into the bathroom. I opened the door and gestured inside.

"Fancy," she said, her voice soft.

The space was just as nice as the rest of the plane, with gold and white décor, a shower on one side and a corner tub on the other.

"The plane carries plenty of water, so don't worry about taking too long," I said. "Is there anything else I can get for you?"

Still in a daze, she spoke. "Just my bag."

"Of course. I'll get it and place it just outside the door."

"Thanks."

With one more nod, I left the bathroom and shut the door behind me. A moment later, a strange noise came from the other side. The door was thick so I couldn't quite make out exactly what it was, but it sounded like a groan or moan, or perhaps a sob. Whatever it was, it was a noise that suggested Emily wasn't happy with how things had gone down.

So be it. She needed to know that what we'd done was a one-off thing, that she shouldn't expect anything else from it. It might've hurt her to know that the man who'd taken her virginity wanted nothing to do with her in a romantic sense, but that was life. Really, I was doing her a favor.

As I left the hallway and returned to the main area of the plane, I considered that the sex hadn't at all been me merely doing her a favor—there had been much in it for me, too. Not only had I slept with a beautiful young woman but I'd done the deed of sticking it to her asshole, idiot father. With a simple few minutes of fun, I'd ruined his precious daughter's innocence for any man who might have her. On top of that, I was certain that once Emily had time to get over whatever rejection she was feeling, she'd be pleased to realize that she'd had such a chance to stick it to her dad.

I couldn't take the smile off my face as I opened the hatch to the belly of the plane and descended the ladder. I was a man used to getting what I wanted, but rarely did it happen so quickly.

I spotted Emily's bag with the pink trim in the luggage area. Once it was in hand, I returned to the main cabin and to the back hall, preparing to place the bag against the door. A bit of turbulence hit at that moment, however, causing the handle of the bag to thump hard against the door. The shaking only lasted for a couple seconds, thankfully.

"Are you OK in there?" I asked.

"Fine." A few beats of silence followed. "Hey. Can you open my bag and take out my little kit? It has my shower stuff in it."

"Of course."

I took the bag into the bedroom and set it onto the bed, unzipping it and taking a look inside. What caught my eye first was the zipper pouch on the inner flap of the bag that contained Emily's underwear. My eyes settled on a black, lacy thong. I couldn't help but imagine her wearing nothing but the skimpy pair of underwear, a sly smile on her face, her hands cupping her full, round tits.

Just like that, I was hard again. Part of me wanted to march right over to the bathroom and throw the door open, strip down and climb into the shower with Emily, and ravish her once again. As enticing as the idea was, I put it out of my head as quickly as I could. Sleeping with her again might send the wrong message. I needed to play things smart.

I spotted her bathroom kit, taking it out of the bag. I zipped the luggage back up and stepped over to the bathroom. The hush of running shower water sounded on the other side, and I gave the door a firm knock so she could hear me.

"Emily? I have your kit."

"Can you bring it in? I just jumped in the shower."

I opened the door, a blast of steam greeting me as I stepped into the bathroom. Just as I'd anticipated, the shower screen was closed, Emily's slender, curvy figure blurry on the other side. The erection that I'd finally managed to get down was returning with a vengeance.

"Got it here," I said, starting toward the sink. "I'll set it—"

I didn't get a chance to finish before the shower door opened, another burst of steam coming from inside. I turned, and as the cloud dissipated, Emily's figure became more visible. The steam cleared away, leaving me with a perfect view of her standing beneath the shower, water cascading down her glistening, wet body as she ran her hands over her head. Her hair was soaked, clinging to her neck and drawing attention to her stunning face. Her long legs were firmly planted, one hip cocked to the side.

The way she looked in that moment reminded me of some sort of classical statue, as if the most skilled sculptor in history had tried to capture Aphrodite in marble. I couldn't help but stare like an idiot, my cock pulsing to life.

Finally, Emily stuck out her hand toward me. I wanted to take it, to pull myself into the shower, push her up against the wall, and give her the screwing of a lifetime.

"Hey." Her voice over the sound of the shower brought me back into the moment. "Can you just hand me that? I don't want to have to get out."

"Yeah. Sure."

As I stepped closer to hand over the bag, a thought occurred to me. Emily might've been new to the world of sex and seduction, but there wasn't a chance in hell she was clueless to the effect the a gorgeous, soaking wet, naked woman had on a man. I wanted her like mad, and it took all the restraint I could muster to simply step over and hand her the bag.

Surprise flashed over her face when I did. Clearly she had expected me to not be able to resist her. "Thanks," she said.

"I'll be out there if you need anything else."

With that, I pulled my eyes from her body, hurrying out of the bathroom and shutting the door behind me. I breathed a sigh of relief once I was out, the temptation at least out of sight. I hurried into the main room, finding my glass of red wine where I'd left it and taking a sip as I eased into the seat.

This was already shaping up to be a bit of a mess, I realized. The plan had been to take her virginity and be done with it. But already I was finding Emily hard to resist. Her subtle way of trying to seduce me left me quite certain I could go back into the bathroom and give her what we both wanted.

Thankfully, the door to the front of the plane opened. Estella, the copilot and a Virgin Islands native, stepped out.

"Hey, *jefe*," she said, shutting the door behind her. "Sorry about the shakiness a bit ago. Hit a little patch, you know?"

I waved my hand through the air, dismissing the idea. "Don't worry about it."

She smiled slightly, bowing her head. "John's got the flight under control, so I figured I'd come back here and see if there was anything I could make for you or our guest."

I grinned. I'd hired Estella not just for her piloting skills, but for the fact that she was an excellent chef.

"Yeah, some food sounds great. Something simple, maybe?"

"Simple." She leaned to the side, giving the matter some thought. "Picked up some flank steak that I've been meaning to put to good use. How about that with a little chimichurri? Beans and rice and tortillas to round it out."

"Sounds perfect. And make a little extra for our guest."

Estella winked. "You got it, *jefe*."

She marched past me, disappearing into the back of the plane. I finished my wine, the matter of Emily still weighing on my mind and pushing me to pour another glass. I did, sipping as I stood by one of the plane's larger windows, the clouds rolling down below, the brilliant blue sky above.

I felt a little like an ass. There was no doubt in my mind that Emily had been hurt by what had happened. Her attempted seduction in the shower was possibly her way of trying to find out if she was anything more to me than a one-and-done piece of meat. She was a grown woman and was more than capable of making her own decisions. All the same, no one liked to feel used.

What was done was done. We'd slept together and I wasn't about to risk making the situation between us more complicated by doing it again. My beef was with her father, and if Emily had her feelings hurt in the process of my getting revenge, then that would be regrettable collateral damage.

I felt like shit. And even more disturbing, I felt a tinge of regret.

Nothing to be done about it. I had a month ahead of me with a gorgeous woman, and I was going to have to play it smart. There would be no room for error, or desire.

CHAPTER 8

EMILY

I felt like a freaking idiot. I wasn't the most skilled girl in the world when it came to seduction, but how the hell had I screwed up all but offering myself to him on a silver platter? What was the deal? Had I been good enough to deflower, but not good enough for another session in the shower?

Tears formed in my eyes as I finished washing myself. The worst part was that I had no idea why I'd even done it. We'd just had sex, did I really want it again that badly?

The more I thought about it, the more the real reason for my clumsy seduction attempt dawned on me. I'd felt strange after Logan and I had slept together, mainly because of the sudden and cold way he'd turned off his emotions.

I wasn't stupid. I hadn't expected him to pull out a damn diamond ring and propose to me on the spot, nor did I want that. I'd slept with him for two reasons—the first was to piss off Dad. I still needed to break the news to him, but as far as I was concerned it was mission accomplished.

The second reason was that, well, I'd *wanted* to. After so much time reading about sex and watching movies about it, I wanted to know what it was really like. And the verdict was... it'd been pretty damn good. Logan, as mad as I was at him, had been an excellent lover. My first time hadn't hurt much at all, and there'd been no doubt in my mind during it that I was in the hands of someone skilled.

But showing him my body like that and having him turn me down had been hard to swallow. I felt rejected, used and silly.

The worst part was that I couldn't blame Logan for anything. We hadn't done anything that I hadn't eagerly walked into. Heck, he'd gone out of his way to make sure I'd been cool with everything we'd done together. If I'd wanted to stop it, I could've done so with a single word.

Still, he didn't have to be such a jerk afterward. What possible motivation could he have for being so cold to me so soon after we'd had sex? It slowly began to dawn on me with horror the possibility that he was some kind of ladies' man, the kind of guy who slept with women for fun and to have another notch on his damn bedpost. The guy was a billionaire, and no doubt used to getting what he wanted, when he wanted it, on his terms.

Why would I be any different?

Part of me wanted to stay in the shower forever, to spend the entire flight in there. It was a silly thought, so I turned off the water and reached for a towel. I dried myself off, taking my time. Every second I spent in the bathroom was one that I didn't have to be around him.

When I was ready, I wrapped one towel around my hair and the other around my body, heading into the bedroom. My bag was on the bed, and I opened it. Right away, my eyes went to the lacy black thong in my underwear pouch. I took it out, holding the panties in front of me, a small smile on my face. No doubt Logan would love the sight of me in these. I almost wanted to put them on, then march into the main part of the plane and really give him something to stare at.

I wanted to do that not for the purpose of seducing him, but for a different reason—to show him what he wanted but couldn't have. Sure, he'd turned me down in the shower, but I saw the way he'd stared at me, the way his mouth had opened, and his eyes locked onto my body. Maybe he'd be able to resist me once, but not twice. I wanted to tease him, to dangle myself in front of him but not let him take me.

God, what had Logan awakened in me when he'd taken my virginity?

I pushed the idea out of my head as I stepped into my panties. Once those were on, I went for a matching bra, along with some simple blue jeans and a comfortable, navy-blue hoodie. There was something about the idea of being dressed sexy underneath while comfy on the outside that was very appealing to me, like I had a secret I was keeping from Logan.

I dried my hair a bit more, putting it into a simple pony-tail before leaving the bedroom and returning to the main space of the plane. My stomach tensed as I stepped into the room, knowing that Logan was there. He was seated at the small dining table off to the side, his laptop open in front of him, a small scattering of papers to his left. He was busy at work, glancing over to his laptop before jotting notes down onto the papers.

Suddenly, a smell greeted me—the delicious scent of cooked steak. I noticed that there was a plate to Logan's left, a neat spread of steak along with some beans and rice and tortillas, a little dish of dark green sauce next to the plate.

It smelled really, *really* good.

Logan kept his attention on his work, not so much as turning his head to greet me.

I went to the bar, taking out a bottle of mineral water and cracking it open before sliding into a seat on the other side of the aisle. Logan stayed focused, the gentle scrawling of his pen on paper blending with the low roar of the engines.

We sat without speaking to one another, tension building in the air by the moment. At least, tension on my end. For all I knew Logan was so engrossed in his work that he hadn't even noticed I was there. I sipped my water, casting glances out the window onto the carpeting of fluffy, white clouds, the shimmering blue ocean peeking through the breaks.

"There's more if you want it." Logan's deep, powerful voice snapped me out of my daydreaming.

"Huh?"

Slowly, he set down his pen before turning to me.

"Food. Flank steak with chimichurri. It's excellent. And there's plenty if you want some."

My stomach growled at the mention of food. "God, something to eat sounds great. I wasn't hungry before, but I guess I worked up an appetite—"

I stopped myself, my face going red. Logan regarded me with a blank expression before chuckling to himself, then turning his attention back to his meal and work.

Without another word, he pressed a nearby button. The door to the front of the plane opened seconds later, a trim, pretty Latina woman who appeared no older than thirty-five stepping out, a warm smile on her face.

"Hello there, *señorita* ! I'm Estella. Something I can get for you?"

Her English was perfect, aside from a slight accent. The

fact that she spoke Spanish, however, gave me an idea.

"*Tu hablas Español, si?*" I asked.

Estella's eyebrows raised in surprise. "You speak it?" she replied.

"Since I was a little girl. My nanny's from Mexico."

Logan perked up. I could sense that he realized that a conversation had started that he wasn't able to understand or participate in.

Good.

"That's so lovely to hear. I have to say, you speak it beautifully."

I smiled. "That's so nice of you to say."

She matched my smile with one of her own. "Anyway, I made some food for the boss, and there's plenty if you'd like some."

"Chimichurri, right? I'd *love* some."

"And to drink?"

I opened my mouth to say water, the only drink that Dad allowed me to have most of the time. No calories in water, after all. Before I said the word, a thought occurred to me.

"Is there Coke back there?"

"Sure is. Even got the good Mexican kind in the glass bottles with the real sugar."

My mouth watered at the idea. "One of those, please. And extra steak."

"You got it."

Estella winked before heading off. I turned my attention to the TV viewing area—a small, cozy little space with two rows of couches situated in front of a decent-sized flatscreen TV. I moved over, plopping onto one of the couches and picking up the very complicated looking remote.

"Hard to make heads or tails of that thing," Estella

spoke in Spanish, approaching with a plate of sumptuous-looking steak tucked next to fresh beans and rice. The meal was served with a portion of delicious green chimichurri and a small stack of foil wrapped tortillas. She placed the spread in front of me before popping the top off the bottle of Coke with an opener.

"My Dad... he doesn't really let me watch TV. No idea how to use this thing."

Estella set the drink down, a quizzical expression on her face. I could guess what she was probably thinking—*why the hell would a dad not allow his adult daughter to watch TV?* If that was indeed the question on her mind, she didn't ask it.

"This thing's got all the streaming stuff—Netflix, Amazon, HBO, Disney... here." She pressed a few buttons on the remote, turning on the TV and bringing up the menu. "Just use the arrows, then press this button to select. The button that looks like a little house takes you back to the home screen."

With that, she handed over the remote. I held it for a time, staring at all of the icons on the screen, each one representing a different streaming option.

"You OK?" Estella asked. "Want me to show you again?"

I shook my head, coming back into the moment. "No, it's not that. It's just... I've never done this before."

"Watched TV on a plane?"

"No, not that. I've never just sat in front of a TV like this with the remote in my hand being able to *pick* whatever I wanted to watch."

Estella cocked her head to the side, regarding me as something quite curious.

"Well, you can watch whatever you want for the entire

flight and no one's going to give a damn, especially not me or Mr. Stone. Though, I might suggest these." She opened a small compartment to the side of the couch, the top popping up and revealing a pair of fancy-looking headphones. "Press the button on the side and you can turn them on. The round button next to that turns on the noise-cancelling. Mr. Stone tends to get, ah, a little animated when he's on his business calls, so you'll get some use out of that."

I couldn't stop beaming. "Thanks, Estella."

"Of course. Let me know if you need anything else."

With that, Estella turned to leave. A thought occurred to me as she did, my eyes lighting up with excitement as it dawned.

"Hey, Estella?" I asked in Spanish.

"Yes?"

"There's a full kitchen back there, right?"

"About as full of one as you can get on a private plane."

"Does that mean there's... ice cream?"

Estella laughed. "You bet there is. A few different flavors, too."

"When I'm done with this, if I still have room, would it be possible to have some?" As I spoke the words, I realized that a tinge of hesitancy was in my voice, as if Estella were going to snap at me for daring to ask for a treat.

Estella cocked her head to the side. "Let me ask you, when's the last time you've had ice cream?"

I opened my mouth to speak but then froze. I had no idea.

"Um, not really sure. Oh, wait! My nanny snuck some in a year or so ago. It was really good, leftover Ted and Jerry's."

"*Ted* and Jerry's?"

"That's what it's called, right? The brand with the two

guys on it?"

Estella let out a lighthearted laugh. "Pick out something to watch. I'll be right back."

She turned and left without another word. Confused, I picked up the remote and selected Netflix. I couldn't believe how many shows were there, thousands and thousands of whatever kind I wanted to watch. After a little browsing, I picked *Emily in Paris*. It looked lighthearted and cute and a little glamorous, with plenty of romance. And it didn't hurt that I shared a name with the protagonist.

The title screen came on and right as I was about to reach for my headphones, a big bowl of ice cream appeared in front of me. I sat up, unsure of what I was seeing.

"Ever had chocolate chip cookie dough ice cream before?"

"Never in my life. But it sounds amazing."

"My mother used to say, 'life is short, eat dessert first.' Not sure if I agree with her one hundred percent, but in this case, I think it's definitely in order."

With another wink and smile, Estella left and headed to the back of the plane. Without waiting another second, I grabbed the bowl and took a bite.

It was delicious. The sweet creaminess of the vanilla ice cream was the perfect complement to the chewy bits of cool cookie dough. I couldn't help but let out a moan of pure pleasure.

"You alright over there?" I glanced over my shoulder to see Logan looking up from his work.

"Fine. Don't you worry about me."

With that, I went right back to ignoring him as I slipped on my headphones, pressed play, and took another bite. Why shouldn't I have dessert first? After all, I'd already had a hell of a main course.

CHAPTER 9

LOGAN

"Mr. Stone, we're about thirty minutes from landing." The pilot's voice snapped me out of my work focus. I glanced up, my eyes landing on Emily as she watched another episode of her program.

She was pissed. That much was obvious.

I'd noticed it the instant she'd emerged from the back of the plane after her shower, the way she'd stormed past me, her wet hair leaving behind the most intoxicating scent I could imagine.

It was fine with me. Perhaps she had a right to be upset after I'd taken her virginity and given her the cold shoulder. We had a month to spend together, and if she wanted to pass it with a sulking silent treatment, that was her prerogative.

Still, I couldn't help but notice how distracting she was. Even something as simple as the way she ate a big bowl of ice cream while laughing along at her TV show was impossibly charming. Her light, lilting giggle punctuated by the occasional snort was adorable. And though it was clear she was attempting to pointedly exclude me by speaking in

Spanish with Estella, I was impressed at how easily the previously isolated Emily was able to make a friend.

I didn't get much work done on the flight, truth be told. Again and again, I found myself looking over at Emily, my gaze moving over her body and settling on her gorgeous face. It was impossible not to stare, to watch as a smile spread across her face at some on-screen joke.

She was irresistibly charming. The fact that she didn't know how charming she was only increased the effect.

The TV automatically paused any time the pilot made an announcement. Emily took off her headphones and turned in my direction.

"Does that mean we're about to land," I said, preempting her question.

"We're almost there?"

"That's right."

"Wow, time flies when you're binge-watching."

"I wouldn't know, never been much for TV."

"Why am I not surprised?"

I chuckled, shaking my head as I closed my laptop and began putting away my things.

"Watch the window," I said. "Quite a view."

She narrowed her eyes a bit, and I could sense that she was bristling at my command. Even so, she rose and sat down in one of the passenger seats, fastening her seatbelt and turning to look out of the window.

I did the same, sitting in the row behind her. Amid the seemingly endless blue of the Caribbean Sea, the smattering of the Virgin Islands provided a sharp contrast with their verdant greens.

"Where are we landing?" she asked, her eyes still on the window.

"Near Charlotte Amalie on St. Thomas," I said. Largest

city in the U.S. Virgin Islands. From there, we'll sail to my island."

She didn't reply, instead taking in the view as we drew closer and closer to the ground. It wasn't long before I could spot the port of Charlotte Amalie. A pair of massive cruise ships were in the bay, a very common sight from above.

We descended further, and I could make out a tense expression on Emily's face. No doubt the novelty of flying hadn't settled in just yet. As we descended, I felt the overwhelming urge to take her hand once more, as I'd done on the way up.

I decided against it. Emily was still upset with me, and there was no doubt that she'd reject my offer of comfort.

We touched down, a gasp sounding from her as the wheels connected with the pavement. The plane raced down the runway, the rolling, green hills surrounding the airport a blur as we moved.

"Is this normal?"

"It's normal. We speed up, then we slow down."

She didn't have anything to say after that, instead choosing to have a white-knuckle grip on her arm rests. The plane soon slowed down, coming to a stop near the private airfield's terminal. A chime sounded to let us know that the flight was over.

"That's it?" she asked.

"That's it. We're here safe and sound."

A breath of relief escaped from her. Emily quickly unbuckled her seatbelt and stood up, stretching and shaking the anxiety from her limbs.

"Wow. You do this all the time?"

"All the time. When you fly as often as I do, you don't even think about it."

She pursed her lips and glanced away.

The speaker came on once more. "Welcome to the Virgin Islands, Mr. Stone and Ms. Marone." The voice on the intercom wasn't the pilot's, but Estella's. "It's a beautiful seventy-four degrees, with not a cloud to be seen. The private car is pulling up now, and as soon as the stairs are secure, we'll have the doors open and you both on your way. A pleasure flying with you as always, Mr. Stone."

I watched out of the window as the stairs pulled up to the door, the runway staff taking a moment to put every-thing into place. Estella came out from the cockpit, eagerly walking over to Emily, both speaking in Spanish as they chatted about one thing or another. I could sense from their gestures that they were discussing the flight.

The door opened moments later, a rush of warm air tinged with a bit of humidity coming into the cabin and intermingling with the chilly dryness inside. I was beyond eager to take in some sun, to have a little time on the water.

"Ready?" I asked, rising and coming around to offer my hand to Emily.

She regarded my hand with skepticism. "Ready." Instead of taking it, she turned brusquely away and headed toward the door.

Estella and Emily chatted quickly in Spanish, finishing the conversation with a warm hug. Estella led Emily the rest of the way to the door and gestured down the stairs. I followed behind as we descended.

The sun hit me right away, a pleased smile spreading across my face as I closed my eyes and let the warmth hit me. After a rough New York winter and chilly spring, a little bit of paradise was just what I needed.

About halfway down the stairs, Emily stopped so abruptly that I nearly walked right into her.

"Something wrong?"

She said nothing at first, simply looking forward.

"It's... I don't know. It just hit me that I'm thousands of miles away from my dad. I'm not free. But this is the closest I've ever been."

I didn't reply at first, letting her words hang in the air. It was a candid admission, considering she was still upset with me. It was also one to which I couldn't relate. Ever since I was a young man I came and went as I pleased. Sure, I was responsible for the company, but it was *mine*. Answering to anyone was something I simply didn't understand.

"The views get better from here," I said. "Come on, we've got a bit of a trek in front of us."

We reached the ground, the staff already waiting with our bags. A sleek, black Land Rover awaited us. I nodded to the crew to load the bags inside. Once more, Emily held her personal bag close, as if someone might pluck it from her at any moment. I was curious as to what was inside but didn't want to pry.

Once the bags were loaded into the back of the car, I took the keys from the staff member and went around to the passenger side to open the door and help Emily inside.

She paused once she realized what I was doing.

"I'm more than capable of getting into a car on my own, you know."

I chuckled, stepping back and sweeping my hand toward the interior of the car.

"Then don't let me stop you."

Seconds later, I was behind the wheel. I opened a compartment just above my head, letting a pair of Ray Bans fall out and into my hand. I slipped them on, started the engine and took one more look at Emily to make sure she was OK. She sat with her bag on her lap, her arms folded over top of it.

"Ready?" I asked.

She nodded without saying a word. I pulled forward, taking us onto a winding road offering a sweeping view high enough to see a large part of the island of St. Thomas and the ocean beyond.

"Let me give you the lay of the land," I said as I drove. I pointed toward the water. "That's Charlotte Amalie, the largest city in the Virgin Islands. Now, when I say, 'largest city,' don't think of New York. Charlotte Amalie is around eleven thousand people, meaning you could tuck it into Brooklyn and not notice it for a week. That's the port and our destination. Our first one, at least. We'll be taking my boat to the island from there. Whenever we want to get out and about and have some fun, we will come back here to St. Thomas."

She said nothing, and I could tell that Emily was content to silently take everything in on her own terms. No doubt that going from her isolated life with her father in Long Island to paradise was something she'd need a little time to wrap her head around.

We drove on. I put some classic rock on the player, The Rolling Stones flowing from the speakers as we made our way to the port. The city was a resort paradise. American tourists in Bermuda shorts, flowered shirts and Panama hats packed the streets, locals mixed in among them. The Virgin Islands were a popular destination for the wealthy, and it was clear just by looking at the tourists that they had money.

"We can come here if we're looking for something to do," I said. "Lots of restaurants and cafes and places to shop. I have most of my supplies airlifted in, but now and then I'll take the boat over to do my own shopping and take in the culture."

It wasn't a long drive at all to reach Charlotte Amalie. I drove to the docks, dozens of boats of all shapes and sizes floating in the harbor, the place alive with activity. I parked, another squad of staff there to take out our bags and bring them to the harbor. A lovely breeze hit us just as we stepped out of the car that made me want to get out of my heavy business clothes and change into something linen.

Speaking of clothes, as we made our way to the harbor, I couldn't help but imagine what Emily might choose to wear once we arrived. I pictured her dressed in a skimpy bikini, her olive skin glistening with oil as she lounged in the sun. I was going to give her space while she stayed with me, but the mere idea of her dressed like that was enough to make me want to pounce on her the moment we reached the boat.

"Here we are," I said, gesturing to a modest-sized boat, a motor sailor with the word *Serendipity* written on the side. I nodded to the staff, instructing them to load the bags into the boat.

"This is nice," she said, approaching the boat as it bobbed in the water, placing her hand on the side.

The *Serendipity* wasn't that big; about the size of two large trucks placed in front of each other.

"I can't believe you have a boat. I mean, my dad has one, but it's about half this size, just something big enough to take out fishing."

"If you like this, you'll love the other one."

She turned to me, cocking her head to the side in confusion. "The... other one?"

I chuckled, casting a glance at the staff as they stowed the last few bags. I tossed the car keys to one of them.

"This is the way I get back and forth between Saint

Thomas and my island. My *other* boat, the one I use for cruising, is at my place."

Emily regarded me with more confusion, her mouth opened slightly. I couldn't help but chuckle.

"Come on," I said. "The ride over to the island isn't long, but I'm ready to get there and relax."

She nodded again, that overwhelmed expression still on her face. Emily was so overwhelmed, in fact, that she actually took my hand when it was offered to her as I helped her onto the boat. Once aboard, she sat down on the U-shaped couch that half-circled the back end of the deck, putting on her seatbelt as I got situated at the controls.

Once the harbor staff gave the all clear, I started the boat, the powerful engine growling to life as it warmed up. The *Serendipity* was easy to drive, was similar to handling a large truck. After a little maneuvering, I was out of the harbor and on the open ocean.

A big smile spread across my face as I drove. I was a city guy at heart, and nothing could compare to the magic of New York. However, there was something to be said for being out on the ocean, the sun bathing you in warm light, the hush of the waves carrying the salt rich air all around you. I savored it, allowing the pleasure of the water to momentarily push aside the distraction of what might have been the most beautiful woman I'd ever seen in my life.

It didn't take long at all before our destination was in sight.

"See that?" I asked, pointing up ahead at a white object in the distance.

Emily squinted, focusing on the object. "Is that a *yacht*?"

I nodded. "That's the *Endeavor*, my main ocean vessel.

One of the finest ships on the sea if I do say so myself. It's parked at my estate. We're nearly there."

She nodded, not taking her eyes off the middle distance.

"That whole island... it's yours?"

"It is."

Emily shook her head in disbelief as we drew closer. The estate was visible before too long, the multibuilding complex causing a feeling of relaxation to wash over me just at the sight of it.

"Let me tell you about the place," I said, putting the boat on autopilot and turning to face Emily. "It's more a complex than a house. It's eight buildings in total, but three of them are for logistics—bedrooms for the staff, a warehouse for supplies, and a garage. The main building has ten bedrooms and twelve baths, a pool, and just about everything else you could possibly want. There's a path that makes its way across the entire island, with a branch that leads to the very top. The island isn't huge—about three square miles in total, a little over twice the size of Central Park. But that's more than enough space for my needs."

I pointed toward the center of the island, a tree-covered rise smaller than a mountain but bigger than a hill.

"Very nice views up there, and the perfect distance from the house for a hike or jog. There's a hot tub, live-in chef, private grotto... plenty to keep you busy. I also have a private arrangement with Amazon, so whatever you need can be delivered nearly as quickly as anywhere else in the country."

Her mouth hung open as the estate grew larger, the sandy strip of private beach cutting under the palatial form of the main building.

"There are rules, however," I went on.

"Rules? What kind of rules?"

"You're mine for the next month," I said. "In case you needed a reminder. While you're allowed to go anywhere you like on the island, you're not allowed to leave without my permission."

She laughed. "Well, duh. Where would I go? I can't even drive a car, let alone steal a boat."

"That makes matters a little easier, then. Anyway, you'll have your own bedroom, and free rein of the house. You can go wherever you like, aside from my private office. It's locked, so you won't be able to enter. Even so, you're not allowed inside under any circumstances without my explicit permission."

She said nothing, but I could tell her mind was racing with possibilities of what might be in there. Fine with me, she could wonder all she wanted.

"The head of household matters is a woman named Pearl Shepard. She's worked with me since I've owned the island, and she's about as capable a manager as they come. You need anything, she's the one to talk to. Roberto Sanchez is the head of security. Barring any unforeseen happenings, you won't need to speak to him. Just know that there is a staff of four security guards on duty at all times. If anything strange happens, or you feel unsafe for any reason, he's the man to inform."

I considered my words after I spoke. Charles was planning something for certain. For all I knew, Emily was in on it with him. Nothing to be done about it at that exact moment in time, but I'd need to have a meeting with Roberto sooner than later.

The boat brought us closer to the shore, allowing a better view of my yacht.

"This is insane," Emily said, rushing over to the side of the boat to get a better look at the massive vessel.

"She's just over three hundred feet long, three stories high, and like the estate, has just about every amenity you could want. There's a helipad, a pool and hot tub, and eight bedrooms below."

She said nothing, her silence letting me know just how impressed she was.

"Where can you go in that?" she asked. "I mean, it's like a floating palace."

"Wherever I want. She stays in the Caribbean, mostly, though I'll take her up and down the east coast quite often. We've even gone all the way to Europe once. Let me tell you, if you're going to spend two or three weeks at sea, *Endeavor* is the way to do it. Don't worry—we'll take her out for a spin during your month here."

Just the sight of *Endeavor* was enough to put me in a relaxed frame of mind. Nothing back in New York required my attention to be onsite, so it was more than feasible to do a little work at sea.

I turned my focus to the dock, spotting a tall, imposing figure awaiting me. By his height and powerful frame, I could tell right away that it was Roberto. He waved me in, and within a few minutes I was moored.

I hopped off the boat and onto the deck, turning to assist Emily.

"Roberto," I said, offering my hand for a shake. "Good to see you."

"Likewise, my friend."

We shook, his big mitt about as large as mine.

Roberto Sanchez was one of my most trusted employees. A former lieutenant in the Mexican Special Forces, I'd used my contacts to scoop him up within a month of his retirement when I had need for a head of private security. He was forty-three, built like a brick wall, his hair long and curly, the same ink-black color as the thick moustache under his nose. He was all angles, built like an action figure. He did good work for me and was one of the few people I trusted with my life. As such, he was one of the most well-compensated members among the thousands of men and women on my payroll.

He was gruff as they came, too. Roberto crossed his arms over his barrel chest, furrowing his brow at the sight of Emily.

"This the girl?" Roberto's English was perfect. Aside from the Northern Mexican accent on his words, there was no indication he wasn't a native speaker.

"Hi," Emily said, offering her hand. "I'm Emily Marone."

Roberto sized her up once more. No doubt he, like me, was keenly aware of how gorgeous she was. The consummate professional, however, he gave her the sort of once-over that made it clear he wanted to know if she was trouble.

"Roberto." He took her hand and shook it in a professional and polite manner. He didn't say another word before turning to me. "The staff will come for your bags, Logan."

"Excellent," I replied. "Let's get inside. I'm desperate for a little rest and relaxation."

With that, we started toward the house. Emily made her way in front of me, my eyes going right to that perfect ass of hers.

With a wry smile, I considered how rest and relaxation weren't the only things on my mind. I could behave myself, sure. But with a woman like Emily, I had to ask myself the question of *how long?*

CHAPTER 10

EMILY

Everything felt so damn surreal. Logan and Roberto, both huge, hulking men, strode just behind me as we made our way toward the enormous estate, the green of the island, the white of the beach and the blue of the ocean combining to paint a perfect picture of paradise.

I could hear Logan and Roberto speaking in low, quiet tones to one another. I couldn't quite make out what they were saying, other than that the subject of their conversation seemed to be Logan wanting to make sure the security of the island had been bolstered.

It was strange. Did Logan really think that I was going to try to escape? I'd told him that I had no idea how to drive, well, *anything*. Did he not trust me? Or was there some other reason why he wanted to make sure that security was boosted?

Either way, the conversation ended when Logan's phone rang. He clapped his hand on Roberto's shoulder to signal that he was happy with whatever they'd talked about, then slipped his phone out of his pocket and took the call.

"This is Stone. Sure, go ahead."

With that, he slowed his pace until he was well behind us, far enough that I could only hear the uttering of his conversation and not the words. I spotted Roberto ahead and decided that this would be a good time to get to know the man who was either in charge of my safety, or in charge of keeping me prisoner on the island—depending on how one chose to look at the situation.

"Hey," I said, hurrying up to his side. "How are you?"

Roberto turned his head slowly. Like Logan, he was the sort of man who didn't do anything in a rushed manner. Even behind his pitch-dark aviator sunglasses, I could sense that he was sizing me up in the way he likely did with everyone he met, giving them a once-over and determining whether or not they were a threat.

No doubt he decided that a woman half his age and height was nothing to worry himself about, at least for the time being.

"I am well, thank you."

"You speak Spanish, right?" I asked, switching over to that language.

Another skeptical look. "Yes, I do." He didn't give away anything more than a direct answer to any of my questions.

"I've been speaking it for years, ever since I was a little girl. I'm excited to have so much opportunity to practice it."

He grunted, his eyes fixed forward. The noise suggested without words that he didn't give a damn whether or not I was excited about practicing my Spanish. I decided to try another angle.

"So, this whole thing with me living on the island... it's weird. Nice, but weird. I'm sure that you've got a ton of stuff on your plate managing security normally, and having another person to worry about probably only makes your job harder. Is there anything I can do to, well, maybe make it easier?"

He said nothing at first, the silence dragging on long enough for me to wonder whether or not he'd simply decided to end the conversation.

"You're an unknown factor," he finally said. "Follow the rules of the house, stay out of the way of my men, and we'll get along just fine."

The certain way he finished the sentence sent the message that this was the end of our little getting-to-know-you chat. Roberto seemed to ease up a bit, suggesting that my efforts in trying not to be a pain in his ass had done a little good. I made a mental note to work on him a bit more, see if I could get on his good side.

I smiled at Roberto one more time before falling back a bit, taking the opportunity to admire my surroundings. The estate was stunning. A sandstone path led from the dock all the way to an enormous gate, behind which was the complex itself. The style of the buildings was what I'd consider palatial, with columns and high roofs and arched doors. There were modern touches, however, like the floor-to-ceiling windows that looked out over the property.

I breathed in the salty air, closing my eyes and smiling as the sun warmed my face. Sure, the place was just as much of a prison as my home in New York, but it didn't *feel* that way. Rather than being confined to my room for most of the day, I had the run of the island. I could wake up with the sunrise and start my day on the beach with a dip into the sea.

Freedom was what I wanted. In the meantime, my month with Logan was shaping up to look pretty damn good.

The gates opened as we approached, leading into a

gorgeous courtyard garden that seemed to function as the middle grounds between the buildings of the estate. The main structure, a three story mansion, was straight ahead past the garden and fountain. To the left and right were smaller buildings, along with a shimmering pool and a warehouse-like structure that appeared to be a garage.

Once we reached the center of the garden, just before the circular fountain of dark granite, the flowers and trees surrounding us, Logan finished his call. He tucked his phone into his pocket before saying something else to Roberto, who responded with a nod before giving me one more skeptical look and then leaving.

"I have to get to work," he said.

"Work on vacation?" I asked. "That's no way to relax."

Logan let out an amused snort. "When you're in my position, you don't get vacations, only different office locations. The staff is around if you need anything. Remember, Pearl is the woman in charge of non-security estate affairs. You need anything, ask her."

He didn't wait for a response before turning and leaving. I watched as he ascended the white steps up to the main building, the tall, arched doors automatically opening. Logan stepped inside and was gone, leaving me alone.

The second he was gone it dawned on me just how out of my element I was, not to mention how little information Logan had given me about the estate. Logan was in his office, and Roberto was nowhere to be found. I turned toward the dock in the distance in just enough time to watch as a small team of three finished loading our bags into the back of a Jeep before heading off to only God knew where.

I was alone in the middle of a freaking private island, no idea which room was even mine.

Pearl. Logan had said she was the head of household affairs. Maybe if I could find her, or at least one of the other members of the staff, I could get some help finding my way around the place. My mission in mind, I started off through the garden.

I couldn't believe how beautiful the space was. Flowers of all colors surrounded me, the wind hushing through the branches of the palms overhead. The garden was laid out in a neat and symmetrical design, reminding me of French gardens that I'd seen in travel books Marta had given me. I loved it. I imagined curling up on one of the hanging benches with a book and letting the hours pass, not a care in the world.

Not knowing where else to go, I left the garden and headed to the right, taking the path between the main building of the estate and the smaller structure beside it, which seemed more like a modest-sized house. Through the windows I could see a sleek, modern kitchen and other well-appointed rooms. But I didn't spot a single soul.

It was actually quite peaceful. Dad's place was always so busy with staff running here and there, Dad storming through the halls shouting into his phone and slamming doors. Being alone, knowing that I was one of a handful of people on an entire island, not to mention thousands of miles away from my father, was enough to bring a sense of calm over me that I hadn't known in a long, long time.

I made my way around the smaller building, coming out onto a quaint veranda that wrapped around the back half of the structure. The view looked over the beach in the middle distance, the waves crashing onto the shore with a quiet hush.

Right away, I noticed that the sounds of the beach wasn't the only noise in the air. A soft, melodic humming came from somewhere nearby. It didn't take me long to spot the source—a young woman was sitting on a swinging bench, pushing herself forward with her foot as she worked on something, a pleasant smile on her face.

I moved toward her slowly, not wanting to startle her. Whoever she was, she was totally focused on what she was doing. As I moved closer, I saw that she had a sketchbook on her lap, her right hand moving in quick, precise lines as she drew. She sat like that without noticing me, rocking back and forth and humming to herself as she sketched.

I wanted to get her attention. At the same time, I didn't want to surprise her. Not knowing what else to do, I cleared my throat and smiled.

The woman turned her head toward me. In spite of the distance between us, I noticed that her eyes were a brilliant ice blue—the same color as Logan's. Before I had any time to think about it, a huge, broad smile spread across her face. She set down her pencil and book and sprang from the swinging bench, spreading her arms wide as she hurried over to me.

"There you are!"

I didn't have a chance to react or respond before she threw her arms around me, pulling me into a tight hug. She squeezed me with enthusiasm, hard enough to wonder if she knew her own strength. I let out an *urk!* which seemed to signal to her that it was time to let go.

She did, and it took a moment for me to catch my breath.

"You're stronger than you look!"

The smile stayed on her face, her expression not flinching a bit.

"Sorry, Logan says I can get a little too excited sometimes. It's just that he told me you were coming and I've been sitting here anxiously waiting to meet you."

As she spoke, I noticed that there was something slightly strange about her, something about her eyes. She smiled innocently, almost like a little girl. Her eyes were big and eager, not a trace of distrust or skepticism behind them.

"Wow," I replied. "Then I feel like you've got me at a disadvantage."

She cocked her head to the side a bit, her forehead crinkling in mild confusion.

"You've got me... what?"

She didn't understand what I was saying.

"I feel like... you know more about me than I know about you."

At those words, the smile returned to her face.

"Oh, I get what you're saying." She followed her words with a light, lilting laugh. "You probably think I'm so weird, just running up to you and giving you a great, big hug when you don't even know who I am."

"Are you Pearl?" I asked.

As soon as the question left my mouth, I knew that it was wrong. The young woman in front of me, as friendly as she was, just seemed a bit *off*—not a trait I'd expect in someone who was in charge of running an entire estate. Not to mention the matter of her striking resemblance to Logan.

"Pearl? You think *I'm* Pearl?" Another laugh followed, her hand going to her mouth. "I *wish* I was as smart as Pearl. She's *so* good at her job. She has *so* much stuff in her head all at once..." she shook her head in disbelief. "I have no idea how she does it all." She smiled again. "I'm Marianne, Logan's little sister. And you're Emily, right?"

"That's me." I allowed myself an easy smile, a bit of

relief taking hold now that I knew who I was talking to. "So nice to meet you, Marianne."

Marianne was so excited that all she could do was squeeze her hands into fists and let out a happy squeal. Her eyes lit up, as if she'd realized something.

"Do you want to see what I'm drawing?"

"I'd love to."

"Come on!" She took my hand and guided me over to the bench where she'd left her sketchbook. Once there, she picked it up and held it in front of me with two hands.

The drawing was amazing. It was of one of the trees ahead, the palm rendered in perfect, photorealistic detail, all the way down to the texture of the leaves and the palm fronds. I couldn't believe what I was looking at.

"Marianne, this is *incredible*. How long did it take you to do this?"

She pursed her lips and looked away, giving the matter a bit of thought.

"Hm. Well, I just woke up from a nap an hour or so ago. Then I had my lunch. Then I came out here. So... twenty minutes?"

"You made *this* in only twenty minutes? That's so good!"

Marianne's eyes lit up even more. "You really like it?" Without a moment's hesitation, she ripped the page out of the book, folded it in half, and handed it over. "Then you can have it! I mean, if you want it, that is."

I took the drawing, giving myself another second or two to admire how incredible it was before folding it back in half and tucking it into my pocket.

"Thank you so much. I haven't seen my room yet, but I have a feeling I'm going to need to decorate it. This'll be perfect for that."

"I'm glad you like it. If you want me to draw anything else, just let me know, OK?"

"I will."

Before either of us could say another word, a voice spoke from behind me.

"Now, Marianne, are you being nice to our new guest?"

Marianne's eyes lit up once more. "Of course, I am!"

I turned around to see a stout, serious-faced woman with swept-back graying hair. She stood with her hands on her hips, the universal pose for "no nonsense." She projected an air of authority, intelligence, and competence. There was no doubt in my mind that I was looking at Pearl.

"You're Emily, I assume," Pearl said coming over to me and offering her hand.

"That's right. And while we're assuming, are you Pearl?"

A small smile broke the seriousness on her face that let me know she wasn't all business.

"You got it," she said. "Pearl Shepard—the caretaker for this oversized estate where you've found yourself. Pleasure to meet you. So, I'm going to guess that our humble host didn't bother to show you around the place?"

I chuckled. "Sorry to laugh. Just that there are a lot of words I'd use to describe Logan, but *humble* isn't one of them."

Pearl laughed along with me. "Nothing like a little comedic irony to start the tour. So, the crew has your bags in your room. I'll finish up the tour there since I'm sure you're ready for a little rest."

"You're right about that. But I'm really eager to see this place."

"Then come with me, I'll show you around." She glanced over my shoulder at Marianne. "You mind giving us a little privacy, Mary-Moo? I'm going to show Emily here to her bedroom."

Marianne's eyes flashed. "I can see her later, right? Oh! Tonight's movie night! Can she watch with us?"

"We'll have to see how she's feeling. Emily came all the way from New York, so she might need a little relaxing on her own."

"Movie night?" I asked.

Marianne nodded eagerly. "That's right. Every Friday night. And I get to pick whatever I want." She grinned with pride. "Oh! And there's popcorn and soda too. But you don't have to eat that; the staff are really nice and they'll make you whatever you want. Last time, I had nachos with extra cheese."

My stomach grumbled at the mention of nachos. "That sounds so fun. Let's do it!"

Marianne let out a squeal, clasping her hands together in excitement. "It's going to be so much fun!"

"Let's not overwhelm Emily," Pearl said, putting her hand on my upper arm and leading me away. "We can talk about movie night later."

"So nice to meet you, Marianne!" I said, waving as Pearl and I made our way around the corner.

"You too, Emily!"

With that, we left the veranda and started back toward the garden. Pearl waited until we were a little bit of distance away before speaking.

"That was sweet of you, the way you were back there."

"She seems really nice. I was happy to meet her."

"You're right about that—Marianne's as nice as they come. But, as I'm sure you noticed, she's a little different. Mary-Moo's twenty-five, but here..." she touched the side of her head with her fingertip, "...she's only around twelve or so. No one's really sure what happened with her. She grew up like a normal girl, nothing physically wrong. But around the age when she should've begun to grow into a woman, her mind just stopped."

She shook her head, as if the mystery of the situation still puzzled her.

"Logan, who's over a decade older than her and was already high up in the company when we realized what was going on with Marianne, vowed to take care of her no matter what. When their parents passed, he became even more adamant about it."

Her words settled in my mind. Logan, who seemed like such a standoffish jerk at times, clearly had a heart big enough for his disabled sister. The revelation made me immediately view him in a different light.

"So, she lives here?"

"It depends. Logan likes to keep her close, but Marianne loves it here on the island. And with a staff here to attend to whatever she needs, it makes sense to not take her out unless it's necessary. Speaking of which, might as well start the tour here." Pearl swept her hand toward the house we'd just passed, the one that the veranda was attached to. "This is Marianne's place."

"She has the whole house to herself?"

"Sure does. She's pretty independent, for the most part. Mary-Moo can do all the important stuff on her own. But now and then she'll need a hand with things, so we're never too far away. Just over there." Pearl pointed to the building on the other side of the garden, a tall, three story structure that was just as big as the main building. "Those are the staff's quarters. As you can see, the big man takes good care of us. Logan can be... well, I'm sure you know how he can be." She chuckled in a good-natured sort of way. "But he makes sure we all have plenty of living space and whatever else we need."

We returned to the garden. I was still stunned by the sheer size of the estate.

"You alright over there, little lady?"

I smiled, coming back into the moment. "Just trying to wrap my head around all of this. I thought the house where I grew up was big, but you could put it right on the island and not even notice."

"That's Logan. He's a hard worker but he enjoys the finer things. Come on, I'll show you the rest of the place."

She guided me up the stairs of the main building. Once at the top, Pearl turned and gestured. Where we were standing allowed for a panoramic view of the property, all the way down to the dock where the *Endeavor* was moored.

"You've got the garage over there," she said. "Pretty nice cars inside if you're into that kind of thing. That building over there's for gear and storage. Over that way is the guest house, though *house* is hardly the right word for it, it's more like a small hotel. Then you've got the pool house."

"I can't believe how big this place is." I felt silly saying the words, but it was how I felt. Everything was so much bigger than the bedroom where I'd spent most of my life up to that point.

"It's good to be a billionaire," Pearl said, nodding toward the doors to the main building behind us. "And it's good for those of us who work for him."

"Really? What's Logan like as a boss?"

"He's tough and demanding. Not everyone can hack it working for Logan. But if you can prove yourself to him, he'll take very good care of you. He pays well, and there's benefits out the wazoo. And..." She trailed off, as if not sure how to phrase what she had next on her mind.

"What is it?" I asked. "Sorry, kind of being nosy."

"No, it's fine. You have a right to know what sort of man you've hooked yourself up with."

She had no idea how accurate those words were. Pearl opened the front doors.

"Logan can seem like a hard man. Hell, he can seem like a real prick at times. And I tell him when he's out of line. I'm probably the only member of the staff who has that right with him. But he's different than you might think. He actually gives a damn about us, and not just as employees. He always gives time off for family matters or anything else that might come up."

"That's sweet of him."

"You have no idea."

With that, the tour of the main building began. Pearl showed me everything—from the massive, industrial kitchen to the movie theater downstairs, to the private grotto and up to the rooftop party area. The place was like nothing I'd ever seen before, a true palace on an island. We reached my room at signaling the end of the tour. It was a perfect, little one room suite with a sitting area, a huge bed, and a balcony with a view of the trees below and the ocean beyond, a pool right below me.

"This work for you, kiddo?" Pearl asked.

"This works," I said with a grin, ready to get the month started, the ocean breeze gently blowing in past the linen curtains. "This works just fine."

CHAPTER 11

LOGAN

I t was her scent.

It was day two of Emily living at the mansion, and though I'd only seen her in passing, I couldn't get her out of my mind. She flitted through the house like a spirit, the only traces of her being a vanishing glimpse around a corner, or her laugh echoing down the hall.

But most of all, it was her scent that drove me wild.

I'd step into a room and it would be there, lingering in the air, that faint aroma of lilacs and lavender and something sweet. I didn't know if she wore perfume, but something told me it wasn't that—it was something more natural.

On one hand, I was relieved that the estate was big enough where I could go an extended period of time without seeing her. After all, how the hell would I be expected to get any work done with such a distraction? On the other hand, I found myself strangely... missing her. I couldn't think of the last time I'd so keenly felt a woman's absence. Typically, it was the other way around—women with whom I'd had brief flings trying their best to get me to make time for them.

Being on the other side of such a situation was odd. Minutes ticked by as I watched the waves roll in, the third floor of my office affording a sweeping view of the water and sand below, all the way to St. Thomas in the far distance.

A knock sounded at my door, the noise snapping me out of my daydreaming. The firm rapping let me know right away that Roberto was there.

"Come in."

The door opened, Roberto silently stepping inside and shutting the door behind him. His expression was blank and impassive, all business.

Something was up. I straightened in my seat and gestured for him to take one of the chairs across from me. Roberto sat down, placing his hands on his knees and sitting up straight, as if awaiting my command.

"You wanted to speak with me?" I asked.

"I did. I'll get right to the point. My men have spotted a strange boat that we believe has been making circles around the island. I don't like the looks of it."

"A boat? What kind of boat?"

He leaned over, reaching into his bag and taking out a manilla folder. He rose and set it on the desk. I wasted no time opening it and taking a look inside.

The folder contained five photos. The craft looked to be mostly inconspicuous, a simple motorboat that appeared to me like a United States Coast Guard vessel.

"Coast Guard?"

Roberto shook his head. "That's what they want you to think. Look closer. Look at the men on the ship, and the identifying markers."

Holding the pictures in front of me, I brought them closer to my face. A knowing grin spread as I noticed what he was referring to. The logo, which at first glance appeared to be that of the Coast Guard, was actually quite different, but almost impossible to tell when one glimpsed it. The crew's aviator glasses made them look like Coast Guard members, but their casual clothes gave away that they were anything but.

"Hard to tell right away, right? It was only thanks to one of the men who was able to spot that the logo was off that I even noticed it. I gave the real Coast Guard a call, but the boat was long gone before they showed up."

I tossed the pictures onto my desk, sitting back and weaving my hands together over my middle.

"So, we've got a boat impersonating the Coast Guard, trying to get close enough to scope us out."

"That's right. You thinking what I'm thinking?"

I let out a snort. "Marone." The name hung in the air like a bad smell as I thought the matter over. "Alright. First of all, who was the staff member that spotted the boat?"

"Esteban."

"Give him a thousand dollar bonus. That's the kind of work I want to see rewarded."

"Consider it done."

I tapped the desk in consideration. "No doubt Marone's scoping us out. I had a feeling he was going to pull something. Just didn't think he'd do it so soon."

"The girl?" Roberto asked. "You think she's in on it?"

"My gut says no." I glanced out the window for a long moment before turning my attention back to Roberto. "What's your take on this?"

"Someone's doing recon—of that I have no doubt. And they likely already have the information they were looking for. My suggestion is to make that information useless."

"How do you mean?"

"I know a crew of five trustworthy security agents on St.

Thomas. You give the word and I'll have them here before the day's out. We might not be able to stop Marone from trying anything, but we can sure as hell have a surprise waiting for him if he does."

"Make it happen. Find out their rate and pay them that plus twenty percent. I want them here and eager to work."

"You got it, *jefe*. And is there anything you want me to do about the girl? We're going to be keeping a team close, especially if she goes to the beach or on a walk."

"Do that. But give her as much space as you can. I don't want her to feel like a prisoner."

Roberto nodded. "Sure thing." A small, knowing smirk appeared on his face. Roberto was the picture of professionalism, but now and then he'd let his more human side show. "Have to admit, *jefe*, I'm a little surprised that you're not volunteering for personal bodyguard duty."

"And what's that supposed to mean?"

He chuckled. "Just saying, couldn't help but notice the tension between you two."

I pursed my lips for a moment. "Let's focus on the task at hand, Roberto."

He laughed, rising from his seat and taking the folder off the desk. "I'll take that as me being on the mark. Don't worry—secret's safe with me. That is, if you're planning on keeping it a secret."

Roberto chuckled, leaning forward and giving my desk a tap as he prepared to leave.

"I'll keep you posted on any changes."

I nodded, not saying a word as he turned to leave, shutting the door behind him. I sat in silence for a time once Roberto was gone. It wasn't that I was upset that he'd pointed out the tension between Emily and me. Roberto and I had that kind of friendship—not to mention that it was his job to notice such things.

No. The issue was that I wasn't keeping my feelings in check. It'd been not even two days since Emily and I had met and I was already letting too much slip. The worst part was that *I* wasn't even sure how I felt. She was stunning, sure, but what else was there?

I spent the rest of the afternoon and early evening in the office taking care of New York work matters, only breaking to spend a little time in the gym. Pearl brought my dinner to me in my office, as she so often did, and I quickly polished off my braised short ribs with my eyes on my computer monitor.

"You know," Pearl had said when dropping off my food, "there's a whole gorgeous dining room down there that doesn't ever seem to get used. Hell, I'd be happy with you taking dinner in the nook even, instead of wolfing it down while working."

I chuckled. "Nooks are a luxury that I don't have time for. How's our new guest?"

"Settling in nicely. And she's already thick as thieves with Marianne."

The statement sparked a bit of warmth in me. My sister might've had all she needed here on the island, but all the same I was pleased to know that she had some company other than her sketchbook and my staff.

"Great to hear."

I'd gone back to work, the sun setting with wild colors over the ocean behind me as I finished up for the day. When seven rolled around, I made the executive decision that a ten hour workday was more than enough. I stood and stretched, trying to decide how to spend the rest of my evening, settling on a little time in the library with some whiskey and a good book.

I made my way down the stairs, the automatic lights of the hallway flicking on as I walked. It didn't take long to reach the library on the second floor, and as I approached the door, I heard the sound of quiet conversation.

I drew closer to the door, finding myself hoping to find Emily in there. As I stepped inside the library, however, I only saw my sister. Marianne stood in front of one of the many tall shelves, moving her finger over the spines of the books placed there.

"Would she like this... maybe. Wait! She said that she's barely read anything... I bet that means she hasn't even read Harry Potter. Oh, that's such a good idea."

I smiled, watching Marianne zip here and there, plucking books off the shelf and tucking them into the huge stack under her arm. My sister often spoke aloud to herself, it was her way of keeping her thoughts in order. I was content to watch her for a time, but when she put one book too many under her arm and nearly dropped the whole stack, I hurried into the library to help her.

"Easy there, sis," I said, putting my hand on her shoulder and using the other to steady the books. "Looks like you're biting off more than you can chew."

Marianne blushed, an innocent, bashful expression appearing on her face, the smile that always reminded me that she was different.

"Sorry, Ev," she said. "Just got a little excited, I guess." Her eyes flashed. "It's just that Emily said she's barely read any books! Well, books like these, anyway." She cocked her hip to the side and turned her arm, showing me the spines of the books.

I tried to get a sense of what they were. I took one off

the top and examined the cover, which depicted a couple, both seeming to be no older than their late teens, in an embrace in front of a full moon. The boy's eyes glowed a deep red, trees surrounding them.

"*Wolf Fever*," I read aloud. "I don't even want to know what this is about."

Marianne grinned. "It's *so* good. It's about a girl who moves to the forest to escape her mean mom and gets protected by a pack of werewolves."

I chuckled. "Classic literature, huh?"

She narrowed her eyes. "Don't make fun. Anyway, Emily should like these."

"Are you taking them to her?"

Marianne gave a crisp, affirmative nod. "I sure am. But Emily said she's a fast reader, so I figured that means I need to bring a lot."

"How about something a little more sophisticated?" I asked, turning my attention to the shelves. "Ah, here we go, *A Tale of Two Cities*. Good book, not too hard to read."

"Yeah, not hard for *you*, maybe. But didn't you hear what I said? Emily wants romance stuff. She said she usually only reads old books when she's not working on her own."

That got my attention. "Her own what?"

"Her own book!" Marianne's eyes flashed. "Oh, shoot. I wasn't supposed to say anything about that."

Too late, she already had my interest. "Emily's working on her own book? What's it about?"

Marianne shook her head. "No way. I already screwed up by telling you about it. I don't want her to get mad at me."

"I doubt she'd be mad at you, Mar."

"Not going to work. When I promise to keep a secret, I

keep it." She turned back toward the shelf. "Oh! *Nightwing Lover*! She'll love this one!"

Caught up in her excitement, she reached for the book so quickly that the stack under her arm became unbalanced, falling out of her grasp. I moved in quickly, grabbing the stack and squeezing it from the top and bottom to hold it in place.

"Oh, shoot!" Marianne regarded what had happened with wide eyes. "I almost dropped it!"

"Good thing big bro was here, huh?" I replied with a wink.

"Yeah, good thing! That would've been a huge mess."

In that moment, a plan occurred to me that would allow me the chance to see the woman I'd been thinking about nearly nonstop for the last two days.

"How about this, Mar," I began. "You're taking these to Emily, right?"

"Right!"

"Then why don't I help you? Grab whatever books you think she'll like, and I'll carry them there with you."

Marianne smiled broadly. "That's a great idea! If you're helping, I can bring her even more books!"

With that, she went back to work. I set down the stack of books on the nearest side table as Marianne collected more, fixing myself a whiskey neat as she did. I sipped and watched, listening as my sister spoke to herself, sharing her thought process for why she was choosing the books she was.

"There!"

When she was done, she had a whole other stack of books. I did a quick guess, and between the two it appeared that she'd gathered nearly two dozen books.

"Now, I'm sure Emily is a fast reader," I said. "But do

you really think that she's going to read about a book a day while she's here?"

Marianne shrugged, not put off in the slightest by my words. "Maybe. But this way she's got more than she needs."

"Can't argue with that. Come on, let's bring them to her."

Marianne picked up one stack and I grabbed the other. Together, we headed in the direction of Emily's room. To my surprise, with each step we took closer to where she was, I found myself growing more excited, like some teenage boy getting ready to pick up a girl for their first date together.

It was strange. I couldn't remember the last time, if ever, a woman had made me feel that way.

I put the emotion away as we stepped up to the door. Marianne, the stack of books barely balanced under her arm, rushed over and knocked.

"Hey! I'm here! You *have* to see all of these awesome books I got!"

"Alright, give me a sec."

I could hear her moving about in there, the excitement returning. The door opened seconds later.

I wasn't prepared for what I saw.

She was dressed in nothing more than a pair of very short cotton sleeping shorts that showed off her perfect, shapely long legs, along with a tank top. Her nipples poked through the thin fabric, letting me know right away that she wasn't wearing a bra. Her hair was in a messy bun, and there wasn't a drop of makeup on her face.

In spite of all that, or perhaps *because* of it, she looked so stunning that it took all the restraint I had not to ogle her. I wanted her like mad, my cock shifting to attention.

"Logan!" Emily's eyes flashed at the sight of me.

Surprise showed on her features at first, followed by annoyance. "What are you doing here?"

I laughed. "Don't be so excited to see me."

She opened her mouth to speak. Before a single word came out, however, she glanced down at what she was wearing. Emily gasped, ducking behind the door and returning with a robe. She pulled it on, but the short length barely did anything to cover up her body.

"Look at all these books we have!" Marianne, oblivious to the subtext of what was happening, held up her stack. "Oh man, you're going to love these. Let me get them set up and I can show you what I brought!"

Marianne hurried into the bedroom, leaving Emily and I face-to-face. A touch of awkward silence hung in the air.

"Everything to your liking so far?"

"It's great. I mean, better than great. The bedroom is amazing, the views are out of this world and...," she grinned. "I especially love your Netflix account."

That got a laugh out of me. "You mean you didn't have one of your own?"

Emily shook her head. "Nope. Only allowed to watch approved documentaries and G or PG movies. And trust me, there are only so many times you can watch *Blue Planet* before the magic wears off. Marta managed to smuggle me a few racier things here and there, though."

"Well, you're more than welcome to watch whatever you want here. And Marianne can give you a grand tour of the library. Though, as you can see, she had us bring about half of it up to you."

Emily smiled. "That'd be great."

"Speaking of which, thanks for spending some time with her. I try to take good care of her, but as you can tell, she's a little starved for friendship here."

She shook her head. "It's my pleasure. She's a really sweet girl, not to mention an amazing artist. She showed me some more sketches and... *wow*."

"The sketches are great, but did she show you the gallery yet?"

"The gallery?"

Right at that moment, Marianne appeared to take the other stack of books from under my arm.

"Hey, Mar," I said. "How about tomorrow you take Emily over to your place and show her your gallery?"

Marianne's eyes lit up as if she couldn't imagine a more fun thing to do.

"Yes! I'd love to!" Another thought seemed to occur to her, my sister's excitement going up another level. "And I heard you both talking about Netflix... maybe tomorrow we can have a sleepover at my house? I can show you the gallery, we can have the staff make pizza, and we can watch a movie. I want to see *Bridesmaids*! But then again, that might be a little adult for you."

Emily laughed. "I think I can handle it. And that sounds awesome. I'd love to do that."

"Great! Now, can I show you some of these books?"

"You sure can."

Marianne shot me a pointed look that made it clear that this was girl time.

"Let me know if you need anything," I said. "And good night."

Emily smiled, her expression suggesting that the conversation had gone a little better than she'd been expecting. Marianne already in the middle of explaining one of the books, I shut the door and stepped away.

There was no denying it—Emily was getting under my skin. As if her beautiful body weren't enough, the way she treated my sister brought my attraction to another level.

Two damn days and I already couldn't get her out of my head. I wasn't protecting myself like I should, but damned if I could help it.

CHAPTER 12

EMILY

"Come on! You both have to see this!"

The following night the pizza was in the oven, Netflix was loaded up in the movie theater, and everything was set for a fun night with Marianne. The day had been perfect too, most of it spent either on the beach or in the library. I was still getting my head wrapped around my new freedom, but I was settling into it nicely.

"Easy, sis." Logan spoke in a tone of dry amusement, as Marianne pulled him down one of the halls of her house. "You're going to take my arm out of the socket if you're not careful."

I was still majorly on the fence with Logan, and not even close to forgiving him for how he'd treated me on the day we'd met. All the same, I knew for certain how I felt about his relationship with Marianne. He loved her and would do anything for her. However busy he might've been, whatever was on his mind, he always made time for her, always made sure she had his full attention.

It was enough to make me view Logan in a different light. He might've appeared cold, but the love he had for his sister caused me to wonder what other parts of his personality he was hiding away behind that hard, prickly exterior.

"Come on!"

Marianne's house was adorable. The rest of Logan's property was done in the same sort of sleek, modern style with the occasional flourish, but Marianne's house was pure coziness, with farmhouse colors and furniture, pictures of inviting landscapes on the walls.

"Here!" Marianne stopped in front of a set of doors, her chest rising and falling as she caught her breath. "Geez, Logan! I think you're getting fatter!"

"Pardon?" Logan raised an eyebrow in mild confusion.

"You're like trying to drag a boulder!"

I couldn't help but laugh, bringing my hand to my mouth. Logan shot me a glance of wry amusement.

"Anyway," Marianne said. "I was originally going to just bring you here to the gallery, Emily. But I decided that it was time for me to show Logan what I've been working on, too."

Logan crinkled his brow in mild confusion. "And what is it that you're working on, exactly?"

Marianne reached over and gave him a playful shove. "I can't *tell* you, that would ruin the surprise! But if you get your big butt in here, I can show you!"

With that, she opened the door and stepped inside.

"You too, Em! I mean, your butt's not as big as Logan's, but you get what I'm saying."

Logan and I shared a look of amusement at his sister's words.

Things between Logan and I had been strange. I'd made the decision to give him the cold shoulder after the way he'd treated me when we'd slept together. As time went on, however, I was finding it harder and harder to do.

Of course, how goddamn hot he was didn't help matters. Logan was dressed casually, in khaki-colored linen pants, black loafers and a navy-blue button up shirt. He was the perfect blend of island cool and New York professional, and it was nearly impossible to take my eyes off him.

"Come on," he said to me. "Let's see what my sister has to show us."

Without waiting for my reply, he headed into the room. I followed.

The studio was beautiful, the back wall one big window that looked out over the ocean, the sun setting in the distance with gorgeous colors over the water, the palms spread out before us, the water sparkling as though it were magical. The other walls were covered in paintings, all of them hidden behind cloth. A table in the middle of the room was packed with painting supplies. An easel was in the center of the space, the painting it held also covered.

"This place is amazing," I said. "But... can I look at any of these?"

Marianne shook her head. "I can show you all my projects later. I like to keep them covered when I'm working —it makes it easier to focus on what's in front of me. And with what I'm working on now, I want it to have all of my attention."

Logan stepped over to the easel, taking the fabric cover and lifting it a bit.

"How long are you going to keep us in suspense for, Mar?"

Marianne's hand shot out, giving her brother a quick rap on the knuckles.

"Not so fast!" she exclaimed. "I need to introduce it."

Logan dropped the cloth, another amused smile on his face. "Fine, fine."

Marianne took her position in front of the easel, clasping her hands behind her back and squaring her shoulders. When she was ready, she cleared her throat and began.

"I don't paint people very often," she said. "People can be complicated, and hard to draw. Not to mention that not everyone wants to sit still for a painting. So, for this piece, I decided to paint the only person I know so well that I didn't *have* to have him sit down—I know his face by memory."

She turned to Logan and smiled.

"It's you!" she said, beaming. "I think it's my best painting ever. Well, so far, at least." Marianne glanced away for a moment, as if giving the matter some serious thought. The smile returned to her face, and she gave a crisp nod, seemingly deciding that yes, this was her best painting ever.

"You did a painting of me?" Hesitancy edged his words.

Concern appeared on Marianne's face. "Are you mad? I mean, no one else has to see it. I just thought it'd be nice, you know?"

Logan offered an easy smile, placing his hand on his sister's arm.

"Not mad at all. Just surprised."

Marianne grinned. "That was the idea. I wanted it to be a fun surprise!"

My eyes went to the easel, curiosity building by the moment. I'd noticed in the main house that there weren't any pictures of Logan, Marianne, or any other family members. Logan didn't seem to be sentimental in that way at all. The idea of him having a painting of himself seemed odd. All the same, I couldn't wait to see what Marianne had created.

"I can't wait!" I said, clasping my hands together.

Out of the corner of my eye, I could see that Logan was

still hesitant. He stood with his brow furrowed, his hand on his chin.

"Alright! Without further ado..." She took the cloth by the top and lifted it, exposing the painting.

On the canvas, he was dressed in a sharp suit, standing before a half-finished background of New York, the setting his office. He seemed aloof. One hand was on his desk, the other tucked into his front pocket. Everything about him in the painting seemed intense and unapproachable.

At first, I found myself wondering if it was an uncharitable depiction. The more I looked at it, however, the more I realized that it was truly accurate. Logan was as cold and unapproachable as he appeared in the painting. His power, not to mention his good looks, had been captured excellently. But Marianne had caught something else, too. It was that intangible wall that Logan put out, the way he could instantly construct a barrier between himself and anyone else with just a look or a word.

I knew that wall all too well.

Silence hung in the air. It wasn't long before worry appeared on Marianne's face.

"Do you guys... not like it?"

"No!" I replied. "It's not that at all. I mean, it's incredible. But good art makes you think. And this is definitely good art."

Marianne grinned with relief. "OK, great." Her concerns partially relieved, she turned to Logan. "What about you?"

More silence followed. Logan kept his eyes locked on the painting. Whether or not he was doing it intentionally, his hand was in his pocket the same way that Marianne had painted.

Finally, he spoke. "Why do I look so angry?"

Marianne appeared confused. "Angry? Do you think you look angry in the picture?"

"A little bit." I could sense that Logan was measuring his words carefully, not wanting to make his sister upset. "It's that look on my face."

Marianne smiled. "Oh, that?" She laughed a bit, as if she'd thought of a private joke. "I call that your stress face."

"My what?"

"It's how you always look," she said. "Even when you're here on the island supposed to be relaxing."

Logan said nothing, his eyes staying on the painting.

"Your resting stress face," I said with a smile.

Logan didn't laugh. He didn't even acknowledge that I'd said anything. Tension filled the air by the moment.

"Do you like it?" Marianne asked barely above a whisper.

A small, forced smile appeared on his face. "Sorry. Like Emily said, good art makes you think. It's beautiful, Mar." He stepped over to his sister and gave her shoulder a squeeze. "You did well." Without waiting for a response, he glanced over at me. "Good night to you both."

Logan turned and left. I watched him go and listened as the sound of his shoes on the tile floor faded into the distance.

Once he was gone, Marianne sighed, shaking her head. "You know what I wish?" she asked.

"What's that?"

"I wish that Logan were happier."

I didn't know what to say to that. Her words lingered in the air, my gaze staying on the painting.

"OK!" Marianne exclaimed, clasping her hands together. "It's *Bridesmaids* time! Come on!"

She didn't give me a chance to react before grabbing me

by the hand and pulling me out of the room, only stopping to throw the curtain back over the painting. We hurried down the hall, outside to the garden, then back into the main house. Fifteen minutes later, we were seated in the big basement movie theater, pizza and soda in front of us and *Bridesmaids* playing on the huge screen.

I'd seen the film before, and while it was just as hilarious the second time around, I couldn't help but think about Logan. The painting had evoked a sense of just how unhappy Logan seemed. It was strange—the man was successful and wealthy and powerful but lived a life that seemed oddly isolated. That is, aside from his sister.

He had all the ingredients for a happy life. Instead, he spent most of his time tense, a wall between him and everyone else. Not to mention how his livelihood involved dealing with scuzzy pricks like my dad.

The way he treated Marianne, along with the occasional glimpses of humor and warmth that would slip through his stony, stoic façade, made me certain that there was something more to him. I knew that he was capable of kindness.

I had a hell of a lot to think about.

CHAPTER 13

I was in the middle of reading the next morning when a booming knock sounded at my door, the rapping loud and sudden enough to make me nearly spill my coffee. I gasped, turning around ready to scold whoever had given me such a scare.

I didn't have a chance. The door opened and Logan entered, a leather briefcase thrown over his shoulder.

"Morning," he said.

I sat stunned, setting down my book and regarding him with an expression of disbelief.

"I get that you're probably a little out of practice with these sorts of things, but you have to know that it's not OK *at all* to barge into a woman's room like that. Don't tell me you do this with Marianne?"

He shrugged. "She's never in her bedroom with the door shut."

"Well, next time when you knock, wait for me to say something. What if I'd been in the middle of changing?"

As soon as I spoke the words, the idea of Logan coming into my room while I was in a state of undress occurred to me. To my surprise, it didn't make me feel weird or uncomfortable. Quite the opposite, actually.

"Fine. I'll wait next time." His voice was tinged with irritation, and I could tell from his tone that Logan was in normal form. "Anyway, we don't have time for questions of etiquette. There are important matters we need to discuss."

"Important matters? Like what?"

He slipped off the briefcase he'd brought it, setting it down onto the bed.

"I have something for you."

"What kind of something?"

He didn't make me wait long. Logan opened the metal clasps of the briefcase before reaching inside and taking out another bag, this one white and plastic.

"Forgive me if I didn't go to the trouble of giftwrapping it. Figured you wouldn't mind."

Logan prepared to set the bag onto my desk but saw that my book was in the way. He craned his neck, checking out the cover. A surge of embarrassment ran through me as I realized that the cover, along with the title of "Embrace of the Vampire Prince," gave the book away as YA romance.

"What're you reading?"

I flashed him a wry smirk as I closed the book and set it aside. "Haven't you invaded my privacy enough for one day?"

He let out an amused sort. "Fair enough."

Logan set the bag down and I was able to make out the word 'Apple.' Curious, I reached inside and grasped the box within. I pulled it out slowly, seeing that it was a laptop.

"What is this?" The words came out of my mouth dumbly.

"There's a picture of it on the box," he said.

I pursed my lips. "I see that. But what's it for?"

"You're a writer, correct?"

"I am. How did you—" I stopped myself before finishing the question. No doubt he'd gotten the information from Marianne.

"A certain someone who isn't good at keeping information to herself. I hope you're not upset with her."

"No, not at all. But why did you buy this?"

"I figured that it'd be a lot easier to do your work on this instead of writing by hand, assuming that's what you do."

"That *is* what I do. Not many other options when your dad doesn't even let you have a phone, let alone a computer."

I picked up the laptop box and looked it over. Right away I noticed that it was brand new and top of the line.

"Is this the fanciest one?" I asked.

"It's a Pro." He shrugged. "Figured it would be smart to just get you the best one. I'm more of a Windows guy, but those are supposed to be pretty good." He nodded toward the box as he spoke the words.

"You're right about that. Maybe a little overkill for writing."

"You never know. You might want to do cover design or photo editing down the line. Better to have the power and not need it than need it and not have it."

The gift was a lot, maybe even a little excessive. But it was a gift, nonetheless. Logan was being his usual icy self, but he'd done something *nice* for me.

Right away, I was suspicious.

"What's going on here?"

Logan cocked his head to the side, seemingly confused by my question.

"I'm sorry?"

"You went out and got me one of the best laptops on the

market. And since I'm guessing there's not an Apple store anywhere around here, had it specially shipped in. And you did all of this for... what? So I could have something to write my book on? Just to be nice?"

"I thought it would be more convenient for you," he said. "If you're going to be here on the island for the next month, that strikes me as the perfect time to work on any projects."

I noticed that he sidestepped the question of whether or not he'd done it to be nice, framing it in terms of pure practicality.

"If you don't have any need for it, I can easily return it."

"No, this is... perfect, actually."

"Glad to hear it. But I hope that you're not just saying that for my sake. If it's not to your liking, let me know."

I decided not to answer him with words. Instead, I opened the box slowly. After removing a bit of plastic, I revealed the silver laptop inside, taking it out and holding it in my hands.

"It's... fancy. And pretty light, actually."

I cleared the surface of my desk, placing the laptop in front of me and turning it on. As it booted up, I moved my fingertips over the keyboard, imagining what it would feel like to type my novel on it.

"This is amazing, *way* easier than writing everything by hand."

"Just so you're not surprised, internet access on the island is limited, it's a security measure. But you should be able to access streaming."

I turned away from the laptop as it performed its first time loading business.

"Thanks, Logan. You didn't have to do that."

"It was my pleasure. Anyway, I'll leave you to it." He

began to turn but stopped himself. "I nearly forgot... the laptop wasn't the only business I wanted to discuss with you."

"What's up?"

A tinge of tension formed on his face, as if he was about to share something with me that he wasn't certain about.

"We're going to be having a guest to the island in a short time."

"A guest?"

"That's right. Marta will be coming."

I couldn't believe what I'd heard. Shock and excitement ran through me in equal measure. My father had made it perfectly clear that Marta would not be joining me during my stay on the island.

"Marta? Marta's coming here?"

He nodded.

"That's amazing! When?"

"Not quite sure exactly. She said that she has to put some affairs in order around the house, be there to take care of some business for your father. I'd say in five days or so."

I couldn't hold back my excitement any longer. I let out a squeal, jumping from my seat and throwing my arms around Logan.

I hugged him hard enough to feel his solid body and the outlines of his muscles. The sensation of his body against mine brought to mind our lovemaking, how good he'd felt on top of me, inside of me.

Logan didn't hug me back. Instead, he placed his hands on my shoulders and gently, but firmly, pushed me away. Rather than put total distance between us, he kept me close, looking deeply into my eyes with those icy blues of his.

His expression was grim and grave, not a trace of warmth or humor.

"I'm only going to say this once—if there's something going on here, if this Marta woman is coming to facilitate a rescue or some other sort of backhanded bullshit, there will be consequences. And the outcome for you will be dire."

It was a threat, and a serious one. His tone was low and deep, and there was no question whether or not he meant his words.

I should've been scared. Hell, I *was* scared. But I felt something else, too. Logan was close enough that I could feel the heat from his body. His big hands gripped my shoulders, holding me still.

I was turned on. My pussy clenched, and I was wet from the moment I'd hugged him. I wanted to respond, but I knew speaking even a single word would betray my desire. My eyes flicked down to his lips, part of me wishing that Logan would lean forward and kiss me hard and deep.

Instead, I nodded. He nodded back, taking his hands off my shoulders. Logan cast me one more hard look before turning and leaving, shutting the door behind him.

The second I was alone once again, I let out a deep breath that I didn't even realize I'd been holding in.

Logan was sexy as hell, but he was dangerous as they came. I couldn't forget that.

As strange as it might've seemed, that combination was what made the man absolutely irresistible.

And I wanted more.

I spent the rest of the evening getting to know my new laptop. It was a total thrill. Dad never let me have anything modern in the way of technology other than a basic cell phone with just about every feature disabled other than a

GPS tracker so he could keep tabs on me at all times. I could only use it to call emergency services. Having a brand new MacBook at my fingertips opened up a whole new world for me.

I spent hours in Word typing up my handwritten pages and transferring them into something more legible, not to mention easier to edit. After nearly two years of sneaking around scribbling my words onto scrap sheets of paper after Dad had gone to bed, being able to sit at a desk and just type was something else, something wonderful.

After I'd done enough work for one day, I clicked over to the internet to see what I could find. Just like Logan had said, most of the internet was blocked for security reasons. I was able to check some news and a few other pages, but for the most part, the internet was on lockdown. I decided to reward myself with a little streaming, bringing my new MacBook over to the bed and curling up in the blankets with a little more *Emily in Paris*, watching until my eyelids grew heavy.

When it was time to go to sleep, I closed the laptop and plugged it in on the desk. I was already excited for the morning when I could wake up and get started once again on my novel. Maybe I'd even take a little walk along the beach for inspiration.

After changing into my sleeping clothes, I opened the window, allowing the sounds and smells of the sea to flow into the room. There was something about the ocean, the sea air and white noise of the water that put me to sleep as quickly and soundly as any pill.

Once under the covers, I closed my eyes, a smile on my face as I drifted off within minutes.

"How are you already having trouble with this thing?"

Logan, as usual, seemed annoyed. He stood next to my desk, one hand in his pocket, the other on his chin, his eyes on the laptop. Some warning error was on the screen, one that I couldn't make heads or tails of.

Was it broken for good? I had no idea. What I *did* know was that the fancy-as-eff laptop that Logan had just bought for me was no longer working less than a day after I'd powered it up for the first time.

He let out a grumble of mild annoyance.

"Took a bit of doing to get this here, you know. Apple doesn't ship to the Virgin Islands. I had to pay a private courier to bring it here."

"I'm just as upset about this as you are," I shot back. "But you don't need to guilt me about it. Not to mention that I'm pretty sure it wasn't my fault."

He brought his eyes to mine, raising an eyebrow.

"Not your fault, huh?" he asked.

"What?" The word shot out of my mouth. "It's not an excuse! I mean, there's a really good chance this thing was just broken out of the box. I was typing on it and then *bam* —error screen."

Without acknowledging my words, Logan stepped over to the computer and tapped a few keys. Nothing happened; the error screen stayed there just as surely as if he hadn't done anything at all. He then closed the laptop and turned toward me.

"Making a mistake is one thing," he said. "Making excuses, not owning up to it, that's another."

I wanted to speak up for myself and tell him that he was being out of line. But the way he looked at me, the slow steps he took in my direction, made my mouth stay shut.

"What am I going to do with you, Emily?" he asked,

continuing toward me. "Ever since I took your virginity on the plane, you've been alternating between giving me the cold shoulder or serving up attitude."

I gasped at the way he brought up what had happened on the plane so directly.

"You know what I think you need?" He stopped right in front of me, gazing down with his electric blue eyes.

"What?" the word came out of my mouth in a whisper.

Logan grinned. With surprising speed, he reached around me and clamped his hands onto my ass, squeezing me tightly. I gasped, my eyes going wide as he pulled me against him, letting me feel his hardness.

"You need discipline."

His hands still on my ass, Logan leaned in and put his lips on mine, kissing me with intensity and passion, his tongue passing my lips and finding mine. I moaned through the kiss, letting Logan's touch and scent and everything else cast its spell on me.

After several wonderful, sensual moments, he put his hand on the small of my back.

"Go over to the bed."

"Why?" I asked with a challenging, teasing tone. "What's going to happen over there?"

"Discipline. Now, go, unless you want your punishment to be even more severe."

My pussy was throbbing by this point, soaking through my panties. I stepped over to the bed and prepared to sit.

"No," he said. "Turn around."

I did as he asked.

"Take off your pants."

My eyes on his, I hooked my thumbs underneath the waistband of my sleeping pants and pulled them down.

Although I had a simple pair of white hipster panties on underneath, Logan seemed most pleased by what he saw.

"Get onto the bed, on all fours."

I was totally in the grips of his command, eager to give myself over to him. The smile still on my face, I turned around and climbed onto the bed, sticking my ass out toward him.

"Like this?" I asked, looking back over my shoulder.

"Like that."

He stepped over to me, placing his hand on my rear and giving it a good squeeze before moving his touch all over my body, traveling between my legs, taking a moment to tease my pussy through my panties before returning to my ass, a gasp pulling into my lungs as he did.

"Are you ready?" he asked.

"Yes." I was ready—ready for everything he wanted to give me.

Logan placed his hand on my right ass cheek, a tingle of anticipation running through me as he prepared to give me the spanking I apparently deserved. I grinned, feeling his hand rise and pull back. Then, with a *whoosh* though the air, his hand rushed toward my rear and—

The rumble of my phone on my nightstand brought me back into the world of the living. It'd been almost a week since Logan had given me the laptop, and as the real world unblurred around me I realized that I'd just awoken from yet another one of the dreams I'd been having since that encounter.

I sat up, running my hand through my hair and shaking my head. Every damn night I'd dreamed about him, each one the same theme—he was in my room upset with me for one reason or another. Eventually, every time, we ended up in bed.

Though this latest dream was a little different. The spanking, the *discipline*—that hadn't been there before. I'd never been one to fantasize about such things, but there was something about Logan, something about imagining him taking control that turned me on like mad.

The phone. I pushed the dream out of my head as I remembered that a text had been what had woken me up.

Logan had given me a phone a few days ago. Like the laptop, it was Apple, top-of-the-line and limited in use. It allowed me to stay in touch with Logan, Marianne, and Pearl which meant that one of them had sent the text that'd woken me up.

My body still groggy, I reached over and grabbed the phone. Sure enough, there was a text from Logan.

Get up and get dressed. Marta is arriving at the dock in one hour.

The words on the screen filled me with such excitement that I didn't even care that Logan was talking to me like he was my boss. I replied with a quick "*OK!*" before tossing my phone onto the bed and hurrying into the bathroom to shower.

With Marta there, I knew the place would feel a little more like home. I just had to deal with the matter of the man I couldn't seem to get out of my head.

CHAPTER 14

LOGAN

"This is a bad idea, *jefe.*"

It was a beautiful day on the island. I, along with Roberto, Marianne, and Emily, was gathered on the dock watching the boat carrying our newest guest to the shore.

Roberto was right—bringing an unknown like this Marta woman to the island was a dumb idea. But there I was, going along with it.

"I understand," I replied, my voice low enough that only Roberto could hear it. "And your caution has been noted and appreciated."

"But you're bringing her here anyway."

"I'm bringing her here anyway."

Roberto let out a small sigh, shaking his head as he rubbed the back of his neck.

"I'll make sure we keep an eye on her," he said. "I'll immediately report to you if anything is out of the ordinary."

"Excellent. Any news on the mystery boat?"

"Nothing so far. Scared off for now. But if they went

through the trouble of bringing a boat all the way over here to spy on us, they're almost certain to come back."

I nodded, keeping my eyes on the vessel as it approached the harbor. Emily was beyond giddy, seeming on the verge of bursting with each foot closer the boat drew. Marianne was infected by her excitement, her hands clasped together by her face.

Roberto was tense, as if half-expecting a team of gun-wielding mercenaries to burst out of the boat and open fire. I understood how he felt. He and I had met a few days ago, Roberto having done what he could to poke into this Marta's history.

He hadn't found much at all. Marta Maria Perez was born in 1978 in Ciudad Netzahualcoyotl, located on the outskirts of Mexico City and one of the largest slums in the world. Her parents both died before she turned eighteen, and she had no brothers and sisters. How she'd ended up in the United States was hazy. Her records stopped when she was eighteen then started again when she was twenty and working for Charles Marone. She'd been in his employ ever since, and as far as Roberto could tell was totally loyal to him.

That was a problem. Total loyalty to Charles could very well mean that she would try to relay information back to him about what was going on with Emily. Another possibility was that Marta's *true* loyalty was not to Charles, but to Emily. That's what I was hoping for. Either way, Marta would have no way to contact Charles, I'd make sure of that.

The boat pulled up to the dock, the captain bringing it to a stop and hopping out to moor it. As he did, Marta emerged from below deck. She was short but solidly built, her hair dark, her face pleasant and friendly. My first thought was how much she reminded me of Pearl.

"There's my *chica!*" Marta burst out of the boat and onto the dock, Emily letting out an excited squeal as she ran over to give her a hug. They embraced, and I watched as Emily introduced Marianne.

So far, so good. No reason to suspect that Marta was anything other than a trusted friend and employee of Emily's.

The captain brought out Marta's bags, and I nodded to Roberto. He nodded back, knowing what needed to be done. Together, we approached the group.

"Logan," Emily said, stepping aside for me to join them. "This is Marta Perez."

Marta looked me up and down, a small smile on her face. I could make out the intelligence in her eyes. Right away, I noted that she was likely more than met the eye. She was unassuming—mousey, even. Maybe her appearance was a reflection of her true nature. Or, perhaps it was a good way to throw people off, the ideal look for a mole.

"It's so good to finally meet you, Mr. Stone," she said, offering me her hand. "As I'm sure you can guess, you're the talk of the staff at the Marone estate."

I extended my hand. "A pleasure to finally meet you." I decided to sidestep her later words. Gossip was of no interest to me. She took my hand and shook it.

I glanced over at Emily. The happiness in her shining eyes was impossible to ignore. Since she'd arrived on the island, she'd been neither happy nor unhappy. Marianne had even told me that she'd overheard her crying. Now, a familiar face before her, Emily seemed content for the first time since I'd met her. Sure, bringing Marta to the island presented a major security concern. All the same, it was a small price to pay to brighten Emily's mood.

"*Dios mio.*" Marta turned toward the estate, shaking her

head in disbelief. "Emily said that this place was something special, but to see it in person..."

"Looking forward to having you here," I said. "You'll have plenty of time to enjoy the island. For now, I'll have Emily show you to your room. I'm sure you'd like a little time to get settled after your journey."

Marta sucked her teeth, waving her hand through the air. "Aye, *es nada*. Not a chance in hell I'm going to be spending my first day here lounging around like a *tourista*. You brought me here to work, and that's what I'm going to do." She turned to Emily. "Show me my room, then show me the kitchen... mole' is on the menu tonight."

"Yes!" Emily said, her face brightening even more.

"Mole'?" Marianne was confused.

Emily smiled. "It's this amazing Mexican dish—a thick, creamy sauce with chocolate mixed in. It's Marta's specialty."

"*One* of Marta's specialties," Marta replied, raising her finger. "Don't try to make me out to be a one-trick pony."

We kept on, Marta, Emily and Marianne behind us, the three of them eagerly chatting away.

Roberto, who was walking next to me, glanced back over his shoulder. "Still not sure about this."

"Appreciate your concern, but I've made my decision."

"Understood. Before I shut up about the subject, I've got a couple of my boys at the gate for the check, if you still want to do that."

"Sure do."

Up ahead, I spotted the two guards at the front gate of the estate, both standing with their hands clasped behind their backs, their eyes hidden behind dark sunglasses, guns tucked into their belt holsters.

"What's with the guards?" Emily asked.

"Security protocol," I said. "We check every guest to the island, without exception."

Emily stood firm and still, an indignant look on her face as the guards approached.

"You're serious? You're really going to check Marta? What the hell do you think she's going to do, take everyone out with a secret pistol and swim me across the water to the mainland?"

I said nothing, not wanting to indulge her outburst. Instead, I turned my attention to Marta. She nodded, but I could sense she was none too happy about what was going to happen. The guards approached, one of them taking Marta's purse to look inside, the other giving Marta a pat down.

Emily didn't take this in silence. She stormed over to Roberto, letting out a tirade of words in Spanish. I didn't speak the language, but even so, I was able to pick out a few less than civilized words, like *puta* and *pendejo*. Roberto seemed more amused than anything else.

"It's fine, *chica*," Marta said. Behind her, another guard quickly went through her bags. "I'm not above the rules. Lucky to even be here to begin with when you think about it."

Emily stopped tearing into Roberto and turned her attention to me. She shot sharp daggers in my direction, not taking her eyes off me even for a second. More than anything, I was impressed. Emily might've been sheltered, but she sure as hell was feisty and protective when it came to her people.

I liked it.

There was still the matter of loyalty. Emily was loyal to

Marta, no doubt about that. But to whom was Marta loyal? Was she really as innocuous as she seemed, or was she working for Charles in another capacity besides his daughter's caretaker? That remained to be seen.

One by one, the men finished. As they did, they nodded in my direction, letting me know that Marta was clear.

Emily put her hands on her hips, her eyes sharp in anger.

"Happy?" she asked. "You've made sure she isn't packing heat or smuggling drugs. Can we go in now?"

Marta said something quietly to Emily, placing her hand on Emily's arm.

"Yeah. Let them in. Marta can have the bedroom across the hall from yours, Emily. Roberto, mind showing them to their rooms?"

He gave me a knowing nod, a silent signal to let me know that he was aware that his duty *also* meant to keep an eye on Marta for anything suspicious. Emily let out a harumph, putting her arm through Marta's as the two of them made their way onto the grounds.

Marianne stayed with me, a despondent look on her face.

"You OK, Mar?"

She sighed. "Yeah. It's just... why did you have to do all of that? Why did you have to make Emily mad?"

How to explain to my sister the sort of danger I worried Emily was in? She had no idea of such things.

"I'm only protecting her, making sure she stays out of danger."

Emily's face shifted from upset to concerned.

"Danger? What kind of danger? From whom?"

"You know how sometimes there're matters that I can't

really explain, just that you have to trust me? This is one of those times."

"Oh. OK."

Of course, there was more to why I couldn't tell Marianne the truth—giving her the whole story would mean telling her that Emily was there against her will. Not a chance that she'd understand that. Hell, part of *me* didn't understand how a woman like Emily could be in the position that she was in, a bird being passed from one gilded cage to another.

Marianne's mind didn't work that way. Her eyes only saw beauty.

But now she was worried. I had to say something.

"There are bad people out there, Mar. And I think, *think,* I don't know for sure, that some of these bad men might want to hurt Emily. More than anything, I want to keep her safe."

Marianne's eyes lit up in shock.

"What? People want to hurt her?"

"Maybe. It's hard to say. But I'm not going to take any chances."

Without missing a beat, Marianne hurried over to me, pulling me into a hug and resting her head on my shoulder.

"I'm sorry. I got mad at you, but I should've known that you would never be mean on purpose unless you had a really, really good reason."

I patted her on the back. "It's fine. You were worried about Emily, your heart was in the right place."

Marianne let go of me, regarding me with excited eyes.

"I have an idea! How about you and I have lunch together? Emily and Marta probably want to spend some time alone, right?"

"That's right. And I'd love to."

Marianne gave me another hug, this one accompanied by a kiss on the cheek.

"Come on! I'm starving!"

She grabbed my hand and pulled me toward the estate.

I had plenty on my mind. But in that moment, all I cared about was spending time with my sister. Everything else could wait.

CHAPTER 15

EMILY

Intensity and anger burned in Marta's eyes. Her hand shot out to grab me, her fingers wrapping around my arm and holding me so tightly that it almost hurt.

"Tell me now," she said, her voice a sharp whisper. "Has that *tirón pendejo* hurt you? Tell me, and don't hold back."

We'd just stepped into her bedroom, and Marta hadn't waited a moment after the door was shut to accost me. Her mood had been so cheery up until that moment; her sudden change in attitude took me by surprise.

"Marta... it's OK." I placed my hand on hers, removing her grip from my arm.

"That man, he's a brute," she said, letting her hand drop back to her side. "I can spot pieces of *mierda* like that from a mile away." She let out a frustrated sigh before turning away from me, picking up her bag and setting it on the bed and pulling it open with three quick jerks of the zipper.

I was conflicted. On the one hand, I understood why Marta was acting this way. For all she knew, I'd been kidnapped and held prisoner on some faraway island, held as a toy to be played with by some sadistic billionaire.

On the other, well, while there were lots of ways I'd describe Logan, a "piece of *mierda*" wasn't one of them.

"It's not that bad," I said. "Logan's been OK so far."

Marta let out another sigh. "That's one of the ways men like him will act, you know? Charming and suave at first, sure, but it's all a way to hide what's underneath." She pulled out a few pieces of clothing, bringing them over to the nearby dresser and plopping them into an open drawer. Then she yanked open the curtains on the window just to her left, revealing a sweeping view of the garden, the rest of the estate, and the rising peak of the middle of the island. "All the same, it's hard to argue with a view like this."

I smiled, happy to see that her defensive attitude had cracked a bit.

"It's not that bad at all," I said, coming over to her side. "I mean, there's *this*. Not to mention the beach." I gave Marta a playful elbowing. "I hope you brought your bikini."

Marta laughed, shaking her head. "With this body? Not a chance." The serious look on her face returned, as if the idea of her in a bikini brought to mind the idea of *me* in a bikini. "Tell me, has he touched you? Has he tried to seduce you?"

"Marta!" I turned away from her right away, not wanting to let her see me blush. My heart beat a little faster with nervousness. There wasn't a chance in hell I'd be able to tell her the truth—not only had Logan and I slept together, but I'd also done it willingly, *eagerly*. At the same time, the thought of lying to Marta was enough to make me sick to my stomach.

But I had to.

"That's how these kinds of men are," she said. "They have money and power and think it means that they can take whatever they want, including the innocence of a young girl."

My gut tightened at the word. Only Dad used the word "innocence" to refer to my virginity. Hearing it out of Marta's mouth didn't make me feel good at all.

"It's not like that," I said. "Logan... he's been good to me. Now, I'm not saying he's a good *person*—I don't know him nearly well enough to come to that kind of conclusion. But he hasn't made me do anything that I didn't want to do."

I was pleased with my words. They weren't entirely honest since I was sidestepping the question of whether or not Logan and I had slept together. My words were the truth, however. Nothing that had happened between Logan and me was anything that I hadn't eagerly consented to.

"Good," Marta replied. "And now that I'm here, I'm going to make sure he doesn't get what he wants." She raised her finger. "Make no mistake, there's not a chance in hell that this prick isn't scheming noon and night to take what he wants from you. Trust me—I'm certain that your innocence and how he can take it for himself is more important to him right now than some stupid company. Men like him are all the same.

I appreciated Marta's concern for my well-being. All the same, at times it seemed like it was my father speaking through her, his wants coming out of her mouth. I still trusted Marta more than anyone else, but with each moment that passed I was more certain that I needed to keep the truth to myself.

"I can't pretend to know what's been on Logan's mind," I said. "But for the most part, he's been leaving me alone, spends most of his time in his office, really. I'm starting to get the impression that he's a workaholic more than anything else."

Marta gave an affirmative nod. "That's good to hear. Let him stay in that office of his worrying about emails and spreadsheets and whatever else. Every moment he's busy with work is a moment he's not pawing at you like some horny dog."

I couldn't help but laugh at her description.

"Oh! And he lets me have so much more freedom here. He's not like Dad, monitoring my every move and not letting me even watch TV." My eyes lit up. "Have you heard of *Netflix*?"

Marta chuckled. "*Dios mio*, Emily, sometimes I forget how much that asshole of a father has kept you sheltered. Of course, I've heard of Netflix. You know those silly little Korean soaps have been my guilty pleasure for years."

"I still can't wrap my head around how I can watch *anything* I want. And it's not just TV! There's this huge library downstairs with just about every book you could ask for."

Marta smiled. "That makes me so happy to hear. I swear, your father would keep you illiterate if he could. You ask me, it's a total crime the way he keeps that brilliant, creative mind of yours locked away from sharing what you can do with the world. Makes me sick to my stomach."

"Speaking of which, let me show you what I'm *really* excited about. Come on."

I gestured for her to follow me out of her bedroom, the two of us making our way over toward my room.

"Oh, *chica*, don't tell me you found some secret S&M dungeon or something. This place is big enough that he could have three of them."

I laughed as I opened my bedroom door. "Don't worry—he doesn't have one of those, at least as far as I know."

We entered my room and Marta stepped over to the window, taking in my view of the beach and ocean.

"This is quite the vista," she said, putting her hands on her hips and looking out. "Don't get me wrong, I'm happy with the view of the garden. But this is something else."

As she spoke, I stepped over to my new laptop and opened it.

"Check it out," I said. "Logan got me this."

Marta turned her attention away from the view toward my computer.

"That asshole bought you this?" she asked. Marta came over to the computer and picked it up, looking it over.

"He got it for me to work on my book. Marianne let it slip that I had a novel I've been writing, so he got me this so I don't have to write it by hand."

Marta set down the computer, turning to me with a hard expression on her face.

"This is not good, Emily," she said.

"Huh? Not good how?"

"You remember what I said, how a man like him would do anything to take your innocence?" she swept her hand toward the MacBook. "Giving gifts like this is a classic way for a man to butter up a woman. Don't get me wrong, *chica*, I know that you're sheltered and a little on the naïve side of things. But you need to learn how the real world works."

"Marta... I don't know if this is like that."

"Oh, but it is. It's a good thing I'm here now. I can watch out for you."

There was something off about Marta, something sharp and even a little bitter.

"Are you OK?" I asked. "I'm happy you're here, but all the same you seem a little irritated."

Marta sighed, as if my words had caught her off guard.

"No, you're right. I don't mean to come down on you so hard. It's just that I've been worried sick about you for the last week knowing that you were here with some strange man doing God knows what with you. And it doesn't help that I'm a little worn out from the trip."

I stepped over to Marta, opening my arms and pulling her into a hug.

"I get it. And like I said, I'm so happy that you're here."

Marta returned the hug, patting me on the back. "Same here, Emily. Now, if you don't mind, I need a little rest."

"Sure. Take a nap, and when it's time for dinner, I'll let you know."

Marta smiled, squeezing my hand one more time before leaving. Once she was gone, the door shut, I turned my attention back to the view.

Something was off with Marta, and the more I thought about it, the more I found myself wondering if there was more to it than just fatigue and worry. She'd sounded like Dad at times, worrying about my "innocence" and convinced that I was some helpless woman on the verge of falling prey to whatever man wanted me.

All the same, Marta was right about me being sheltered. I took my eyes from the view and regarded the laptop. I'd been so wrapped up in the gift at the time that I hadn't stopped to consider if there had been more to it other than something given to me out of the kindness of Logan's heart. What if it had merely been a way of buttering me up, trying to get me to trust him more so that I'd easily give myself to him again?

It was all too much to think about. My stomach grumbled, and I decided that a little snack would take my mind off everything racing through it. I left my room, stepping over to Marta's and peeking inside. She was already on the bed, her eyes closed as she rested. I shut the door softly before heading down the hall.

Minutes later I approached the kitchen. It wasn't near dinner time yet, so the staff wasn't around. I pushed open the door and stepped inside.

Logan was alone in the big kitchen, seated at the island in the middle, half of a sandwich in one hand and a tablet in the other. He brought his eyes up from whatever he was reading.

"Hey, there."

"Hey."

I entered the room, my footsteps echoing through the space. The kitchen was unbelievable—packed with top-of-the-line appliances, the equipment rivaling what one might find in the back of a chic restaurant.

"Just came in for a little snack."

He raised his sandwich a bit. "Great minds think alike."

I paused. "Sorry if you wanted some alone time. I can leave."

He shook his head. "Not at all. Just catching up on the news. You want me to call the staff in to make something?"

"Nah. Cooking for yourself is underrated."

He gestured toward the fridge and pantry. "Help yourself. I'm not much of a chef, so it's sandwiches for me."

"That sounds kind of good, actually."

I went over to the fridge, taking out some cold cuts and cheese, along with mayo and mustard. Once those were out, I found some bread and with all the ingredients in hand, went to work.

Logan picked his tablet back up, but I could feel his gaze flicking over to me as I assembled my sandwich. Truth be told, I kind of liked it. His stare burned in the best way possible, my pussy clenching at the idea of him looking at me.

"How's your maid?" he asked.

I cleared my throat, keeping my eyes on my food in order to not make the sexual tension between us even worse.

"She's not my maid. Marta was my nanny when I was younger, but now, she's my friend."

"Fair enough. How's your friend?"

"She's fine." The words came out perhaps a bit sharper than I'd intended. But I didn't care. I didn't want to give him the wrong idea about anything.

He chuckled.

"What's so funny?" I asked.

"Just wondering why you're being so defensive with me."

In the middle of spreading the mayo on my bread, I set down the knife and looked up at him with a harsh glare.

"Are you kidding? How about the fact that I'm your prisoner here? How about the fact that, as long as I'm here, I'm less a person and more a tool to be used in some petty squabble between you and my father?"

Logan said nothing for several moments, his eyes on me as he let the silence linger in the air. Logan appeared to have no issue with tension. More than that, he seemed skilled at using it to his advantage.

He set down his tablet and his sandwich, then got up from his seat and walked over to me, his eyes still locked on mine as he made his way around the kitchen island.

He waited until he was near to speak, close enough that I could feel the heat from his body.

"Is that what you think is going on here?" he asked. "Is that what you think I did on the plane?"

He didn't raise his voice in the slightest, he didn't have to. Logan was so close to me that he could speak in a low tone and I could still easily hear him, the deepness of his voice resonating in my bones. I was turned on, my breaths short and shallow.

"Yes." I couldn't say anything more than that.

"Funny that you think that I used you, when I know you'd be more than willing to do it again." He leaned in, close enough that I was certain he was about to kiss me. "Am I wrong?"

My heart was thudding in my chest, my pussy throbbing and soaking wet.

I opened my mouth, wanting to tell him that he wasn't wrong, that I wanted him like mad.

He didn't give me the chance.

He winked, then stepped away from me. Logan reached across the island and took his tablet, tucking it under his arm and leaving the kitchen.

When he was gone, I stood there stunned, my chest rising and falling.

He was right. All I wanted was for him to touch me again. And what was worse, he knew it.

CHAPTER 16

LOGAN

I'd pushed my luck the other day in the kitchen. I'd come close, *very* close, to giving in to what I wanted. It'd taken all the restraint I had to resist grabbing Emily by the hips and bending her over the kitchen counter, shoving my cock into her deep and bringing her to orgasm again and again.

It was what she wanted, and it was what *I* wanted. However, one of us had to be strong enough to resist.

I'd woken up that morning in a state of total arousal, the dream I'd had during the night playing in my head with the clarity of a movie. The dream had been of Emily sitting in my bedroom in nothing but a matching black lace bra and panties, her legs crossed and a seductive smile on her face.

I'd stepped over, my cock at eye level.

"You know what I want," I'd spoken in the dream. "And I know what you want."

She'd responded without words, placing her hand on my cock through my slacks, stroking me slowly until I was hard as steel. A seductive, teasing expression stayed on her face, her hands working deftly to open my zipper and button, reaching in to retrieve my manhood.

Emily began by kissing my end, as she'd done on the plane. This time, however, she took more of me into her mouth. She parted those plush, full lips and wrapped them around me, flicking me with her tongue as she traveled up and down, her eye contact unbreaking, her eyes smiling with pleasure.

I'd let her please me this way for a time. But there was only so much foreplay I could take before I had to simply take what I wanted. I'd guided her off my cock, slipping my hands under her arms and turning her around. Her ass was perfect, round and heart-shaped, and I'd been unable to resist simply ripping off her panties and tossing them aside.

I'd placed my hand on her ass, spanking her firmly, gasps pulling into her as my palm made contact. I measured my strength, spanking her just hard enough so as not to cause anything more than the slightest sting. When I took my hand away, a red imprint was left on her cheek, a sign that I'd claimed her.

Emily was bent over on all fours, her rear pointed toward me as I took my cock into my hand, placing the end at her entrance as I prepared to push myself into her. She squirmed and moaned, pressing her ass against me. I teased her a bit more, dragging my head along her opening, pressing it into her clit.

"Are you ready for me?" I'd asked.

"So ready. Please, *please* don't make me wait a second longer."

I didn't. I pushed into her, watching as her lips spread and my cock vanished inside, inch by inch.

Of course, that was when I'd woken up. My eyes opened and I didn't need to turn and look at my nightstand clock to know that it was six-thirty—the same time I awoke every morning.

Sex dreams were double-edged swords. While they could be fun as hell, it always seemed like they stopped right when the good parts were about to happen.

Back in the present moment, I tossed off my clothes in the bathroom and stepped into the shower. While washing, I found my hand traveling down my body to my cock, as if I were being guided by unconscious forces to pleasure myself. It was a tempting idea. Images from the dream were still fresh in my mind, and I was certain it would take no time at all to finish to the mental image of Emily looking up at me with my cock in her mouth.

I decided not to do that. Ever since the near-encounter in the kitchen, I'd gone out of my way to put some space between myself and Emily. There were too many uncertainties with the current situation and making it all more confusing with sex wouldn't be a smart long-term plan.

I dressed in a simple gray T-shirt and jeans, stepping into a pair of white sneakers as I headed out of my bedroom. I was hungry for something good for breakfast. The last few days I'd been taking meals in my office in order to avoid Emily. Now that it was day three of this strategy, however, I realized how much I wasn't enjoying skulking around my own house like a trespasser. Sure, it might've been a challenge not to give in to what I wanted with Emily, but it needed to be done.

Lively chatter sounded from the kitchen as I approached. I stepped inside to see a small group there. Emily, Marta, Marianne and Pearl were gathered around the kitchen island, all chatting with big smiles on their faces, a huge platter of pastries in the middle of the island. A carafe of hot coffee was off to the side, my mouth practically watering at the idea of a fresh cup.

"Morning, ladies," I said as I entered, grabbing a mug out of the nearby cabinet and heading over to the carafe.

A scowl appeared on Emily's face, no doubt she was still salty from my rejection the previous day. She looked stunning as always, wearing a spaghetti-strap top and a pair of short jean shorts that showed off her long legs.

Just as it was impossible not to notice how stunning and sexy Emily looked, it was equally as impossible to not spot the hard, withering expression from Marta.

She was canny enough to have picked up very quickly on the sexual tension between Emily and me – and clearly, she wasn't happy about it.

"Morning!" Marianne sprang from her seat, throwing her arms around me for a quick, tight hug. "Did you sleep OK?"

"Intense dreams," I replied, stealing a sideways glance at Emily. "But other than that, I slept just fine."

Marianne's face lit up at my words. "I had a really intense dream, too! It was about the hill in the middle of the island. I have the *perfect* image in mind for a sketch I want to do today."

"Sounds like you've got your morning planned. What about you, Emily?"

"She's going to the beach," Marta said, her tone sharp. "And I'm going with her."

"That's nice to hear," I replied. "But I'm sure Emily's more than capable of speaking for herself."

Tension thickened in the air at my words, but I didn't care. I wasn't about to be spoken to like that in my own home. Marta didn't care for my response one bit, shooting me another withering stare.

"That's right," Emily spoke up. "As Marta just told you, we're going for a little dip in the water."

Pearl chimed in as she took my coffee mug from my hands, pouring a healthy measure of coffee into it from the carafe. "Now, it's supposed to be extra sunny today. Em, I noticed that you don't have a decent sun hat."

"I've got a ton!" Marianne said. "She can use whatever hat of mine she wants."

"There you go," Pearl said. "And make sure you're wearing sunscreen."

Marta's hard expression broke, a small smile forming. "I said the same thing to her. Emily gets so excited about whatever she wants to do that she often forgets about practical matters."

Emily laughed. "I feel like I'm here with two moms. But thanks, both of you. And I appreciate it, but I can look after myself."

Pearl handed me back the mug. "Have something to eat. I know you're not big on breakfast, but I went a little nuts with the Danishes this morning."

The spread before me looked enticing, for sure. There were a good dozen Danishes, all with colorful filling from blueberries, cherries, and peaches. Part of me wanted one, but the greater part knew how I'd feel if I were to eat something so sugary first thing in the morning.

"I'll have one after dinner," I said. "Not sure one of those'll sit well before my workout."

Pearl chuckled good-naturedly. "Alright, alright. But I'd better see you eat at least *one* before the day's out."

"Sure, sure."

I was in the middle of a sip of coffee when the kitchen door opened, Roberto stepping inside.

"*Buenos dias,*" he said. Roberto had a thermos in his hand and made a beeline for the coffee carafe.

The group said good morning to him, Pearl wasting no

time putting one of the Danishes on a small plate and offering it.

"Have some breakfast, Roberto," she said. "Logan gave the excuse of not wanting anything before his workout. You, on the other hand, need something substantial in your stomach."

"Not going to see me turn down Pearl's fresh pastries," he said. "But let me take it to go—I need to get my day started *pronto*."

"One, actually *two*, Danishes to go coming right up," Pearl replied.

Roberto seemed more serious than usual. Something was on his mind. The rest of the women had fallen back into conversation, so I took the opportunity to get more information.

"Something wrong?" I asked.

"It's probably nothing," he said. "Just got a feeling, so I wanted to get out there and check with all of the guards individually, maybe do a long sweep of the beach."

Marta's focus broke away from her conversation as soon as Roberto mentioned the beach. Her gaze lingered on him for a moment before turning her attention back to Emily and Marianne.

"Sounds like a good plan," I replied. "Don't think we can be too careful about anything after what happened with that boat."

"My thoughts *exactamente*," he replied as he turned the cap on his thermos.

Pearl came over, placing a box of pastries into his other hand. "This better be empty within the hour; there's three in there."

"*Three?*" Roberto asked. "You trying to give me a belly?"

Pearl laughed, giving Roberto's flat middle a playful swat. "You ask me, you could use a little meat on your bones."

Roberto chuckled, shaking his head. "Anyway, I'm off. I'll check in with you when I'm done with my patrol."

"Sounds good. Keep me posted."

Roberto nodded before heading out. Once he was gone, I turned my attention back to the other conversation as I took a sip of my coffee.

"Marianne," Pearl began, "I think a trip to the beach sounds pretty fun. Why don't you go with those two?" Pearl was always trying to get Marianne to socialize, to spend less time alone painting and drawing.

"No!" Marta shot out the word, her tone harsh enough to make me raise an eyebrow.

"No?" I asked.

Marta cleared her throat, collecting herself. "It's just that Emily and I are going to be doing a little catching up on things back in New York. It'd be boring for Marianne."

"I don't know about that," Marianne replied. "I love gossip. But I really want to get started on this picture I have in mind. I feel like if I don't get it down soon, I'll forget it."

"You can come with us, go get ready!" Emily offered. "It'll be fun."

Marianne's eyes lit up. "Yeah? OK, I can work on my picture later, I guess."

Marta said nothing, a strange expression on her face. The group gathered some pastries for the road, Marta giving me one last look before the three of them headed out. Once they were gone, I wasted no time turning to Pearl.

"That was weird," I said. "You agree?"

She nodded. "This Marta woman... I don't know. She's friends with Emily, I get it. But friend or not, she's been jumpy since she showed up. And the way she reacted at the idea of Marianne going to the beach with them was beyond strange."

"She didn't want company. Just wanted it to be her and Emily."

"Right. Maybe it's nothing, but like you I'm trusting my gut. Might not be a bad idea to check on them."

"Yeah. Not a bad idea at all."

"Let me know what you find out," Pearl said. "I know it's only been a little over a week, but I've grown quite fond of Emily."

"I'll keep you posted."

I took my coffee to go, heading out and returning to my bedroom. Once there, I opened a locked safe in the back of my closet, removing a silver pistol and tucking it into the back waistband of my pants. Packing my gun seemed insane to me, but if I needed it, I wanted to have it easily accessible. Along with that, I retrieved a walkie-talkie that could be used to get in touch with Roberto.

If anything was going down on my island, I was going to know about. And if so, there wasn't a chance in hell I'd let any harm come to Emily.

I'd kill anyone who tried.

CHAPTER 17

EMILY

"**W**hat do you think, *chica?*"

I couldn't get over the fact that I was laying on a blanket on the beach, wearing a *bikini*.

While I'd packed a couple swimsuits for the trip to Logan's, all of them were according to Dad's rules, which meant that everything was a one-piece suit, with a skirt that covered my thighs. The swimsuits Dad made me wear had always struck me as those that women wore in old, black-and-white pictures from the early twentieth century. The only thing missing was a white swim cap.

It went without saying that no male guards could be around to see me swim at home. With all of the hassle it took, I only bothered taking a dip in the pool a handful of times a year.

Marta, knowing the swimsuit rule was likely one of the first I'd want to break, had gone to the trouble of picking out a few bikinis for me and packing them in her clothes. So, there I was, lounging on a gorgeous beach, clad in nothing but a black bikini that showed off just about every bit of my body.

"It feels... wrong. But in a good way." I flashed her a grin. "Dad would *kill* me if he saw me like this."

"Well, your papa isn't here to scold you for not dressing like a little Amish girl. He would throw a fit for sure, but it can be our little secret." Marta, seated on the towel next to me, followed up her words with a wink.

It was true that I felt like a very bad girl dressed in my skimpy bikini. All the same, as I lay there on my towel soaking up the warmth of the sun, I could definitely see the appeal of such a swimsuit. Every part of me felt kissed by the tropical rays above. Instead of being covered up and constricted, I was open and exposed.

I loved it.

I sat up, putting on my sunglasses and watching the water crash onto the shore.

"This place... it's something else." Marta shook her head in disbelief as she spoke.

"You're right about that. Still doesn't feel real."

"People like this Logan character live in a way that people like us only dream about," she replied, her eyes on the water. "Even your father, wealthy as he is, would be impressed by all of this."

The mere mention of Dad was enough to make my stomach tighten.

"You want to hear something weird?" I asked.

"What's that, *chica*?"

"I know that I'm a million miles away from my father, but part of me still half-expects him to pop out from behind a tree or a rock and scold me for what I'm doing."

Marta let out a light laugh. "It makes perfect sense. You've lived under his rules for so long that it's hard for you to imagine any other way to be."

Out of the corner of my eye, I noticed Marta pursing

her lips, her expression turning to one of contemplation. I could sense that something was on her mind that she wasn't sure how to say.

I offered her a warm smile. "Come on, Marta. When have you ever been shy about telling me what's on your mind?"

"Ah, it's *estupido*. But it's something I'm wondering about anyway."

"What is it?"

A few beats of silence hung in the air. I sat up, resting my arms on my knees as I turned my head toward her.

"Maybe it's the last thing on your mind, but I'm wondering if you miss your father."

I opened my mouth to speak, but before I could get a single word out, Marta raised her finger to silence me.

"Think about it," she said. "Before you go off, that man, hard as he can be at times is your flesh and blood. People like me would kill to have a parent in our lives. Not everyone is as lucky as you, my dear."

Marta had a point. All the same, her sentiments didn't change how I felt in the slightest.

"I don't miss him. Not even a little bit."

Marta raised an eyebrow in surprise.

"You're serious about that?" she asked. "You don't have the slightest bit of longing for him?"

"Nope. Hell, if I had the choice to never go back to New York, I think I'd do it."

Marta said nothing for a few long moments, eventually shaking her head in disbelief.

"That's strange to hear, *chica*."

"Are you serious? After the way he's treated me since I was a little girl, you're surprised that I'd feel this way?"

"I know your father can be... harsh."

"That's one way to put it. The prick's kept me locked up in that damn house for *years*."

"You know that's not the truth. You're making it sound like your room was a jail cell. He let you leave to go swimming or go for walks and all of that."

"That just proves my point even more, don't you see? He *lets me* do all of the kinds of things that a woman my age should have a *right* to do. I shouldn't have to ask permission to leave the house to get some fresh air or take a swim."

Marta pursed her lips again, and I could sense that she knew she couldn't really argue with that.

"All the same, I know that your father has his parenting quirks, but he loves you... in his own way."

I couldn't help but snort. As I let out the noise, I reached into my bag and pulled out the novel I'd been reading, *IT* by Stephen King. Marianne's YA fiction was fun, but I'd been plowing through those in a matter of hours. A big doorstop like *IT*, something I could sink my teeth into and spend some time with, had caught my attention the last time I'd been in the library.

For the moment, the book was a prop with which to make my point.

"Here's another example," I said, holding the book up. "There's no way in hell Dad would let me read anything like this. And this bikini! You said yourself that you had to sneak it here so Dad wouldn't find out about it. He's completely controlled my life—telling me what I can wear, what I can and cannot do, what I am allowed to *read*. And don't even get me started on how he controls everything I eat.

"But you're a prisoner here all the same, Emily," Marta said, a tinge of confusion in her voice. "You're not allowed to leave at all."

"You're right but again, I'm here because my father ordered it. Between the two flavors of being a prisoner, however, this one tastes a hell of a lot better. Not to mention the little detail that Dad's overall plan with me was to keep me locked away until he could marry me off to some cartel prick who'd treat me as a sex toy and breeding cow, and that's if I'm lucky. Nope—I'll take this prison cell over what my asshole of a father had in mind for me any day." I swept my hand toward the ocean as I spoke.

Marta said nothing. I glanced over to see a strange expression on her face, one I wasn't used to... she appeared *hurt*.

"You OK over there?" I asked.

Marta cleared her throat and shook her head, as if coming back into the moment. The typical toughness returned to her face.

"It's fine, *chica*. I asked you a question, and you gave me an honest answer."

All the same, I felt compelled to say something.

"Listen, I'm sorry. It's just... the subject of Dad and the way he treats me, it's not a pleasant one. I'm not going to apologize for my take on the whole thing, but I shouldn't have jumped down your throat like that."

"It's OK, *chica*."

I could sense that she hadn't been entirely mollified by my words. All the same, if Marta was going to be upset over me not caring for the way Dad had treated me, that was her own business to sort out.

"Look at this!" I said, gesturing toward the water once more. "We're on the beach, the weather's perfect, and there's not a thing in the world to worry about. So, let's relax and enjoy ourselves, OK?"

Marta cleared her throat once more, sitting up.

"Sí, you're right. No need to talk about subjects that don't make either of us happy. Better to focus on the good things."

I smiled at her answer before placing my book on my legs and opening it. I began to read, but it was hard to focus. I kept thinking about Marta, kept thinking about how different she'd been since she'd arrived.

Marta had always been sassy—the type of woman to tell you exactly what was on her mind and not give a damn what you thought. It was one of my favorite traits of hers. But since she'd come to the island she'd been nothing but negative, constantly making comments about Logan, implying that he was somehow worse than my father. I didn't like it at all.

I did my best to push the issue out of my head, instead trying to focus on the good things around me—the water, the sun, the book on my lap. It was hard to do though because out of the corner of my eye, I could see Marta sitting there looking totally uncomfortable, nervous, even.

As I tried to read, I found my attention still drifting. I thought about Marta back at the house, how she'd had a quick, mild freakout at the idea of Marianne coming to the beach with us. It was almost as if she'd wanted to make sure we were alone.

But why?

Once more, I tried to turn my attention to the words on the page. A few sentences in, however, I heard something. It was a strange sound, like a big, angry bee buzzing in the distance. It grew louder and louder.

I set down my book, looking up at the water. Sure enough, a boat was approaching—a red and white speedboat tearing through the waves, drawing closer and closer by the second.

"Who the hell is that?" I placed the book face down on the towel in front of me. "They're way too close to us."

Marta didn't answer. Instead, she rose slowly, sticking her arms into the air and waving them around.

"Hey, hey!" she called out, yelling at the top of her lungs. "We're over here!"

Something was happening. My stomach grew tighter by the second, the urge to get up and run building within. Strange as it might've seemed, my first instinct was to call for Logan. But I knew he was nowhere nearby.

I rose, standing next to Marta and squinting my eyes to get a better look at the boat. It was coming right toward us, three men on board. As they drew closer, one more horrible detail was revealed.

The men were armed.

Each of them had a rifle in their hands. The men were dressed all in black, with sunglasses hiding their eyes and bandanas over the bottom part of their faces.

I had to run. I had to get out of there.

Without waiting another second, I turned and prepared to bolt. Before I could take even a single step, something stopped me, some*one* stopped me, a hard grip on my wrist. I turned, horror on my face as I realized it was Marta.

"What the hell are you doing?" I asked. "Let me go!"

I tried to pull my hand away from her grasp, but Marta held me with surprising strength. Her expression was hard, determined.

"Please, Emily, don't run."

Despite Marta holding me in place, the boatful of armed men drawing closer by the second, I did my best to stay calm. The speedboat's motor grew louder, the sound nearly deafening.

"Marta, please tell me right now what's going on." My voice cracked a bit from the fear running through my body.

"You have nothing to be worried about, *chica*. Those men, they were hired by your father. Don't you see, this is a rescue mission!" She smiled as if that were news that I'd be happy about. A new pulse of fear blasted through me.

I had to run.

"Over here!" Marta shouted, waving with her free hand. "You have to hurry!"

Taking advantage of her momentary distraction, I put my hand on Marta's shoulder and shoved her hard. Marta let out a cry as she let go of my wrist and stumbled backward, and I had my chance. I turned and ran hard, my legs pumping, my feet pounding into the hot sand.

But I didn't get very far. I hit a pocket in the sand, my foot twisting to the side, my leg giving out underneath me. I stumbled forward, landing hard on my elbow, more pain rushing through me.

I rolled over onto my side, watching with bleary eyes as the boat approached, coming to a stop a hundred or so feet away from the shore. Marta ran in front of me, waving her arms.

"Right here! Hurry, before she runs again!"

I struggled to get up, the pain in my ankle too much to put weight on. The men jumped out of the boat and into the shallow water, guns in hand.

CHAPTER 18

LOGAN

"Where the hell are you?"

The growl of the Gator ATV filled the air as I tore down the path toward the beach. From my vantage point on the hill, I'd been able to see the speedboat as it'd driven closer to the shore. At that moment, it was out of sight.

"At guard post C." Robert's voice crackled in through the walkie-talkie. "Luis and I are on our way now."

Guard post C—that was all the way on the other side of the estate. Even if Roberto hauled ass in his Gator, there was no way he'd make it in time.

"Call the rest of the men," I said. "I want them heavily armed and wearing armored vests."

"Will do, *jefe*. Don't go running headlong into trouble now, you hear? You're not as good of a shot as me."

In spite of the severity of the situation, I allowed myself a small smile. Roberto and the rest of the guards may not have been near enough to help, but I was. Not a chance I'd let anything happen to Emily.

I pulled the Gator just behind the bluff overlooking the

beach. Once there, I killed the engine and dismounted, taking my pistol out and clicking off the safety. I'd counted three men, which meant that I'd need the element of surprise if I was going to get through this encounter without being turned into Swiss cheese.

A scream cut through the air and I knew it was Emily. Anger coursed through me, pure rage at the idea of one of those assholes so much as laying a hand on her. I closed my eyes, forcing a moment of calm. I knew the fastest way to end up with a bullet in the head would be to run headlong into the fight like an idiot.

"Over here! Hurry, before the guards come!"

I recognized the voice right away as Marta's. I cursed myself for allowing her onto the island. I'd known deep down that inviting her was a terrible idea. But part of me had hoped that her presence would make things easier for Emily.

It'd be the last time I didn't trust my gut.

Gun in hand, I made my way up the bluff, taking cover behind one of the towering palm trees at the top. From there, I was able to get a good view of the beach. I saw Emily, and Marta nearby waving her arms for the men. Three black-clad goons were in the process of wading through the water. They were armed with rifles, which would be more than enough to do some serious damage.

The men stepped out of the water, making their way slowly toward Emily and Marta. They were a good hundred and fifty feet from me. I was a decent shot and could handle myself in a fistfight, but three men armed with automatic weapons was no joke.

The trio continued toward Emily. Marta rushed to them.

"What the hell took you so long?" she asked. "You *idiotas* were supposed to be here thirty minutes ago!"

One of the men replied in Spanish, his tone suggesting that he didn't care one bit for the way he was being spoken to. The men formed up, preparing to gather around Emily and take her to the boat.

No way I was going to let that happen. Emily screamed as the men drew near.

The distance between the trio and me was less than ideal. However, it was what I had to work with. I raised my pistol slowly, holding it with both hands as I took aim. I pointed the weapon at the man farthest away from Emily, hoping to hit him but not wanting to risk harming her. After expelling all of the air from my lungs, I pulled the trigger slowly.

A *pop* sounded from the pistol, the bullet casing launching from the side and landing in the sand.

"*Pinche puta!*"

I looked up to see that my shot had hit home. The man had fallen onto the sand, his hands wrapped around his thigh where the bullet had struck. The other two men stood confused.

This was my chance.

I sprang from behind the tree, letting out a roar as I ran down the bluff, pointing the gun into the air above where the men stood and firing a shot. The gunshots and the screaming did the job of scaring the hell out of them. Their discipline broke, one of them turning tail at the sight of me and running back toward the water.

The man on the ground continued to cry out in pain as the sand around him turned red from the blood spurting out of his leg. Marta, having seen what was happening, hurried to his side to help him up. Once his arm was wrapped around her shoulders, the pair started in the direction of the boat, moving as quickly as a hobbled man and a middle-aged woman could.

The other man remained. He stood still, clicking off the safety of his rifle and preparing to fire.

He wasn't fast enough. I quickly closed the distance between us, raising the pistol into the air and bringing it down hard onto his face. The connection pulverized his nose and sent blood streaming down the bandana covering his features. He let out a cry, his hands going from his gun to his face. I finished the attack with a quick kick to the gut, knocking the air out of him.

"*Aye, cobarde!*" Marta shouted, now moving through the water with the wounded man. "*Haga algo!*"

The third man, the one who'd taken off running, stopped at her words. He began to fiddle with his gun with nervous hands, but I wasn't about to let him fire so much as a single shot. I quickly glanced down at Emily.

"You OK?"

She nodded, her hands still wrapped around her ankle. "I think so, just twisted something."

"Good. Give me a sec."

I tossed the gun aside, breaking out into a full sprint toward the final man. He managed to raise his gun right as I closed the distance between the two of us, and I quickly grabbed the end and shoved it up and out of the way, a quick shot firing off. The barrel of the gun was hot as hell, my skin burning like mad as I held the gun up.

Ignoring the pain, I drove my other hand into his side, avoiding the armored plating of his carrier vest. The strike hit home, my fist slamming hard enough into him to break a rib or two. He tried to pull off a kick, but it was easily grabbed. His foot in my hands, I yanked him off his feet and into the water. From there, it was a simple matter of pulling the gun from his grip.

"All of you!" I shouted, taking aim at each of them in turn. "You have thirty seconds to get the fuck off my island before you die!"

Marta and the men paused for a moment, my words sinking in along with the fact that their kidnapping operation had been foiled in less than three minutes. I held the gun aloft as the wounded men scrambled to the boat. Once the four of them were on board, I kept the gun pointed in their direction as the engine roared to life and the boat turned.

The second it was over the horizon and the danger had passed, I clicked the safety on the gun and slung it over my shoulder, running toward Emily. She was already in the process of standing back up, but the wince on her face was a sign she felt pain.

"Stay off it!" I called out as I approached. "If you broke something the last thing you want to do is put weight on the injury."

"It's fine. Just twisted something, I think."

"Not going to take that chance."

Despite everything that had just happened, it was impossible not to notice how fucking sexy Emily looked in that black bikini. Maybe it was the adrenaline rushing through my veins, but my cock twitched to life as I approached. I bent down a bit, scooping her off her feet.

"Hey! What the hell!"

The shock only lasted for a moment. Once she was in my arms, Emily looked me up and down. Her lips parted, and no doubt she had the same thing on her mind that I did. I leaned down and kissed her hard.

Our tongues found each other right away. I held her

close, one arm wrapped around her bare legs, the other around her middle. Didn't matter that I'd come close to death—Emily, and her safety, were the only things on my mind.

The growl of another Gator approaching snapped me out of the kiss. I took my lips away, giving myself a moment to appreciate Emily's ridiculously gorgeous face.

I looked up to see Roberto and Luis hopping out of the Gator, guns in hand.

"What the hell happened?" Roberto called out.

Emily still in my arms, I approached the pair.

"Marta was a traitor and complicit in an attempted kidnapping," I replied. "Charles was behind it, of course."

Roberto glanced down at my new gun, then up at the beach.

"We got here as fast as we could."

"I understand. No sense in worrying about what happened, what we need to do now is prepare for another attack. I want round-the-clock boat patrols, and another half-dozen guards for the island. Charles's men aren't going to set so much as another foot on my beach."

"*Entiendo*," Roberto said, turning his attention to Emily. "Are you OK?"

"Fine," she replied.

"We're going back to the house. I want you and all the rest of the men to do a sweep around the island. Get a pair up in the helicopter to make sure we don't have any surprises waiting for us. For all we know, that could've been a distraction for the real invasion."

"Will do, *jefe*. I'll make sure to initiate security protocols for the estate once you're back, get it locked up nice and tight."

Without another word, I nodded at Roberto then loaded Emily into the Gator and started the engine.

The Charles situation had just gone to another level. But in that moment, the stunning woman at my side was the only thing on my mind.

CHAPTER 19

EMILY

"Tell me how you're feeling."

The island was a blur before me as the vehicle rushed away from the beach.

Logan's words sounded distant, as if he were underwater. It was nearly impossible to muster the mental energy to reply.

"Huh?"

He placed his hand on my shoulder, giving me a reassuring squeeze as he drove.

"I said, tell me how you're feeling."

I closed my eyes, attempting to answer the question in the most honest way I could.

"My ankle hurts."

"I know. You twisted it. At least, that's all I hope happened."

The situation with my ankle was easy to sort out in my mind. I fell, it hurt. The rest of what had happened on the beach was another story. Marta's betrayal, the terrifying arrival of the men, Logan rushing in like a freaking action hero... it was all too surreal to even process.

"I'm fine." I turned in my seat, Logan visible in the corner of my eye. He didn't say anything, but I could sense that he didn't believe my answer.

It didn't take long until we reached the estate. Four guards were at the gate, all swarming to the ATV as Logan pulled to a stop. He issued orders to them in a commanding voice, telling them where to go and what to do. Once that was done, he pulled the ATV the rest of the way onto the estate, the heavy gate shutting behind us. I was relieved when it was closed. The gate wasn't just for show; I could tell the bars were solid, likely made of steel.

When Logan killed the ATV engine, I prepared to step off.

"Not yet," he said. "You're not putting a pound of weight on that ankle until I've had a chance to take a look at it."

I wanted to protest, but the tone in Logan's voice made it clear there was no point in that.

"Yeah. Sure."

He stepped over and scooped me up, my body pressing against his. As much as I wanted to walk on my own two feet, I had to admit that there was something nice about the way he held me, something that made me feel as if danger couldn't touch me.

Logan carried me up the stairs of the mansion, the doors opening on their own. The staff was waiting inside, all of them regarding us with worried expressions. Pearl hurried over.

"What the hell happened down there?" she asked.

"I'll tell you all about it later." Logan's tone was firm and commanding. "Right now, I need to get her upstairs."

"Of course." Pearl glanced down at my ankle, noticing

the issue right away. She placed her hand on the swollen spot, a tinge of pain radiating outward from it. "Hurt?"

"Yeah, a little."

She smiled. "Could be a hell of a lot worse. Get up there and lie down."

With that, Logan carried me up the stairs all the way to the third floor, toward what seemed to be the master bedroom.

Logan carried me over to the big bed, setting me down. The covers were soft as silk, the mattress like laying on a cloud. The sensation was enough to bring me the first smile I'd had since the incident on the beach.

Once I was on the bed, Logan gave me a look over with careful eyes, as if wanting to make sure there were no other injuries that he might have missed. Despite all that was happening, I liked his eyes on my body.

"Stay there," he said. "Be right back."

He stepped away, heading into the ensuite bathroom.

He returned a moment later with a small medical kit.

"Wait," I said, watching him kneel down and set the kit onto the bed. "Do you know what you're doing?"

"I know a little bit of first aid. Had to learn it a while back."

He didn't go into any more detail than that, leaving me to wonder where he'd learned such skills and why.

Once more, he examined my ankle.

"How does that feel?"

"It hurts. But not too badly."

"That's a good sign. Now, what I want you to do is rotate your foot. Do it slowly."

I nodded, obeying his command. Slowly, carefully, I began to rotate my foot. A dull ache radiated from the area, but I was able to do it.

"How does that feel?" he asked.

"I mean, not great. But it's not the worst pain in the world."

"More good news. Now, I want you to try and put weight on it."

I nodded, moving my butt slowly off the bed, putting my right foot onto the cool, smooth tile. Once that was done, I repeated the process with the injured left one. At first, it was OK, nothing too horrible. The more weight I put onto it, however, the more it hurt.

"Ow-ow-ow."

Logan quickly raised my left foot off the ground, helping me back onto the bed.

"That's bad," I said. "Right?"

He shook his head, standing up. "I don't think it's broken. If it was, you wouldn't be able to move it or tolerate any weight on it."

"So, what's the prognosis, doc?"

"You'll need to stay off it for a few days and let it heal. We've got a set of crutches around here somewhere. I'll have Pearl look for them."

He sat down onto the bed next to me, my bare leg grazing against him and sending a thrill through me. His nearness was impossible not to notice. Despite what had just happened down on the beach, all I could think about was how good the heat radiating off of him felt.

"Your ankle's one thing. How are you feeling otherwise?"

"I don't know. Need some time to process it."

"I'm sure. Important thing is that you're safe."

Logan placed his hand on my bare thigh. I wasn't sure if he'd done it intentionally, or without thinking. Either way, his touch was enough to send a hot surge of arousal through my body. My pussy tingled, and I squirmed a bit where I sat.

He turned to me. "You alright?"

I wasn't alright. In fact, I was so turned on that I could hardly think straight. Part of me wanted to tell him to take his hand off my thigh so I could compose myself. The other part of me, the greater part, wanted him to move his hand up farther.

"I think so. I'm just glad you're here with me now."

His hand began to move up my leg slowly, inch by inch, his rough palm impossibly sensual against my soft thigh. It wasn't long before his hand was at my hip. With a sharp pull, he brought me toward him, turning me to face him.

Then he kissed me.

The sensation of his lips upon mine was more than enough to melt away the lingering anxiety from what had happened on the beach. His tongue found mine and I let out a soft moan. He squeezed my hip, handling me in that stern, commanding way that I couldn't resist.

The kiss became deeper, our lips forming a tight seal together. My pussy grew wetter by the second, every part of me yearning for his touch and his warmth and his passion. His hand soon traveled from my hip to my inner thigh, my nipples hardening in anticipation of what he was about to do.

Logan inched up, up until he was right on the border of my bikini bottom. Once there, he pulled the tight fabric aside, exposing my pussy. He then touched me in the way I craved, spreading my lips and teasing my clit. His other hand stayed on my lower back, guiding me to lay down.

I fell onto the bed, my chest rising and falling as he

rubbed my clit with his fingertip. I opened my eyes to watch him move onto the ground in front of the bed.

He flashed me a small smile as he moved onto the floor, wrapping his arms around my legs and pulling me toward him. Logan brought his lips to my inner thigh, kissing me slowly, letting me savor each press of his lips against my skin.

He moved closer and closer until he was at my center, the sensation enough to send waves of delight through my body. I gasped at the sensation of his mouth on me in that way, the pleasure something I hadn't been prepared for.

He kissed me, his tongue doing the work on my clit that his finger had been performing only a few seconds ago. I breathed in and out, my chest rising and falling, my hips squirming as the delight built and built until I could take no more. I opened my mouth and let out a cry that filled the room as his tongue danced on my clit, his hands on my thighs.

The orgasm came and went, and when it was finished, Logan wasted no time rising. He reached forward and put his hands on my hips, flipping me over in a manner that was wonderfully aggressive, but not rough enough to hurt me.

Once I was on my belly, I turned around to watch as he disrobed, taking off his linen shorts and T-shirt, exposing his perfect, statuesque body. I paid special attention to his legs, which were thick and powerful as tree trunks.

"Take off your bikini." It was that commanding tone again.

"You're so bossy sometimes," I replied with a grin.

"Take it off. Or I'll take it off for you."

I practically melted into a puddle of pure arousal at his words. I did as he commanded, slipping out of my bikini bottom and tossing it aside, followed by untying the string of my top and removing it. When I was totally bare, he pulled his black boxer briefs down his legs and threw them aside. His cock was solid and stiff.

He knelt behind me, wrapping his huge arm around my middle and pulling my ass up, his head grazing my lips. I couldn't wait any longer. I reached behind me, taking his cock and guiding it to my pussy, pressing my ass back against him until he was inside me.

Logan's thickness stretched me out, filling me in exactly the way I wanted to be filled. Through the pleasure, I turned and watched as his cock vanished into me, his body moving closer to mine until he was buried deep.

"God, you feel so fucking good." He growled the words into my ear, making me moan again from the sensation of his hot breath against my skin.

I pushed my ass up, forcing him into me as deeply as he would go. Logan got the message, pulling back and driving into me firmly, another cry coming from my lungs as he entered again. He pulled back and entered again, then again, then again, my ass shaking from the collision of our bodies, the pleasure ripping through me.

He soon steadied into a slow, deep rhythm. I could hardly believe how good he felt, the richness of the pleasure he instilled in me. He was in total control.

The way Logan made love to me was the perfect blend of sensual and firm. It didn't take long before another orgasm was on the verge. His thrusting grew faster until he released, his cock pulsing inside as my own orgasm exploded through me. My back arched, my limbs stiffening as I cried out, a hard grunt shooting from his mouth as his muscles tensed.

He poured into me, his warm seed shooting deep. I closed my eyes and savored it, not wanting to miss even a single sensation of how goddamn good this man made me feel.

CHAPTER 20

LOGAN

"Someone's a million miles away."

I should've been focused on the moment. Because the moment was a damn good one. Cool air breezed into the bedroom through the open windows, the hush of the waves upon the shore audible in the distance. Then there was the gorgeous, impossibly sexy woman curled up at my side.

Emily had noticed that my mind was somewhere else. In my defense, how could it not be? It'd been less than an hour ago that I'd fought off a damn invasion and attempted kidnapping on my own goddamn island.

Rage burned deep inside. I wanted to kill Charles, to rip him limb-from-limb. My island was one thing—a belonging that could be replaced like any other. What truly caused the anger to boil was how he'd put Emily, his own daughter, at such great risk. All it would've taken was a single bullet to shoot wide.

Emily sat up, an expression of concern on her face.

"Seriously, something's wrong."

That was another bother, how easily Emily made my emotions come to the forefront. I took pride in not being easy to read. The way I felt about Emily, however, caused me to wear my emotions right there on my sleeve.

I wasn't normally one to talk openly about my feelings, and I wasn't planning on starting. All the same, I had to say something to her. She'd gone through it with me, after all.

"Thinking about the attack."

She let out an amused snort. "Logan, why not let me in a little bit? Are you worried? Scared? Tell me." Emily reached forward and placed her hand on my chest, right over my heart.

Scared? Worried? I didn't have time for such frivolous, useless emotions. Anger wasn't much better, but at least that particular emotion had the potential to motivate.

"Just pissed that it happened, pissed that you came so close to getting hurt."

"But I wasn't hurt. You saved me."

"Yeah, I did. But if I had shown up just a few minutes later..."

Emily shook her head. "You *didn't* show up a few minutes later. You showed up right on time. And damn, that was something else to see you at work. Where the hell did you learn those kinds of moves anyway?"

I wasn't in the mood for a conversation about my past.

"Don't worry about it."

She opened her mouth to object, but closed it before saying anything, shaking her head with a smirk on her face, as if she'd been silly to have expected any other answer.

"And letting Marta onto the island," I went on. "That was sloppy and foolish."

"Never in a million years would I have guessed that Marta would do something like that, that she'd betray me to my freaking dad. I always thought she was on my side, you know? I thought she was looking out for me. Turns out I was wrong."

"Could be. Perhaps in her own way she'd convinced herself of the rightness of her actions. Might be that she thought she was doing you a favor."

Emily sat up, running her hand through her thick, dark hair. "It's too much to process."

I sat up with her. "Not to mention that you don't need to worry about anything right now other than getting better. I'll find out the how's and whys of what happened."

Still sitting up, she turned her attention to her twisted ankle.

"Be careful on that thing," I said. "You lucked out by not fracturing it. You go too hard too quickly and you might make it worse."

Without replying, she rotated her ankle slowly. I watched, expecting her to let out a cry of pain. That didn't happen. Instead, she turned toward me and flashed a smile.

"Barely hurt at all."

"That's good. But don't—"

Emily didn't even let me finish my sentence before she slid off the bed and onto her feet. Instead of buckling under the pain, she stood normally.

"You OK?" I asked.

"It hurts a little bit. But nothing crazy. Much better than earlier."

I watched her step around the room. The sight of Emily moving around, completely naked, was almost hypnotic. Her heavy breasts bounced with each step, the muscles of her long, slender legs tensing. She was a thing of beauty. When she was done testing out her ankle, she turned to me with a smile.

"Good as new, I think."

"Maybe. Still, I wouldn't go running on that thing if I were you. Give it a few days before you're back to normal."

Emily came over and sat down on the bed next to me. I glanced ahead at the open door to the bathroom.

"I'm going to take a shower," I said. "Why don't you relax here for a little while. Lie down and rest, at least until I'm done in there. Give your ankle a little time to recover."

She nodded, as if seeing the sense in my words.

"Alright. Only because you asked." She followed up her words with a wink, then scooted back onto the bed and laid down.

I rose, eager to step into the shower. I was still tense from the fight, and a little high-pressure soak sounded like just the thing to work through it. As I stepped into the bathroom, I cast one last glance over my shoulder.

Emily was on the bed curled up, laying on her side in a way that drew my attention to the sensual curve of her hip. We'd only just had sex, but a single orgasm hadn't come close to satisfying my desire for her. My cock twitched to life, stiffening by the moment until I forced my eyes away from her.

I closed the door slowly. My bathroom was huge, perhaps excessively so. A clawfoot tub was at one end, a jacuzzi in the corner on the other side of that. A massive mirror with two sinks was situated on the opposite side of the door.

The real piece de resistance of the room was the enormous shower sauna that took up a third of the space. It was gigantic, big enough for a dozen people, at least, that's what the contractor had told me.

I stepped into the shower, the floor and walls dark wood, a bench going all around. The electronic panel lit up as the sensors detected me, numbers appearing as I waved my hand in front of the control panel. After a bit of tooling with the settings, I had a triple-stream shower going, hot water hitting me from just about every angle.

It was heaven. Not quite as nice as being in bed with Emily, but the shower did wonders to help me work through tension that had taken hold since the attack.

The attack... A fresh wave of anger ran through me as I remembered it. I'd done the right thing by letting those pricks go. All the same, I couldn't help but imagine what could have happened had things gone differently back there. It'd be a simple matter of grabbing one of their guns and popping them off one by one. I'd leave Marta alive so that she could inform her asshole boss of what had gone down.

There was a hell of a lot to do. I'd need to meet with Roberto and discuss the assault and come up with a plan to defend against the next one. On top of that, I'd need to add more guards, make sure they were armed with top-of-the-line weapons, no room for mistakes.

Through the sound of the rushing water from the shower, I heard the bathroom door open. I turned where I stood, my blood running hot at the idea of someone getting the drop on me. But beyond the fogged glass of the shower, I made out a figure I'd be able to spot anywhere.

Emily approached the shower with slow, sensual steps, and as she drew closer, I could see that she hadn't bothered to put her bikini back on. She approached the glass and knocked softly.

"Yes?"

"Can I come in?"

"Yeah. You can."

She opened the door, steam from the heated water

cascading over her perfect body. Emily entered, looking around at the space.

"You've got your own steam room in here?" she asked.

My eyes were locked onto her body. I'd barely processed her question.

"Yeah," I said, coming back to the moment. "Jealous?"

She chuckled. "Extremely. Don't get me wrong, my bathroom is nice. But this is on another level."

I turned, water running down my body and my cock.

"Something I can help you with?" I asked. "And aren't you supposed to be staying off that ankle?"

She raised her foot, rotating her ankle as if nothing was wrong in the slightest.

"Feels better by the minute. Anyway, I thought a shower sounded pretty nice. And..." She trailed off, looking away with a smile on her face.

"And what?"

"And... Well, I thought that there might be something I could help *you* with."

"Is that right?"

She began making her way over to me. "Mmm-hmm. I was thinking that after all you did back at the beach, you could use a little relaxation." Emily closed the distance between the two of us, draping her arms over my shoulders.

"What kind of relaxation did you have in mind?"

"I could tell you. But I'd rather *show* you."

Emily stepped up on her tiptoes, coming in for a kiss. Part of me wanted to resist and tell her we needed to pump the brakes on what was happening between us. But how the hell was I supposed to refuse a woman like her naked in my damn shower?

So, I didn't. I kissed her right back, letting my hands fall onto her perfect tits, then down to the curves of her hips.

"I hope you had more in mind than just a kiss," I said with a grin.

"Someone's presumptuous." She reached down and took hold of my stiff cock, wrapping her fingers around it. "Presumptuous and eager." Emily stroked me for a bit, the pleasure beginning instantly. "OK, so... I wanted to do something. But I'm not exactly sure how."

I said nothing for a moment, savoring how damn good it felt to have her hand on my cock like that.

"Tell me."

"I want to taste you." I nearly came right then at her words.

"Just don't use your teeth and we'll be fine," I said. Emily grinned, standing on her feet for one more kiss. I kissed her back, but her lips only stayed there for a moment before she moved them to my cheek, then to my jaw, then my neck. Bit by bit, she made her way down my body, marking her path with kisses. Soon she was down on her knees, my cock right in front of her face.

She turned her attention to it, leaning forward and placing a kiss on the end. I watched as she opened her mouth, flicking out her tongue and using it to tease me a bit more before sealing her lips around my end.

Emily looked up at me, and the sight of her on her knees with my cock in her mouth was about the sexiest damn thing I'd ever seen. She went down slowly, taking more of me into her. I placed my hand on the back of her head, guiding her down, down until she stopped. Once she hit about the halfway point, her eyes flashed wide and she went back up.

"That was a lot," she said.

"You're doing fine," I said. "Hell, better than fine. Just keep doing what you were doing."

She nodded, then went back to it. Emily brought my cock into her mouth, forming a tight seal as she descended down my length once more. After reaching the halfway point again, she went back up and gave my head another lashing with her tongue.

She soon had a steady rhythm going, her lips going down my shaft, up and down, up and down.

I took her hand as she sucked me, placing it on my balls. Emily got the hint, squeezing me gently as she sucked. The pleasure was intense, and I felt myself grow weak in the knees as the orgasm built.

Right as I was approaching the edge, Emily took my cock out of her mouth and stood up.

"Something wrong?" I asked.

She didn't respond with words. Instead, Emily took me by the hand and led me over to the benches on the other side of the space. Once there, she turned around and sat down, spreading her legs before me.

"That was more of a turn-on than I expected," she said. "Now let's finish together."

I stepped closer to her. "Ask me nicely, and maybe you'll get what you want."

Emily licked her lips. "Please. Please fuck me until we both come."

I took hold of my cock and drove it into her. She moaned loudly, her pussy soaking wet. Emily wrapped her legs around me and I wasted no time driving into her with wild abandon, bringing the both of us closer to orgasm until we released at the same time, my cock draining deep inside of her.

We said nothing for a time, catching our breath and recovering.

CHAPTER 21

EMILY

It was the day after my shower with Logan, and my body still felt electrified. I was seated on my balcony, my laptop open in front of me as I switched back and forth between transcribing my handwritten notes and admiring the view.

A small smile formed on my lips as I lifted my eyes from the screen to watch the waves crash in on the shore. The island was so calming, so peaceful. Part of me never wanted to leave. I found myself not wanting to leave Logan, either.

How the hell could I possibly feel such a way for a man who was essentially my warden? I should've hated him the same way I hated my father. After all, I was just a pawn to both of them, a doll to keep in a box to bring out whenever they wanted.

I gave the matter more thought as I sat there, my fingers hovering over the keys. *Was* Logan truly the same as Dad? Was one really no better than the other? With Dad, it was simple—he was a prick, and a controlling, abusive one at that.

Logan, on the other hand... he seemed different. I tried

many, many times to muster up hate for him, to convince myself that he was evil but it never took. He was ruthless, sure. And after what I'd seen on the beach, I was convinced that he was also dangerous and deadly.

But evil?

Either way, I was only supposed to be there for another couple of weeks. If everything went how my father had planned for it to go, at the end of the month I'd be spirited away back to New York, to return to my bedroom prison until he saw it fit to send me off again. I took one more look at the beach, trying to burn the sight into my memory so that I'd never forget it.

A knock at my bedroom door snapped me out of my daydreaming. I rose, my ankle stinging a bit as I put weight on it.

"Who is it?"

"It's me!" Marianne shouted on the other side of the door. "Oh, and Pearl."

I smiled, making my way over to the door and opening it.

"Morning!" Marianne was all sunshine and smiles, her hair done up and her outfit a cute sundress and sandals. Pearl stood next to her, a tray of food in her hands.

"Morning," I replied.

"Mind if we come in?" Pearl asked. "Brought you a little something."

"Sure."

I stepped aside, Pearl entering and Marianne coming in behind her so excited that she was practically skipping.

"What's on the tray?" I asked.

"It's breakfast, silly!" Marianne replied as she bounded over to the end of my bed and sat down. "You know, the meal you skipped today?"

"Sorry. I guess I got so into my writing that I forgot to eat. Happens sometimes."

"Well, no meal goes skipped in this house," Pearl said. She set the tray down next to my laptop on the little table on the balcony. Once it was placed, she lifted the lid revealing a stack of pancakes, sliced-up fresh fruit, and a mini carafe of coffee. My stomach grumbled at the sight of it, my appetite awakening in full force.

"Now," Pearl said, dusting her hands as she came back into the room. "I'm going to take a look at your ankle. How's it feeling?"

"Fine," I said. "I mean, a little pain, but not much."

"Good. And I assume you've been avoiding jumping jacks and wind sprints like I told you?" Pearl winked as she tapped me on the shoulder, nodding toward the bed.

"I sure have," I replied with a grin.

I sat down next to Marianne, Pearl coming over and kneeling down in front of me. With quick, precise movements, Pearl poked and prodded my ankle. Surges of mild pain shot out here and there.

"How's that feel?" she asked, her eyes on my ankle.

"Not great but not horrible, either."

She nodded. "Just as the big man thought, nothing more than a mild sprain. Still a little purple here, but that's not the worst thing in the world." Pearl pushed herself up to her feet. "You'll be right as rain in another few days. I'd take some ibuprofen for the pain if you have any."

"Don't think I do."

Pearl nodded. "Eat your breakfast, I'll go grab some."

Without another word, Pearl exited the bedroom.

"OK, I don't know about you, but I'm hungry," I said, my eyes fixed on the food outside.

"Eat!" Marianne seemed totally thrilled. "I helped cut up some of the fruit."

I stepped outside, gesturing for Marianne to come with me. I popped a strawberry into my mouth, chewing it as I poured some coffee. I noticed Marianne was watching me out of the corner of my eye, a look of concern on her pretty face.

"Something wrong?" I asked. "Everything has been great so far, if that's what you're worried about."

Marianne pursed her lips, glancing down at her feet. "It's not that. It's just... how do you feel? I mean, not in the way that Pearl was checking. How do you feel in your heart?"

"My heart?" Her words gave me pause.

"I don't mean to be nosy—Logan's always telling me not to step into people's personal business. But you were attacked on the beach."

I realized right away what she was talking about.

"That had to have been so scary. Plus, Marta was your friend. I bet it didn't feel good at all to find out that she tricked you like that."

I once more shifted in my seat. The whole subject was too difficult to think about.

"It doesn't feel good, that's for sure. But Logan saved me. You should've seen him! He was so fast, running in and punching those jerks right in the face!"

Marianne smiled. "That sounds like Logan."

I sighed. "But with Marta... I'm not sure. I'm trying not to think about it, but when I do, I tell myself that she was only doing what she thought was the right thing."

"Pearl always says that the road to hell is paid with good intentions."

I chuckled, letting her malapropism slide. "She might be

right. In fact, I know she's right. I'm just glad that nothing really bad happened."

"I am too."

Marianne opened her arms to give me a hug that I eagerly accepted. When she released me, however, I saw that she had a confused expression on her face.

"Something wrong?"

"Uh-huh. Pearl tells me I'm not supposed to talk about this kind of stuff, but... do you have any women stuff?"

"Women stuff?"

"You know, like for your, um, lady problems."

It dawned on me what she was talking about. I opened my mouth to tell her sure, let me just run to the bathroom. But before I said that I realized that I didn't have anything to give her.

"You know what, I haven't had my, ah, lady problems since I've been here. I've actually been meaning to ask Pearl."

Marianne's eyes lit up. "There's lots of stuff down in the pantry storage. I'll go find Pearl and tell her that we both need them. Is that OK?"

"That's just fine. Thanks, Mar."

With another smile and nod, Marianne sprang from her chair and hurried out of my room, leaving me alone.

One thought was on my mind once she was gone—why hadn't I needed any period supplies? I closed my eyes, trying to think back when my last period was. I didn't know the exact days, but it was definitely over a month ago. Far more than a month ago, actually.

Panic gripped me. I was late, and I'd been having unprotected sex. I knew for a fact that I hadn't been taking the pill every day when I should've been. Marta had always been the one to remind me of that, and without her around...

Shit. Shit, shit, shit.

I stood up, my heart racing as I tried to wrap my mind around my situation. There was no way, no *way* that I could be...

Right in the middle of my panicking, a knock sounded at the door. I took a deep breath, hurrying over and opening it to find Logan standing there.

"Hey."

Even through my worrying, I couldn't help but notice how hot he looked in his navy linen pants and white, V-neck T-shirt.

"Hey," I replied, trying to play it cool. "What's up?"

He narrowed his eyes, as if unsure of how I might react to what he was about to say.

"Want to talk to your father?"

CHAPTER 22

LOGAN

G oddamn, she was the most beautiful woman I'd ever seen in my life.

Emily stood before me with an expression of bewilderment on her face. She had on not a drop of makeup, but with a face like hers that didn't matter one bit. I'd always preferred the natural look, anyway. She wore a pair of pink sleeping shorts and a tight T-shirt that hugged her braless breasts. My cock stiffened, and I wanted nothing more in that moment than to bend her over the bed and fill her full.

"My father?" The worry on her face was intense. It didn't take a genius to see that the mere mention of her father had put her into a tizzy. "Please don't tell me he's here on the island. I don't know if I can handle seeing him in person."

I shook my head. "Nope. If you decide to talk to him, it'll be on Zoom."

"Zoom? What's that?"

I chuckled at the reminder of how sheltered she was.

"Never mind," she said. "When does he want to talk?"

"Whenever you're ready."

She pursed her lips, bouncing her leg up and down as she thought the matter over. Emily folded her arms under her breasts, pushing them up in a way that made it nearly impossible not to stare.

"Can I have a moment?" she asked. "Like, in the bathroom. I need to shower and I haven't even brushed my teeth."

"Sure. Take your time."

"It'll only be a minute," she said. "Just need to think this over. You can wait here if you want."

"Yeah. I'll do that."

Emily flashed me an uneasy smile before rushing into the bathroom and shutting the door. Seconds later, the noise of rushing shower water sounded.

I stepped out onto the balcony, spotting Emily's barely-touched breakfast. A carafe of coffee was there with an empty mug. I poured myself a cup as I leaned onto the railing and watched the surf come in, the conversation I'd had with Charles only a few moments ago still fresh in my mind.

"You've got three seconds to tell me what the fuck happened, Charles."

I'd been in my office, the call coming through my computer. He'd called me with the video turned off—I was almost certain that he didn't want me to see him sweat. Being the coward that he was he probably didn't want to make eye contact, either.

"I don't know. I don't know what the fuck happened!"

I chuckled. "You think I'm going to buy that? If you're going to try to sell me a load of bullshit, at least try to put a creative spin on it."

"There's no creative spin to put on it because I'm telling you the truth, boring as it might be. I have no fucking idea who those men were, and why they were trying to get to my little girl."

"So, let me get this straight—Marta connived her way onto my island working with a team of men whose identities you have no clue of."

"That's what happened. Listen, I'm just as shocked as you are. Marta's been working with me for *years*, longer than Emily's even been alive. She was the last person I figured would stab me in the back like this."

"And you had no clue she had ulterior motives when she told you she wanted to come to the island?"

"Why would I? She'd told me she wanted to be with Emily, to make the transition a little easier to handle. Seemed perfectly fuckin' reasonable to me."

I wanted to chew him out, to keep telling him that he was full of shit, maybe even threaten him a little, until he finally gave up the act and told me what was really happening. However, strange as it might've seemed, part of me actually believed him. He'd called me, and I'd been able to detect the fear in his voice from the first word he'd uttered. Either he was a hell of an actor on top of being a total scumbag, or Charles was telling me the truth.

"Why the hell would I do this?" he asked, as if sensing my conflict. "The whole point of this arrangement was to smooth things over with you, to prove to you that you can trust me. Why would I jeopardize that?"

Another good point. Did it make sense that he'd put his daughter at risk in that way?

"Ah ha!" he said. "See? I can tell by your silence that you're thinking it over. You know I'm right!"

"Don't tell me what I am or am not thinking, Charles. Even if, and I mean *if*, you're not the one responsible for this, the fact of the matter is that a woman under your employ put the lives of me and my staff, not to mention Emily, at risk. One of the first rules of running any sort of organization is that ultimate responsibility lies with the person on top. In the case of my company, it's me. In the case of your household staff, it's you."

"I get it, I do, I really do. And trust me when I say that I'm going to find Marta and get to the bottom of what happened."

"I take it that means you haven't heard from her yet."

"Nope. Dropped off the face of the fuckin' earth. But I've got ways of tracking people down."

"For your sake, I hope you do."

He sighed. "I want to talk to her. I want to talk to my daughter."

"Funny thing about that. Emily hasn't once mentioned any desire to speak to you."

Charles snorted. "Little brat, little ungrateful brat. It doesn't matter what she wants. I want to talk to my daughter and make sure she's OK."

"She's a guest on *my* island at the moment, and I'm not into making my guests do anything they don't want to do."

"Please, Stone, I just want to talk to her."

"I'm going to hang up now. Then I'm going to go talk to Emily and tell her that you want to speak to her. If *she* wants to speak to *you*, I'll call you on this line. Understand?"

With that, I'd ended the call.

I took a long, slow sip of my coffee, my eyes still on the water. The bathroom door opened behind me, and I glanced over my shoulder to watch as Emily strode into the bedroom, her hair slicked back and a towel wrapped around her body just above her breasts.

She didn't give me a single look as she got dressed,

pulling on a pair of light blue panties and stripping her towel off, exposing her beautiful breasts for a moment as she put on a white bra. As much as I was enjoying the view, I decided to give her a bit of privacy as she finished getting dressed.

"Hey." A few moments later, she stepped out onto the balcony. Her hair was still slicked back, highlighting her stunning face. She wore a simple dress, white with a baby-blue floral pattern. Though all I could think about were the bra and panties she had on underneath.

"You think about it?"

She nodded. "I did. First, I want to know what the hell he wanted."

"According to him, he wanted to make sure you were alright."

She let out a loud, but humorless laugh. "Not a chance in hell he gives a shit about that. Well, aside from caring in the way someone would about property they were worried might've been damaged. I kind of wish you'd told him to go fuck himself."

I raised an eyebrow. "That's an expression I don't think I've heard you use."

Emily formed a sheepish grin, as if she were in trouble.

"Something about him brings it out of me, I guess." She cleared her throat and went on. "Really, there's no way he cares if I'm alright. Never cared a day in his life. I've always been more like... like a *prop* to him, something he has to maintain. He's never let me have friends, never let me experience the world. Instead, he's always treated me more like a prisoner or one of those harem women."

She let out another dry laugh, this one somehow even more mirthless than the last.

"You know, the other day Marianne was listening to

music, something I'd never heard before. I asked who it was, and she was shocked I didn't already know. She said it was someone named Taylor Swift."

"One of Marianne's favorites. Not my cup of tea."

Emily's eyes flashed. "See! Even you knew who she was. So, I go on Wikipedia and it turns out she's one of the most famous singers in the world. And I'd *never* heard of her."

Her face turned a deeper shade of red as her anger grew.

"My dad's a liar and a bastard, a real piece of shit." Her words dripped with venom. "Did I ever tell you about the two times I tried to rebel against him?"

"No."

She let out an amused snort. "Tried to sneak out once when I was fifteen. Just wanted to see what the world was like outside of my prison of a house or whatever boarding school he'd shipped me off to. Anyway, he caught me, took away my books, my journals, and even Marta. I was a kid, so I of course tried again a few months later. That time, he took all of that away again, and hit me."

Now it was my turn to feel anger. Just the thought of that prick laying his hands on Emily was enough to make me want to jump on my private plane and kick his ass in person. The conversation wasn't about me, however. I set my anger aside and focused on her.

She kept her eyes on the ocean, a single tear trickling down her face.

"You don't have to talk to him." I wiped the tear away with my thumb, gently turning her toward me. "And when I say that I mean you don't have to talk to him ever again."

Her eyes widened as it dawned on her what I was saying.

"You don't mean that. You don't know what you're saying."

"I wouldn't have said it if I hadn't meant it."

Emily pursed her lips and nodded. "Thank you. I mean that. Thank you for making me feel safe."

The anger subsided for a moment, replaced by the sentiment that I'd actually done the right thing back when I'd accepted Charles's barbaric proposal. Emily hugged me tightly, and I returned the hug, wrapping her in my arms and holding her close.

After a few moments, she stepped back.

"You know, I think I actually do want to talk to him."

"Are you sure?"

"I wouldn't have said it if I hadn't meant it." She offered a small smile and a wink as she echoed my words back to me. "You can listen in, if you want."

I shook my head. "This is between you and your father. Come with me."

CHAPTER 23

EMILY

Fear and anxiety gripped me as Logan and I walked upstairs. I wasn't sure where we were going, exactly. But with Logan at my side, I felt like I could do anything.

I was nervous as hell at the idea of talking to Dad. I knew he was a liar, that he'd lie to me again without thinking twice about it. However, I needed to make sure that Marta was alright. No matter what she'd done, Marta was the only person who'd ever loved me, the only mother I'd ever known.

Together, Logan and I approached the double doors that led to his office. My heart skipped a beat as I realized where we were standing.

"I thought this room was off-limits?"

"Not right now. Best place in the house for a private meeting. Come on."

He pushed the door open, revealing a massive room with towering windows up to the ceilings and a massive oak desk situated so that it looked out onto the ocean. Bookshelves were neatly arranged on one side of the room, a fireplace with a huge TV over it on the other. A small bar was in one corner, a meeting area of four wing-backed chairs and a black table in the other.

It was an impressive room in a house full of impressive rooms.

"Come here," he said, nodding toward his desk. "I've got Zoom open, let me show you how to use it."

I stepped around the enormous desk with him and in front of the computer. Logan gave me the basics in using a computer to conduct a video call.

"Do I have to look at him?" I asked, pointing at the video button. "I want to talk to him, but I don't know if I can handle looking into his eyes while he spits out one goddamn lie after another."

"I felt the same way, and that's why I turned off video. Just click here and... done."

A touch of calm ran through me.

"OK," Logan said. "I'm going to step out. But know that if you want to, you can end the call at any time. Tell him to fuck off and click the phone icon here."

"Thank you," I said. "I just need to do this all on my own."

He nodded in understanding. "OK. I'll be in the kitchen when you're finished. Call when you're ready by clicking here—his number is the last one in the list."

Logan prepared to move away. Before he did, however, I threw my arms around him and buried my face into his chest. He placed his hand on my back, and I felt so small in his grasp. I also felt protected, as if he'd do anything for me. Logan had put his own life in danger to make sure I was safe.

He squeezed me one last time.

"Good luck."

With that, he left me alone in the enormous room at the

enormous desk. I watched as he made his way to the other side of the room and left, shutting the door behind him. When I was ready, I clicked the button to call.

The phone rang a few times, and part of me hoped that Dad might not answer.

"Hello?" he asked. "Emily, is that you?"

I cleared my throat and spoke. "It's me."

A sigh of relief came from the other side. "Thank God. Em, you have no idea how worried I've been since I heard what happened. Hearing that you're safe and sound makes me so happy."

His voice was syrupy sweet, slathered with enough fake concern to make me want to puke. It was a good thing that I'd chosen to not do a video call—there was no way I would've been able to handle seeing his face while he said those phony as hell words.

"Why is the camera not on?" he asked. "Em, I want to see your face. Please."

I tensed, the idea of looking at Dad's face enough to make my stomach turn. My first instinct was to tell him to screw off, that I never wanted to see his face again.

"Please, Em."

"Fine." I leaned forward and hit the video button. My father's face, his features painted with an expression of over-the-top concern, appeared on the big TV over the fire-place. I could see myself in the corner, the camera attached to the computer on Logan's desk.

My stomach tensed as I looked upon my dad. Just seeing him was enough to make me never want to go home again.

"There you are," he said. "Good. You're looking fine. It's just... after what happened..."

"Yeah. I know. Speaking of which, where's Marta now?"

Anger tinged his face. "Marta? Why the hell do you care about her? She tried to kidnap you, remember? She put your life in danger. If I were you—"

"Well, you're not me. And I want to know where she is."

Dad shrugged sadly, shaking his head. "Em, your guess is as good as mine. Whatever happened with her on the beach, she'd planned it all on her own. I had nothing to do with it if you're wondering."

Dad's words didn't sit well with me. It was almost as if he was overselling the story he was weaving.

"But I have to wonder," he said. "Why didn't you get on that boat with her?"

"Huh?"

"You heard me. Marta, a woman you love and trust, gave you the chance to leave the prison where that prick Stone is keeping you. I would've thought that you'd been eager to get away. Why didn't you leave?"

"Are you kidding? Three men with guns pulled up to the beach while I'm wearing nothing but a bikini and demanded that I go with them, and you're honestly wondering why I didn't?"

His eyes narrowed. "A bikini? You know you're not supposed to be wearing clothes like that." The words seemed to escape from his mouth, his voice carrying the judgmental, controlling tone that I was used to.

"I was wearing what I *wanted* to wear," I shot back. "And that's got nothing to do with the story."

"I think it's got everything to do with the story. If your choice of beachwear is any indication, it sounds like Stone's giving you far more freedom than you ought to have. Makes sense that you'd use it to dress like a whore."

"What's wrong with you?" I asked. "I almost died and all you care about is what I was wearing?"

Dad formed his lips into a stern line, as if working past the anger he felt at the idea of me dressed in a bikini.

"You're right, more important things than that. Though we *will* discuss that matter when you're back at the house."

Just the mention of being back with my dad was enough to make me sick to my stomach.

"Why didn't you go with her? Why didn't you take the chance to escape Stone?"

"I told you why. And besides, you've always told me to be wary of people like that coming for me. You always told me that there were men who wanted to get ahold of me, and if they did, I'd wish that I was dead."

"You should've gone with her, Em. Let me ask you this, how many people are there on the island with you? There's you, and there's Stone. Who else?"

"What? Why?"

"How many guards? I'm sure a man like Stone keeps plenty of private security. How many are there?"

I had a rough idea of the answer—probably a dozen guards, plus the staff of ten or so that took care of the property. Then there was Marianne and Pearl. However, there wasn't a chance in hell I was going to give him any concrete information. The longer the conversation went on, the more certain I was that he was lying right to my face about his involvement with the attack, and that he was fishing for information that would make the next one successful.

"I don't know! I'm not going around counting. I spend most of my time in the house or on the beach and that's it. Hell, I don't even know how many guards are at *our* house."

Dad narrowed his eyes once again, tilting his head back.

"You seem different, Emily. You're more insolent than usual. What's going on there with you?" Anger flashed on his face, replacing the skepticism.

The anger on his face was unlike anything I'd ever seen before, and I'd seen Dad angry plenty of times.

"If I'm different, it's because I'm not locked up in some damn house all the time."

My father's eyes appeared almost black as he leaned toward the screen as if to get a better look at me. "You fucked him, didn't you?"

His words made my blood run cold.

"What are you talking about?"

"Don't even try to lie to me. My men told me what happened on the beach, that he came to your rescue like some Prince fucking Charming. They told me he carried you back to his ATV in his arms like you were all his."

His men? So he *had* been lying and he *was* in on the attack.

"You little slut. You know what you are? You're a whore, just like your mother. All the time and money I've put into raising you right didn't matter, and I should've known. Her whore blood runs in your veins, and it's only a matter of time until—"

At that instant, I reached my limit. I was done being talked to like that, done being controlled.

"You know what, yeah, I did. More than once and I plan to do it again. And again, and again, and as many fucking times as I want to!"

The rage built on his face as I spoke, his cheeks taking on a deeper shade of red than I'd ever seen in my life. I knew for certain that if I'd been in front of him, he'd have hit me.

I didn't care. I was having too much fun ripping into him.

"My virginity's gone, long gone. I guess I'm just trash to you now that you can't sell me to the highest bidder anymore, right?"

To my surprise, the rage on his face faded. Dad stared at me blankly for a moment, as if a circuit had shorted inside of him and he couldn't quite figure out how to feel.

Then a smile spread. It was a horrible smile, an *evil* smile. The confidence I'd felt faded away at the sight of it, fear returning.

"You want to know where Marta is?" he asked. "She's down in the basement right now. And she's dead as a goddamn doornail."

CHAPTER 24

EMILY

T he world seemed to fall down all around me.

I placed my hand on my heart, my breath gone, tears welling in my eyes.

It couldn't be true. There's no way that Dad, vicious as he was, would do something like that.

There's no way he would kill *Marta*.

"No." The word came out of my mouth on a whisper. "You're lying."

Dad grinned, seemingly pleased that I was right where he wanted me.

"I've got no problems lying to get what I want, but in this case, the truth will go a lot further. Marta's dead, Emily. And I was the one that ordered it."

The tears that had been gathering in my eyes trickled down. I dropped back into my seat, Dad's grinning face striking me as completely demonic.

"Don't believe me?" he asked, reaching into his suit pocket and taking out his phone. "I've got plenty of pictures. Believe me—when you pay what I did for this kind of work, you want as many pictures as you can get."

There was no doubt in my mind that the phone contained all sorts of horrible images, the kind that would never leave my mind once I'd seen them.

"No!" I shouted. "Please, no."

Dad stopped, the phone in his hand as he turned his attention back to me. "You sure? Because these guys... well, they're the sorts of ruthless fucks that Marta fled Mexico to get away from. I can see why she did; the kind of shit they did to Marta... *wow*."

I was too stunned to say anything.

"In a way, they're almost like artists. The way they can cause so much pain and suffering and *still* keep the poor SOB alive so they can experience it... It's impressive."

"Please, stop."

"What's the matter? You don't want to hear about the consequences of your actions?"

"*My* actions? You're telling me this is my fault?"

"That's right, Em. Marta's mission was to convince you to come back with her. She failed. So, she had to pay the price. I'm not, nor have I ever been, one to reward incompetence. It's a shame that after so many years of loyalty to me that Marta's tenure had to come to an end. But without you, what good was she to me?"

I was too shocked to say a word. More tears poured from my eyes.

"Oh, she cried and sobbed and begged for forgiveness. Poor Marta was so upset that she hadn't been able to get you to leave with her." Dad's horrible grin deepened, and he leaned forward. "I wonder if this would've changed your mind? If you would've known the price Marta would pay for your selfishness, would you have made the same decision?"

"You didn't have to kill her."

"If you'd come back and decided to be a good girl, then you might've been right. When the mission failed, however, I needed to tie up all loose ends. Not to mention that I was pissed when she'd told me how badly she'd fucked up."

Dad let out a sigh, shaking his head sadly before his expression turned severe once more.

"And make no mistake, Emily—I have *zero* qualms about putting you through the same fate. You might be my daughter, but you're a tool to me, something that I'm going to use to get what I want. You're going to have the chance to come home one more time. Do *not* fuck with me again. Fight me, and what happens to you will be far, far worse than anything you can imagine."

With that, the call ended, the screen turning blank.

I sat there stunned, unable to move, to think.

I tried to stand, my legs weak and wobbly underneath me. Nausea gripped me, and I felt the urge to run to the bathroom and vomit. Instead, I gathered what little strength I had and ran out of the office, sobs pouring from me and pain searing through my ankle as I ran downstairs and past the kitchen.

"Emily," Logan called out after me, but I just kept going.

Desperate for fresh air, I ran outside and into the garden. Once there, I kept on running until I reached the beach, the world a blur around me. My ankle throbbed, but I didn't care. More sobs wracked me, memories of the day the men in the boat had arrived flooding back to me. I dropped to my knees in the sand, all the tears and moans of anguish that I'd been holding back letting loose, the ocean before me listening indifferently to my cries.

When I couldn't cry another tear, I let my arms drop to

my sides. I sat, totally numb, watching the waves crash into the shore.

"Emily."

Without another word, he stepped to my side and dropped down to his knees next to me. Logan was calm and even and stoic, just as he always was. I'd had my issues in the past with how cold and detached he could seem, how he would never share his feelings or what was on his mind. In that moment, however, he was a rock. And a rock was just what I needed.

"You don't have to tell me what happened," he said after several moments of silence. "But if you want to, I'm here."

I took a deep breath. He had a right to know. More than that, he needed to know what he was up against so he could make the decision on what to do with me.

"My father admitted that he was the one that set up the kidnapping attempt. And when Marta came back without me..." I trailed off.

"He killed her," Logan finished. He didn't try to mollify me; didn't tell me it would be alright. How could it be? The closet thing I'd had to a mother was gone, and it was because I wouldn't go with her.

Silence hung in the air. I wondered what he was going to say next. Logan gazed at the ocean, and I could only imagine what was going on in his head as he considered what he'd just heard.

"You can't go back. Not a goddamn chance. No way I'm going to let you go back to that murderous bastard."

Calm washed over me at his words. "He said he'd come for me again."

"Let him come," Logan said. "He'll find out what happens when he fucks with me."

Logan's words were braced with complete determination and confidence. I was still scared out of my mind, shaken to my core by what I'd learned and how my father had threatened me. Knowing that Logan was in this with me and had my back went a long way.

He wrapped his big arm around me, pulling me close against his strong, solid body, his nearness, his warmth, wrapped around me like a heavy blanket. I turned, nuzzling my face into his chest and breathing in his scent.

As he held me there, I knew what I wanted. I took my face from his chest and gazed up at him.

"Take me," I said. "Take me right here, right now."

Logan answered my words with an expression of slight curiosity, as if he weren't sure he'd heard me correctly. It appeared I needed to clear the confusion in the air. I inched up, bringing my lips to his and kissing him deeply, my tongue tip touching his.

The kiss sent the message more clearly than any words could have. Logan kissed me in return, placing his hand on the back of my head, weaving his fingers into my hair. I moaned, each moment of the kiss blocking out a little more of the outside world, of the stresses that were weighing down on me.

"Please," I moaned through the kiss. "Please."

Logan took his lips from mine, his broad, powerful chest rising up and down as he pulled his shirt off and over his shoulders. I was turned on as always at the sight of him shirtless, his cock straining against the linen of his shorts. Once his shirt was off, he spread it out onto the sand behind us.

CHAPTER 25

LOGAN

I held her close as she slept on my chest, her body sheened with sweat after our lovemaking on the beach.

And it had most certainly been lovemaking. As I laid there, images from what we'd just done flashed through my mind—her beautiful eyes on mine as I moved in and out of her gently, the hush of her breath, the delicate moans. There'd been a melding of bodies during our lovemaking that hadn't been there before.

I'd come so damn close to saying the words, caught up in the passion. I'd wanted to lower myself, to bite down gently on her hear and whisper those three little words that I'd never said to a woman before in my life.

I love you.

I'd bitten my tongue, however. The urge to speak the words had been sudden and had come out of nowhere. I'd never been a man to get caught up in a moment and simply go with it like that. I'd need to think about it. Not to mention, after that call she'd had with her father dropping a bomb on her like he did, I didn't want my feelings to feel like a burden she had to carry along with everything else that was weighing her down.

It couldn't possibly be love, not so soon. No, what I was feeling was a mixture of strong lust combined with respect, and a little protectiveness on top of that. I'd only known the woman for two weeks, after all. How the hell could I fall in love with someone so quickly, and with such intensity?

So, I'd simply made her come over and over. The sight of her body arching underneath me as I drove into her was one that could never possibly get old. And the sensation of her pussy clenching my cock as she came...

I considered the matter of Charles as I held Emily close. Things were going to come to a head, and soon. He might've been a coward, but he was as ruthless as they came. Not a chance in hell he'd let his daughter slip through his fingers without fight.

That was fine with me. Emily was a woman worth fighting for.

A small, personal plane buzzed overhead, the sound of its engines enough to rouse Emily. She opened her eyes sleepily, a small smile forming on her lips when she remembered where she was, who she was with. The way she looked with that dreamy smile on her face was enough to bring those three words to mind once more. I wanted to say them so damn badly. But again, I pushed them down.

"Thank you," she said.

"For what?" "For all of this. For giving me a glimpse of a life that wasn't simply being my father's prisoner."

I leaned in and kissed her gently, her lips pressing against mine.

"It's a crime that you've been forced to live that way for so long. If I can play a role in stopping it, then I'm glad to do it."

Emily said nothing, once more gazing at me in that way that brought those three words to mind. I pushed them down with a tinge of anger, frustrated at the lack of control over my feelings. I rose, brushing the sand from my body.

"Come on, let's get moving." The words came out with a gruffness that I hadn't intended, yet another slip of my emotions. Emily regarded me with confusion. I leaned down and kissed her again to answer the concern, taking her hand and lifting her to her feet.

"Just don't want you to burn, is all," I said.

The two of us started back toward the house, the sand warm underneath our feet. It was quiet, peaceful. But I knew it wouldn't last. Sure enough, the tense expression that formed on Emily's face let me know that reality would find us before too long.

"You alright over there?" It was a silly question to ask—how the hell could she be anything close to alright after what she'd been through?

"I can't stop thinking about Marta."

I put my hand on her shoulder. "I don't mean to sound callous here, but the best thing you can do is try to move past that. Your father did what he did not just to punish her, but to make *you* suffer too. He wants you to tear yourself apart with guilt."

"Yeah. That's how the asshole operates. He's good at both the physical and emotional kinds of manipulation. All the same, I wish there was something I could do."

I tried to imagine Marta's final resting place. No doubt a man like Charles had no issues throwing her into the nearest body of water, or burying her in the middle of a forest or some such place where she'd never be found again.

"What about a memorial?" she asked.

"A memorial?"

"Yeah, like a little ceremony we could do to remember her by. Nothing big, but maybe something where we set up some flowers, play a little music, and I could say a few words. I mean, I know that she tried to take me from here, but she was acting under orders from my father and most likely under threat of death if she didn't succeed. I really want to do this for her after everything she's done for me throughout my life."

Her attitude perked up a bit as she spoke, letting me know this was indeed the right call to make.

"I think that sounds like a fine idea."

"Not until tomorrow," she said. "I want to take some time to write exactly what's in my heart about her."

"Maybe on the western shore of the island. Sunset sounds like the right time for a memorial."

She nodded.

We reached the house, making our way to the kitchen for a quick snack before hitting the shower. To our surprise, Roberto, Pearl, and Marianne were all there. A platter of sandwiches was on the kitchen island, my stomach grumbling at the sight.

"There they are," Pearl said, an expression of concern on her face. "I thought you could both use something to eat."

I could sense right away that Emily was conflicted. The sandwiches, toasted with melted cheese, looked amazing. I sensed her hesitation, placing my hand on her shoulder. She glanced over at me and I spoke up.

"You ever want to get anything done, food in your stomach's the first step."

Pearl smiled, pushing the plate over toward us. "Before you compliment Logan on his wisdom for that comment, know that he got that one from me."

A small smile formed on Emily's gorgeous mouth. Without another word, she picked up one of the sandwich halves and bit into it, the toasted bread crunching as she did. Roberto, already polishing off a sandwich of his own, regarded me with a look that made it clear he wanted to know what had happened.

"Why do you look so sad?" Marianne asked Emily.

"Mary-Moo, you know it's not nice to pry like that. If someone wants to tell you how they feel, they will."

"It's OK," Emily said, her eyes downcast. "I am a little sad."

With that, she filled in the group on what had gone down. She glided over the more difficult details for Marianne's sake, of course, phrasing things carefully.

"Marta's gone?" Marianne asked when Emily was done. "Forever?"

Pearl's eyes were wide, her hand on her mouth. "That's... Oh, my God." She hurried over to Emily and pulled her into a hug. Marianne, seeming to understand the gravity of the situation, joined them.

"Thanks," Emily said, the women letting go. "I just... this is really hard for me to talk about. But I want to do a memorial tomorrow at sunset."

"A memorial?" Marianne asked. "What does that mean?"

"A memorial is a way to celebrate someone's life," Pearl answered. "We'll get together and talk about the person lost and promise to keep them in our hearts."

Marianne's eyes lit up. "I know a good way to remember someone—I can draw a picture! My memory's really good, and I definitely spent enough time with Marta to be able to draw her. I mean if that's alright, of course."

"That would be great," Emily said, tears forming in her eyes. "It really would."

By this point, Roberto was staring at me hard enough to burn holes in my skin. He wanted to know exactly what had happened, and he didn't want to wait another minute longer. Emily, Marianne, and Pearl had fallen into conversation about the memorial, and that seemed like as good a time as any to fill in Roberto. I nodded toward the door connecting us to the dining room.

"Something tells me that what happened to poor Marta was a little more gruesome than what Emily let on," he said as the door closed behind us.

"You're right about that," I replied, stepping over to the twenty-person dining room table and leaning back against it. "Emily had a hard time giving me details, and I didn't want to pry them out of her. But from what she told me, Charles didn't hold back. Used cartel guys."

"Fucking hell," Roberto said, shaking his head in anger and disbelief. "Bet you anything that *bastardo* forced her into it. Marta was strange the entire time she was here. I could tell she was hiding something."

"You would be correct. Charles admitted as much to Emily But what's done is done. Important thing is that we prepare for whatever Charles has in mind next. He told Emily that he's not done with her, and I believe him."

"So, this means that Emily's staying here for good."

I hadn't thought about it in such direct terms, but it sure as hell appeared that way.

"Maybe, maybe not. That all depends on her. For the time being, she's here until the matter of her fucking scumbag father is resolved."

"Smart call. If he's willing to kill just to make a point, then God only knows what else he might do."

"Seems like she was always more of an object than a person to him. In his eyes, she's spoiled goods."

Roberto flashed me a small smile. "But in your eyes, she's something else."

"Excuse me?"

"Come on, *jefe*," he said, coming over to give my shoulder a friendly jab. "There's something going on between you and her. I've seen you bring women to the island before but this time is different, and not just because she's got a psycho *padre* after her."

I said nothing, but I couldn't argue with him because he was right.

"Let me tell you as a friend, this is a good thing. Emily's got a big heart, and I'm glad to see you open yours for her."

"Thanks." I grumbled the word. Roberto gave me a playful shove, and I allowed myself a small grin as I pushed him away.

"But first thing's first," I said. "We get this island locked down tight. I want more guards, and twenty-four-seven surveillance. Not a thing happens without my knowing."

"That's the easy part. Hard part is how we strike at Charles."

"Maybe we wait for him to strike first. He's vicious, but he's not smart. We play this right, and we can take advantage of how fucking furious he is."

"You may be right. I'll get on it, *jefe*."

With that, Roberto left me alone. I kept my eyes on the shore in the distance, knowing this was going to get a hell of a lot harder before it got any easier.

CHAPTER 26

EMILY

I couldn't have asked for a better night for a memorial. The air was calm, with just the right touch of warmth. The sunset was by far the most beautiful I'd seen since coming to the island. Deep, blood-reds and burnt-oranges surrounded the sun itself, a sheet of dark purple dotted with twinkling stars above.

The beauty of the setting was not enough to suppress the sadness in my heart, however.

The entire staff, all three dozen men and women, had gathered for the memorial. The staff had brought bouquets of gorgeous flowers to decorate, and the stunning, lifelike drawing that Marianne had spent all day creating was situated on a stand next to me.

Marianne, Pearl, and Logan were seated in the front row. It seemed a bit premature to think about, I knew, but as I laid eyes on the three of them I couldn't help but feel like I was with my new family.

"She was the closest thing to a mother I'd ever had," I said. "And I know she loved me like a daughter. Thank you all for coming tonight. If we keep her in our hearts, we can make sure that her memory is never forgotten."

A tear that I'd been holding back fell from my eye as I finished. Logan rose, coming over to my side with a tissue and placing his hand on my shoulder.

With that, Pearl rose and pressed play on the speaker. Gorgeours Arias flowed from the speakers, Marta's favorite kind of music. Logan wrapped his arm around my shoulders, and I placed my head against his chest.

I had no idea what I would've done if Logan and the rest hadn't been there for me. I'd lost Marta, and that was a wound to my heart that wouldn't be healing anytime soon. But I had love and support, two notions that I'd never enjoyed before. That is, aside from what Marta had given me. Even in the end, she'd been trying to take care of me the best way she knew how.

"I'm sorry, Emily." I took my face from Logan's chest to see Marianne standing before me. She looked gorgeous in her simple sundress. "I miss Marta so much, and I'm sure you do, too."

"I do. But thank you, Mar. And thank you for the painting."

She smiled. "It's pretty good, right? I think I might hang it up in my house so we can always have something to remember her by."

"I think that's a wonderful idea," I agreed.

"Listen," Pearl said as she joined us. "I've been to my share of funerals, and I know that eating's usually the last thing on your mind, but there's a reason it's a tradition to always have lots of food—you need to eat and keep your strength up."

"Yeah, you're right."

"Take a seat," Logan said. "I'll put together a plate for you."

Pearl stepped over and gave me a hug, then Logan lead me into a nearby chair. The rest of the staff was at the long table packed with food. Though I wasn't hungry myself, it made me happy to see all of them eating and chatting. Marta would've wanted it that way.

I spotted Roberto in the middle distance. He stood with his hands behind his back, his eyes scanning the scene—no idle time for him. I sprang out of my seat and hurried over to the food table, slipping through the crowd and putting together a quick plate. I made my way to Roberto and handed it over.

"Couldn't have you just standing there watching all of us eat," I said.

He allowed himself a small smile. "*Gracias*, Emily. And my condolences."

I thanked him as I handed over the plate. On the way back to my seat, I noticed Marianne had her phone in her hand, and over and over would check the screen, a worried look on her face. I wasn't normally one to pry, but with everything going on I wanted to be aware of anything out of the ordinary, not to mention if any of my friends were in peril.

"Hey!" I said, walking over to join her. "What's up?"

"Huh?" Her eyes went wide, as if I'd interrupted her right in the middle of something. She fumbled with her phone, nearly dropping it on the ground.

I laughed, helping her steady herself. "You look a little worried. Something up?"

"No. I mean, yes. But I don't want to bother anyone."

Logan approached with my plate, placing his hand on my shoulder as I took the food from him.

"Everything OK over here?" he asked.

Marianne pursed her lips, as if not sure how to say what was on her mind.

"It's... it's huge!" She threw out her hands as she spoke, nearly tossing her phone into the sand.

"Easy, Mary-Moo," Pearl said as she approached, having likely been drawn to the commotion. "Remember what I told you to do when you have something on your mind? Take a deep breath, close your eyes, and focus."

"Right." Marianne did as she was told. When she was ready, she opened her eyes. "There's this gallery in New York City that likes my work! They're really fancy, I think. They're in a part of the city called Chelsea."

"That *is* fancy," Logan said. "Go on."

"They sent me an email that said they found my art on my website and want to do a showing. I said yes! But they haven't emailed me back yet. I keep checking because I'm worried they'll change their mind."

"Wait, you've got a gallery in Chelsea that wants to show your art? Mar, this is *huge!*"

"I know!" she said, as if my words had made her even more nervous. "That's why I'm scared that—," Her phone chimed in her hand as she spoke. Marianne quickly turned her attention to the screen. "It's them! And they sent dates they want me to come!"

My heart beat faster with excitement. Logan, calm and composed as ever, stuck out his hand for the phone. Marianne handed it over.

"The Fordham Gallery, I know this place," he said. "I've actually been there for a showing. This is legit. Congratulations, sis."

I couldn't help myself. I let out a squeal of excitement, nearly launching my plate into the air as I came over to give her a hug. Pearl joined me, the two of us giving Marianne a big squeeze.

"They have a gala planned," Logan said once the commotion died down, his eyes still on the screen. "They're looking for some up-and-coming artists to show off to the art world in New York. Mar, if you present there and make an impression, you might have a career in this waiting for you. Only thing is, it's in two days. We'd have to leave tomorrow."

A couple of hours later, the memorial was over. Marta's picture was hung in Marianne's house in one of the hallways, and it did me good to know that there was always something I could look at to remember her by.

Pearl, Logan, Marianne, and I were in the small but cozy kitchen of Marianne's place, music playing as we chatted about the trip ahead.

"Pearl, you're coming, right?" Marianne asked.

"Kiddo, I'd love to, but someone's got to stick around here and make sure this place keeps chugging along. Besides, I'm way better at home cooking for the staff than I am cramming my big ass into some fancy gown and going to a New York gallery party."

Marianne crossed her arms. "Would you mind helping me pack some clothes?"

Pearl raised her eyebrows. "Right now?"

"Yeah! And you can help too, Em!" Without another word, Marianne sprang out of her seat and hurried out of the room and upstairs.

"I'll keep an eye on her," Pearl said. "And I'm sure you two have a lot to talk about as far as this trip goes."

"Thanks, Pearl," Logan said.

A few plates of food were on the table. I rose, gathering them together to do my part in helping to clean up.

"Thanks again, Logan," I said. "I know I said it a million times, but the fact that you did this means so much to me."

Logan rose from his seat, stepping behind me at the sink and wrapping his big arms around me from behind. It felt so damn good to be held by him like that, like I was so small and so secure all at once. And he must've liked it too; his hardness pressed against me, his cock growing stiffer and stiffer by the moment.

Logan kissed my neck before stepping away.

"Let me help," he said, positioning himself in front of the second sink next to mine and starting on some dishes.

We washed in silence for a time, the scene strangely domestic in its own way.

"The trip," he said finally. "We need to talk about it."

"You're right. You think this is a bad idea?"

"Could be. Your father's in Long Island, which means we'd be bringing ourselves closer to him. At the same time, he's no doubt preparing for another assault on the island. If we're not here, that'd throw a wrench into his plans. Not to mention that Roberto would be coming with us. I trust that man with my life."

"Yeah. He knows what he's doing."

"But there's still more to think about. I'll discuss the matter with him and let him know what we decide."

"Good. Thanks for keeping me in the loop."

We went back to washing and one thought lingered in my mind.

"You're thinking about it," Logan said. "You don't need to worry."

I pursed my lips. "I know. It's just that this thing with my dad is going to come to a head sooner or later, right?"

"Right. And I'd put my money on sooner. But you don't need to weigh yourself down with that. I've got the best private security staff money can buy. If anything, I *want* Charles to make his move so I can crush his ass once and for all."

Logan spoke with total confidence that calmed me down a great deal. I glanced over at him, noticing a small smile on his face.

"What's up?" I asked.

"Huh?"

"You're smiling."

He snorted. "Yeah, I guess I was. Just thinking about... actually, never mind."

I leaned over and bumped him with my hip. "Come on, you can't smile like that and not tell me what you're thinking about."

He said nothing for a few moments, as if trying to decide how much to tell me.

"Alright. Well, Marta's memorial got me thinking about my own mom. Both my parents, actually."

"You haven't talked about them since I've been here."

"It's a hard subject."

"You don't have to say anything if you don't want to. But I have to admit, I'm curious about where you came from."

Logan shifted his weight from one foot to the other, a sign that he wasn't entirely comfortable with the topic.

"I was just thinking about the time when we'd learned that Marianne had a talent for art. We had this old dog named Jasper, this mangy mutt that my dad had adopted before Mar was born. One day, when she was about eight, she just stared at him for hours, following him around the house and not taking her eyes off of him, as if she wanted to burn every detail of him into memory. Then, she sat down and drew him, this damn near perfect depiction. Mom was blown away, convinced that Marianne was destined for great things in the art world."

"And your dad?"

He chuckled. "The old man... he was always more practical minded, art wasn't really his thing. But over the years, as her skill grew and the nature of her uniqueness came to light, he came around. One day, I went into his office to grab something for him and saw that old picture of Jasper, framed and hung over his desk."

He took in a slow, deep breath. "Just thinking about how they'd feel to know how far she's come."

I couldn't help but reach over and take his hand, squeezing it tight.

"I'm sure they'd be thrilled, especially since her big brother is so supportive of her."

"I hope so. I've had two responsibilities in my life—first the company, then after my parents passed, Marianne. Back when I was a younger man, I used to bristle thinking about all of the responsibilities that would eventually be placed on me. But now that I'm older, I realize that such things are what give life its meaning."

"What happened to your parents? If you don't mind me asking."

"Car accident. They were in California on the 405, someone pulled into their lane and sideswiped them and that was that. I was on active duty in the Marines when I got the news that would change my life forever."

"The Marines... that explains the hero complex."

He smirked. "That's right. Anyway, after the funeral, I finished my tour then came back and took over the company while going back to college and watching over Marianne. And that's been my life for the last nearly two decades."

"It's quite a life."

"It is. Funny thing is this life of mine always has a way of surprising me." He glanced over and offered a small smile that I returned.

A buzz sounded out, Logan drying off his hands and reaching into his pocket for his phone.

"Roberto wants to talk about security for the trip."

"Go ahead," I said. "I'll finish up here."

He leaned over and kissed me on the forehead before heading out to meet Roberto.

Once Logan was gone, words he'd spoken came to mind, the ones about responsibility. I placed my hand on my stomach, knowing there was a damn good chance my child, *our child*, was in there. It'd be another responsibility on top of all the others. And, perhaps, one more surprise to change both of our lives forever.

CHAPTER 27

LOGAN

The jet engines roared as we took off, Roberto seated across from me in the plane's back office.

"This is my favorite part!" Marianne called out. "Feels like you're flying into space!"

I chuckled. Marianne had been on cloud nine since the beginning of the day, having woken me up at six in the morning like a kid on Christmas. After a few minutes we were up and on our way. I clicked off my seatbelt and sat back.

"What's the plan?" I asked.

Roberto nodded, leaning over and lifting his briefcase from the ground. He set it on the table and opened it, taking out a manilla folder of information.

"It was tricky to get this all sorted out with only twenty-four hours to spare, but I have an itinerary that should work."

"Excellent. Let's hear it."

"The penthouse is ready for us. I had the building security do a sweep to make sure everything was in order. As long as we're there, we'll be safe."

"So far, so good."

"The hard part will be whenever we're outside of the penthouse. As confident as I am in my skills, I figured a little backup would be in order. To that end, I made contact with an old associate of mine in the city. He recommended two men—Edgar Sanchez and Renaldo Hernandez—to work with me. Wherever you go in the city, the three of us will be there with you."

He opened the folder and passed me two sheets, each with a summary of the men. I looked them over, everything seeming to be in order.

"Sounds good."

"There's a damn good chance that Charles won't even know that we're in town until we're gone. But no way I'm going to be banking on that."

"What if we manage to get him out in the open?" I asked. "If he finds out that we're nearby, he might try something without planning. Could get him into a trap that way."

Roberto nodded in a way that made it clear he'd considered that possibility.

"He very well could. But make no mistake—we'll be ready if he tries anything. And if we get the chance, I'll ice him myself."

"Excellent. Thanks for all of your hard work, Roberto."

"My pleasure, *jefe*. If I get to take out a murdering *bastardo* like Charles, hell, that's almost a bonus in and of itself."

"You serve him to me on a slab and you'll get the normal kind of bonus, too."

Roberto chuckled. "Naturally."

I rose, stepping out of the office and into the hallway.

"OK, you *have* to let me pick. I have the best show ever in mind."

"Are you sure? Because I just looked and there's a new season of *Emily in Paris* up."

"This is *way* better."

I entered the main cabin of the plane, a smile spreading on my face as I laid eyes on the conversation. Marianne and Emily were seated in the TV area, both covered with blankets, a plate of snacks in front of them.

"What is it?"

"It's called *Outlander*. It's this amazing show about a lady who goes back in time and falls in love with this super-hot Scottish guy."

"Mar!" Emily said, a playfully scandalized tone to her voice. "You watch this?"

"Sure do. I want to tell you more about it, but that might spoil it. Logan says I have a habit of telling too much of the plot."

I chuckled. Seated at the table in front of me and to the left was Pearl, her computer open as she typed away.

"How're we doing, Pearl?"

"Huh?" she glanced over her shoulder at me. "Oh, fine. Just trying to get everything in order for the staff, then plan an itinerary for the trip. After that, I've got to get in touch with some local boutiques and see what I can do about last-minute dresses."

"I appreciate your hard work," I said.

"Sure, sure. Still can't believe that Marianne managed to talk me into coming."

"You know you're going to have fun, don't even pretend like you're not excited about it."

Before Pearl could fire off a snarky reply, Emily sprang out of her seat. She turned, her face pale as she hurried past me and down the hall, barely able to get out an "excuse me" as she rushed into the bathroom and shut the door.

"She alright?" I asked.

"Think so," Pearl said. "But... this is the third time I've seen her run to the bathroom like that."

"Could be the flight. Only the second one she's been on, remember."

"No, I mean third time all day today. This morning I was helping her pack and right in the middle of folding something she threw the damn dress onto the bed and ran off to the bathroom. Pretty sure she was throwing up in there."

"A lot to be nervous about."

"That's true. Anyway, big guy, I need to finish this."

"Sure." I stepped over to my desk and sat down, my eyes on the Caribbean below. The sea was vast and endless, and part of me wished that we didn't have to leave the island.

I didn't have much time to contemplate the matter before Emily returned from the bathroom. It was impossible to not notice that something was awry. She emerged from the hallway with her arms folded over her middle, a sheepish expression on her face as if she'd done something that she shouldn't have.

"You OK?" I asked.

"Yeah. Fine." She didn't even pause to say the words, instead blowing past me without making eye contact and hurrying over to the couch, plopping down next to Marianne and pulling the blanket over her.

"Something to eat, Mr. Stone?"

Estella's voice snapped me out of my staring. I cleared my throat and turned my attention to her.

"Uh, sure. I'll take some blackened chicken and rice, a bottle of mineral water to go with it."

She smiled before stepping away and asking the same question to the rest of the passengers. It wasn't long before I had a plate of food in front of me, questions running through my mind. Regardless of what was going to go down during this trip to New York, I had to be ready.

I passed the time with some work on my laptop, figuring there was a good chance I wouldn't be getting much done while I was there.

When the island of Manhattan appeared in the distance, I took a moment to prepare myself.

For better or worse, I knew this trip would be unlike any other.

CHAPTER 28

L ogan's Midtown penthouse apartment was something
else.

The place was huge—three stories situated on the top of
a prewar tower bordering Central Park, the views from
every side of the place sweeping and endless. A huge spiral
staircase traveled up through the middle of the apartment,
the space sleek and modern.

"I always forget how cool this place is!" Marianne
rushed into the enormous main living space of the first floor
and fell back onto the long, white couch, her purse sliding
off her arm. "I mean, I love the island. But this is *New
York!*"

Marianne grinned, her eyes closed as if she had nothing
but her future success in the art world on her mind. I, on the
other hand, didn't feel as comfortable giving myself over to
the fun and excitement of the big city. The view from
where I stood looked out east over Queens and Long Island,
and I couldn't shake the reality that my father was somewhere in the distance.

"Mary-Moo, why don't you get your stuff put away

before you start relaxing?" Pearl asked. "And don't you dare tell me you're thinking of taking a nap after all that snoozing you did on the plane. You've got a show tomorrow, and being an artist isn't just about wearing a pretty dress and showing off your art."

Marianne sat up and smiled. "But most of it is."

Pearl chuckled as she made her way over to the coffee station at the living room bar. "Well, sure. But you're going to need to supervise your paintings while the crew packs them up and ships them over. Lots of logistical work."

Marianne cocked her head to the side. "What's logistical work?"

Logan entered, slipping off his suit jacket and nodding to Pearl to make him one of the espressos she was preparing.

"Logistics is the name for how things get done. For example, if you want to show off your art at a fancy Chelsea gallery, then the logistical aspect is what Pearl mentioned—everything that you need to do to actually get the art over there."

Marianne's face fell a bit before brightening. "Well, that might be fun!"

"I like that attitude," Logan said with a small smile. "I've already done the legwork of getting the art movers organized, they'll be here bright and early tomorrow. You going to be ready for that?"

Marianne nodded eagerly. "I will!"

"Good. In the meantime, you three have an assignment."

"Is that right?" asked Pearl.

Logan checked his watch. "It's a little after one right now. I've made dinner reservations for eight. Until then, the three of you need to take the afternoon and find something to wear for the opening tomorrow. I've been in contact with a few boutiques in town, all with prêt-à-porter clothes, so you should all be able to find something."

"We get to try on dresses!" Marianne said, her eyes lighting up with excitement. "This is going to be so fun!"

I shifted my weight from one foot to the other, anxiety taking hold.

"What about... you know." I didn't want to come out with the exact words, not wanting to scare Marianne.

Logan stepped over to me. "Here in the penthouse, you're as safe as it gets. This building is as secure as a bank vault, with on-staff security and no way to get in or out without explicit permission. As far as when you're out in the city..."

As if they'd been awaiting those very words, Roberto and two other men entered the apartment. Both men were huge and hulking, just like Roberto. One had a shaved head, the other with long, dark hair pulled into a neat ponytail. Both wore serious expressions of all business, their eyes hidden behind sunglasses and their mouths in hard, flat lines.

"Roberto?" Logan asked. "You want to introduce our new friends?"

"Gladly. Ladies, this is Edgar," the man with the shaved head nodded, "...and Renaldo." The man with the ponytail nodded. "Now, as much as we'd love to give you three the run of the city, we're going to err on the side of caution. To that end, each of you will have one of us assigned to you for the next few days while we're here."

Marianne appeared worried. "Is this because of what happened at the beach?" she asked. "With Marta?"

"That's right," Logan said. "But I'm almost positive that

there's nothing to worry about, sis. These guys are just here to make sure this weekend is fun and safe, OK?"

Marianne nodded, but I could see the tinge of fear in her expression.

"We're going to be shadowing you three," Roberto went on. "So, just try to pretend we're not there."

Pearl smiled, her eyes lingering on the two new men in a way that made it clear she was happy with the displays of macho manhood on display. "What if we don't *want* to pretend that you're not there?"

Roberto chuckled. "Easy, Pearl. Try not to chew these poor boys up and spit them out."

Pearl laughed. "I'll do my best."

"Anyway," Roberto said. "There's a pair of cars outside. We'll take one, you three will take the other. I'll be the driver of your car, ladies. Take a few minutes to get settled in, then we'll be on our way."

"Come on," Logan said, an espresso in his hands. "I'll show you to your room."

He nodded toward the spiral staircase and together, we went up. The height of the stairs afforded an incredible, sweeping view of not just the apartment, but the city outside the tall windows. It was like nothing I'd ever seen before.

"This is a big place." Not knowing what else to say, the words came out of my mouth sounding silly.

"A little too big, if you ask me," Logan replied. "I'm here most of the time by myself, and sometimes it can feel a little empty." He chuckled. "I bought this as something of a celebration for myself when I turned thirty, to celebrate my first billion."

I blinked hard at that revelation.

"Marta made me Crème Brulé for my last birthday."

He chuckled at my words, the two of us reaching the third floor and heading down the hall. Logan opened the door to a large bedroom, the window-walls looking out over the south half of Manhattan.

"Hope this works for you," he said, shutting the door as he spoke.

"Should be just fine. And—"

I didn't get a chance to finish. Logan wrapped his arm around my waist and pulled me in for a kiss, the suddenness of it shocking and wonderful all at once. Our tongues met, the taste of espresso on his lips. I fell into the kiss right away, eager for him to take me right then and there.

Instead, he pulled away. The cocky smile that remained on his face suggested that he knew just what he was doing by denying me what I wanted.

"You're such a *tease*," I said.

"This is your bedroom. But if you're in the mood for a little company tonight, I'm right at the end of the hall. Take your time to get settled, and let Roberto know when you're ready to go."

With that, he opened the door and stepped out, leaving me alone and hornier than I'd been in as long as I could remember. It was almost scary how well Logan knew how to tease me, how to push my buttons. The worst part? I actually kind of liked it.

I laid down on the bed to try and get a few minutes of rest in before our big afternoon out. It wasn't long before a tinge of nausea ripped through me, the sensation intense enough to make me sit up and prepare to run to the bathroom.

It passed. I sighed with worry, thinking about all the times I'd been sick on the plane, how there'd been simply no way that Logan hadn't noticed. I'd tried not to make eye contact with him on the way to the bathroom, but that last time I'd been sure he'd been watching me, wondering what was going on.

What did he know? Logan was many things, but dumb wasn't one of them. Then again, I'd told him that I was on the pill.

I sighed, getting up and washing my face. One of the employees arrived with my bags, and I did a quick change before heading out. Marianne and Pearl were ready to go, and it wasn't long before we were seated in the back of a sleek, black SUV taking us through the city. Marianne had her face pressed to the window the entire time, gasping at the towering buildings all around us.

"I don't care how many times I've been here," she said, turning to me and Pearl. "It's always *amazing!*"

"Just think," Pearl added. "If you become a big shot New York artist, you could get your own place and do showings all the time."

Marianne's eyes became somehow wider than they already were.

"Really?"

"I bet you could," I said. "You've got talent, and so much of it. I still get misty-eyed when I think about the portrait you did for Marta."

Without another word, Marianne leaned over and threw her arms around me.

We parked somewhere in NoLita, getting out and taking in the sight of the city all around us. It was a beautiful day, the sky blue and the air nice and warm. Together, we headed into one of the boutiques on the list, a place called "The Show" that appeared to be closed down for a private fitting session just for us.

A smiling clerk greeted us as we stepped into the store,

Roberto hurrying in beforehand and taking a quick look inside as Renaldo and Edgar posted out front. Once Roberto gave us the OK, we entered the shop.

"Welcome," the clerk said, the woman tall and slender and leggy.

As I walked further into the place, my eyes went wide at the display of gorgeous dresses. I stepped over to the nearest one—a long, dark red strappy gown made from fabric so delicate that I worried it might shatter at my touch.

"These are *so* pretty!" Marianne said. "Which ones do we get to try on?"

"All of them!" the clerk said. "And that's what we're here for." She swept her hand toward two equally beautiful young women behind the counter. "Choose whatever you like. We have your sizes, so everything should work."

Marianne smiled. "My name is Marianne Stone. This is Emily Marone, and she's Pearl Shepard."

Pearl hurried over to Marianne's side, whispering sharply into her ear.

"Don't need to tell everyone our life stories."

The clerks didn't seem to notice or care about the interjection.

"Well, I hope you three are in the mood for something good to drink. Want a little bubbly while you try things on?"

"Oh, that sounds amazing!" Marianne said. "Don't worry, Logan says I can have a little every now and then. I *am* a grown-up after all."

Pearl gave me a look that seemed to say, "Don't worry, I'll keep an eye on her."

I went right for the red dress, the clerk taking it off the rack and leading me over to one of the dressing rooms. She helped me into it and my jaw nearly hit the floor when I saw myself in the mirror.

"Pretty glamorous," the clerk said. "But that's just my opinion."

I did a turn, the red fabric twirling around me. I couldn't help but let out a laugh of joy as I watched the fabric spin.

"I love it. But do you have anything a little, um, *sexier*?"

The clerk grinned, a mischievous twinkle in her eye. "Let me see what I can find."

She left and returned a few moments later with something black over her arm.

"No wardrobe is complete without a little black dress. Try this."

I slipped out of the red number and held up the black in front of me. Right away I noticed that there was far less fabric than with the first one. That only made me more eager to wear it. The clerk helped me with the dress, pulling the nearly skintight article over my head and zipping it up. Once it was on, I looked into the mirror.

"Wow." The word fell out of my mouth.

The dress was most definitely sexier than the last. It was tight and short, the hem hitting me in the middle of my thigh, the top lowcut enough to show off far more of my cleavage than anything else I'd ever worn—other than a swimsuit, of course.

"Now, *this* is something that you can make a statement with," she said.

I turned, getting a look at my profile. "It sure is. Not sure what that statement might be, though. Hm. How about something a little between the two? As fun as it is to wear something like this, I don't know if I want people looking at my butt instead of the art."

She chuckled. "I've got a few more in mind."

Just then, another tinge of nausea hit me. I placed my

hand against the wall and closed my eyes, letting the sensation move through me.

"You alright?"

"Fine. Just... I think I need to run to the CVS."

"Sure. I'll get a few more pieces for you to try on while you're there."

I quickly changed back into my street clothes and left the changing area. In the other spaces I could hear Marianne giggling with excitement as she tried something on, along with Pearl calling out "there's no *way* I'm wearing this in public!"

I chuckled, making my way onto the main shop floor. Roberto was there, seated in the waiting area and reading the New York Times. I nodded to him as I hurried to the entrance. When he realized what I was doing, he quickly folded the paper and hurried to my side.

"Something I can help you with, Emily?"

Shit. I needed to get to the drug store and take a test. But there was no way I'd be able to do that without having Roberto on my ass.

"CVS," I said. "Need some, um, Tums."

The skeptical expression on his face made it clear he didn't believe me for a second.

"Sure. I'll escort you."

"That's OK," I said with a nervous smile. "I'm fine on my own. But, um, thanks."

His skepticism only increased. "Emily, as much as I want to respect your independence..."

He didn't need to finish the sentence. I knew there was no way I'd be able to buy and take the test without him knowing.

"Can we walk and talk?"

His expression softened. "Of course. Come on."

Together we stepped out onto the city streets, people all around us, the road to our left packed with cars.

"What's wrong, Emily?" he asked.

There was no getting around it, no lying my way out of this one. I needed a pregnancy test; Roberto was going to find out one way or another.

I paused in the middle of the sidewalk, feeling suddenly overwhelmed by the enormity of what was happening.

Roberto placed his big hand on my arm, taking me out of the path of oncoming pedestrians.

"Come with me, Emily. It looks like you need someone to talk to."

He gestured toward a nearby café, keeping his hand on my arm as we made our way over and entered. I was still in something of a daze, and Roberto did all the work of finding someplace quiet to sit and ordering us something to drink. When the barista came over, she placed a latte in front of Roberto, some tea in front of me.

"That's green tea," he said. "Good for the nerves. Take a sip, take a deep breath and tell me what's going on."

I couldn't get over how kind and accommodating Roberto was being. Like Logan, he was a big, tough-looking man who concealed a heart capable of great empathy. I did as he asked, sipping my hot tea, taking a slow breath, and speaking.

I told Roberto everything, told him about how I'd been sleeping with Logan—this wasn't a surprise to him—and that I was nearly certain that I was pregnant, that *was* a surprise. When I was done, I felt drained, like I needed rest.

Roberto smiled warmly. "A child is a wonderful thing. And if you ask me, *jefe* is due for something like this to get his priorities straight. The love of a good woman and a baby can do just that."

"Do you have a family?"

He nodded. "I do. He took out his phone and scrolled a bit, showing me pictures of a stunning woman with fair skin and red hair, a pair of twin toddlers on her lap.

"That's my wife Marie, my twin boys Jacob and Noah."

"They're beautiful, all of them."

"*Gracias.* My line of work doesn't lend itself to a normal family life, but Logan takes good care of me, which means I can take good care of them, visit for a month or so at a time when I can. It works." He tucked his phone back into his pocket. "I like to throw wisecracks at Logan about his bachelor life, but deep down I think he knows that it's time for something real, something that's not seventy-hour weeks at work. And I'm sure you don't need me to tell you that Marianne would love a little niece or nephew to spoil."

The idea of Marianne spoiling my child was enough to warm my heart, to push aside the anxiety running through me, if only for a moment.

"But what will Logan say?" I asked. "How do I know he won't kick me out?"

Roberto laughed. "Well, if he ever tried anything like that, I'd have him laid out on his *culo* before he even finished the sentence. Logan can handle himself in a fight, but I've got a few moves he doesn't know about."

He leaned forward, his smile turning into a more serious expression.

"Logan isn't like that. He's a hard man, but he's that way because he needs to be. He's been looking out for his sister for years, knowing that he'd always be responsible for her. *Nothing* comes between him and those he cares about. He might be surprised, he might be unsure of how to react. I have no doubt, however, that he'll do right by you, Emily."

He placed his hands on the table. "Let's go take this test,

si? You find out the truth, then we go back to the boutique. If it's positive, we can talk about what to do from there. Ok?"

There was something about the easy way he spoke, his calm tone, his reassuring words that made me quickly feel better.

"Yeah. Let's do it."

We took our drinks to go and left the café. Together, we walked to the CVS on the corner and I purchased a few pregnancy tests.

"We can always wait until we're back at the penthouse, Emily," he said as I made my way to the bathroom.

"No. I want to know now."

He nodded, standing guard outside of the bathroom as I went inside. The test didn't take long at all, and within five minutes I knew my fate.

I was pregnant.

CHAPTER 29

EMILY

I t was the night of the gallery show, and I was in front of the full-length mirror in my bedroom. I'd spent the previous night with Logan, the two of us making love late into the night.

I hadn't told him. The secret was between Roberto and me only for the time being. I'd cursed myself for not saying anything, but I had no idea where to even begin. Not to mention that tonight was about Marianne.

After the show, that's when I'd tell him. We had plans for later that evening after the gallery showing—we'd be taking a late dinner up on the rooftop, the food provided by the Michelin-star restaurant in the lobby of the building. Marianne would likely be worn out from the events, wanting to go to bed fairly early.

It'd be the perfect time. Until then, I had to keep it to myself.

I turned my attention to the mirror, shocked at what I saw. The dress was stunning, a long, sleeveless ivory gown with floral embellishments that all appeared handmade. The gown hugged my curves in a manner that was sensual and elegant at the same time, and the top was just low enough to be interesting but still classy. Along with the dress, I wore a pair of color-matching Sergio Rossi heels. My hair was done up in curls, my eyes dark and my lips a popping red. I almost didn't recognize the woman looking back at me.

A knock sounded at my bedroom door as I stood giving myself a once-over.

"It's me," Logan said, his low voice muffled.

I was the perfect blend of excited and nervous at hearing his voice. Pearl and Marianne and I had spent most of the day running errands and getting ready for the show, which meant I'd barely seen hide nor hair of Logan.

"Come in!"

The door opened and he entered. I nearly gasped at the sight of him.

Logan was dressed in an ink black tuxedo, his hair slicked back and his face clean shaven, patent leather Oxfords polished to a mirrored shine. He looked powerful and handsome and gorgeous.

My pussy clenched as he approached, his eyes moving over my body, a sly smile on his face.

"God, you look amazing." He placed his hands on my hips, squeezing my curves gently through the fabric. "It's very hard to resist the urge to take this off right now and show you just how turned on I am."

I placed my hand on his crotch through his slacks, feeling his hardness.

"You don't need to tell me, I already know."

I closed my eyes as I stroked him, feeling myself growing wetter by the moment.

Logan leaned in and kissed the slope of my neck, goosebumps breaking out all over my body.

"You're going to need to stop that right now," he said. "Or you're going to need to get ready a second time."

He placed his hand on mine, gently moving it away.

"There's going to be plenty of time for that later," he said. "But right now, I'm pretty sure that if Mar has to wait any longer, she's going to blow her top. That's why I'm up here, actually—she very strongly hinted that you're taking a bit too long and asked if I could come move you along."

I laughed. "Alright, let's not keep the star of the show waiting."

He leaned in, planting a soft kiss on my cheek.

"Emi-*lyyy*," Marianne called from downstairs. "Are you ready?"

"Coming, coming!" I replied.

We took the stairs down to the first floor, and right as we began our descent, I spotted Marianne looking up.

"There you are!" she said.

Marianne looked pretty damn glamorous. She'd opted for a stylish pantsuit, the color navy blue with a white shirt underneath, along with black pumps and a few pieces of jewelry.

"Wow," she said as I descended. "You look like a princess."

I smiled, opening my arms and giving her a big hug.

"You look amazing too."

Pearl was seated on the couch, wearing a dark gold gown that complemented her figure perfectly.

"And look at you, Pearl!" I said, coming over to her. "You look so freaking hot!"

Pearl let out a boisterous laugh. "Hey, not going to tell you you're wrong. Kinda feel like it's prom night all over again. Maybe I'll meet a special someone so this night can end the same way that one did, if you know what I mean."

She followed up her words with a wink, which got a laugh out of Logan and me.

"And look at these men, sharp as tacks," I said, turning my attention to Roberto, Renaldo, and Edgar. All three of them were in dark suits which, while sharp, did not hide the fact that they were trained guards.

We headed down, taking the elevator to the expansive lobby. The black SUVs that we'd been taking around the city over the last day awaited us, and together Logan and I piled inside ours. Once we were seated and on our way, Logan reached into the side bar and pulled out a bottle of champagne.

"I hope you all are in the mood for something sparkly," he said.

"You kidding me?" Pearl asked with a grin. "I'll take the whole bottle."

That got a laugh out of us. A tinge of tension ran through me, however. Obviously, I wasn't going to be drinking. How would I play it off without attracting attention?

Logan popped open the bottle and poured glasses for all of us. Outside of the car, the sun had begun to set, casting the streets of Manhattan in wild colors. It was the perfect New York night, something I'd always dreamed about since I was a little girl.

"I'm not big on toasts," Logan said as he poured and passed. "But with the special night we have ahead of us, I'd be remiss if I didn't say a few words."

He held his glass in front of him, the look on his face suggesting he wasn't quite sure where to begin.

"Anyone who's met my wonderful sister, Marianne, learns right away what a light she is, what a warm presence she gifts upon anyone lucky enough to know her. What many who've met her *don't* get a chance to learn is how damned talented she is. I know this, and so does everyone in this car. But tonight, the world is going to find out about you, Mar. I couldn't be prouder to be a part of this amazing night."

He started to raise his glass, Marianne leaning over to hug him with such intensity that he nearly spilled it. Logan let out a laugh, wrapping his arm around his sister and giving her an eager hug right back.

Logan raised his glass. "Cheers!"

We all said the same, tapping our glasses together. I waited until everyone was sipping to bring my glass to my lips. Maybe a single sip wouldn't matter, but I wasn't about to take that risk. I formed a hard seal with my lips around the glass, letting the drink flow against my mouth without ingesting any.

"Delicious," I lied.

Ten or so minutes later, we pulled in front of the gallery in Chelsea. The neighborhood was gorgeous, tall condos flanking us on both sides, people packed on the sidewalks, the evening alive with activity.

"There it is!" Marianne slid over to the other side of the car, putting her hands against the glass. "I can see my paintings from here!"

The front of the Fordham Gallery was glass, and inside I could see that the place was crowded with well-dressed men and women, all of them looking like the elite of the city. On the walls were several paintings, many of which I'd recognized from Marianne's room.

We parked in front and stepped out, the staff leading us to the front doors. On the sidewalk was a sign for the showing—"Marianne Stone: Sketches from a Future Master."

"The title was my idea," Pearl said with a wink. "And

it's true, right? Imagine what this girl's going to be putting out in a decade or two."

The staff opened the front doors for us and the moment we stepped inside, Marianne was the center of attention. A crowd formed around her, tears in her eyes.

"Thank you... thank you so much for coming!" the music over the speakers quieted down, the crowd silenced. "I... this means so much to me to see so many people here tonight. I'm so used to working in my room alone that I forget sometimes that there're people out there!"

Light laughs sounded from the crowd.

"I can't wait to get to know you all more and tell you about my art. So many of these pieces mean a lot to me, and sharing with you is like sharing a part of myself. So, enjoy!"

The audience applauded, and Marianne melted into them, answering questions.

Logan moved to my side, smoothly taking a pair of wine glasses from a server's passing tray.

"This is really something, isn't it?" he asked.

"It really is."

We said nothing for several moments, both of us looking over the pictures. My gaze lingered on Marta's drawing, longing tugging at my heart.

"Marianne and I aren't all that different," I said. "Both of us are learning about the wider world in our own ways."

"That's right," Logan agreed. "And you're both thriving. There's two women in my life now with amazing futures in front of them. I can't wait to see what you two can do."

I couldn't resist leaning over and kissing him. As I took my lips away, I spotted the stares of a few young women in the crowd, a naughty bit of satisfaction forming in me as I knew that they were all realizing at the same time that *the* Logan Stone was taken.

Or was he? Everything was so confusing on that front.

"I'm going to make the rounds," he said. "Got a few clients here I'd like to check in with. Come find me later."

He leaned in and placed one more kiss on my lips before departing.

Warmth and happiness in my heart, I began to make my own rounds through the gallery. Marianne was in the middle of explaining one of her paintings, Logan networked with clients, and Pearl was enjoying a drink from the bar while flirting with one of the servers. Roberto and his guards were posted throughout, trying their best to remain inconspicuous.

I stopped in front of one painting, a drawing of the beach. It was in the corner of the gallery, giving me a peaceful quiet to admire it. I found myself thinking of that first day at Logan's, how overwhelmed I'd felt. If only I could've guessed what the next few weeks would hold.

I prepared to step away when I felt something hard press into the small of my back. Confused, I began to turn.

"Stay perfectly still," a voice spoke. "Make a single sound and I'll kill you and your baby."

CHAPTER 30

LOGAN

"Something wrong, Mr. Stone?"

Where the hell was she?

John Lyman, the billionaire real estate mogul whose account my company managed, stood before me with a curious expression on his face. No doubt he'd noticed that my attention was elsewhere. I'd been trying to spot Emily in the crowd during my conversation but couldn't find her.

"Sorry, John," I said. "Just looking for my date, worried she's getting bored."

The smile returned to his face. "I saw her, such a gorgeous young woman. I don't want to pry, Logan, but I couldn't help but notice the way you two looked at one another when you arrived. Is she more than just one of the many models I've seen hanging on your arm over the years?"

I chuckled at how obvious I was being. "You know, she just might be."

"In that case, go find her. I won't keep you any longer."

"Let's set something up for this Monday at nine-thirty," I said. "On Zoom. I want to make sure we're on the same page for the next quarter."

"Perfect. Have fun, Logan."

John reached over and patted the side of my arm, offering one last warm smile before rejoining the crowd. Marianne was easy enough to spot, her tall, slender figure zipping from here to there as she eagerly explained her work to the many guests.

But Emily was another story. I scanned the place top to bottom, not finding her anywhere. Minutes passed, too many of them. Roberto was posted near the entrance, and I sidled through the crowd to him.

"Have you seen Emily?" I asked.

He shook his head. "Was just looking for her. Haven't spotted her for ten minutes. I asked Marianne to run into the ladies' room to see if she was in there."

Tension gripped my gut. "What about outside? Any chance she stepped out?"

"Got my boys out there, they would've seen her."

"Something's wrong."

He pursed his lips, nodding slowly. "Yeah."

"Call the guys in. We'll take a pass through the gallery, see if we can spot her."

"Got it. We'll meet here in five minutes."

Without another word, we broke and moved through the gallery, Roberto taking the right and me taking the left. I hurried as quickly as I could without attracting attention, not wanting anyone to get the sense that something was wrong.

Halfway through my scan, I spotted something on the ground in front of Marianne's beachfront picture—Emily's white clutch. I picked it up and looked around.

She was gone. There was no doubt in my mind.

I made my way back to the entrance, Roberto waiting for me. He shook his head as I approached.

"Something happened," I said. "We need to move —*now*."

"Fucking hell," he growled under his breath. "What about Marianne and Pearl?"

"Bring the guys in here, tell them to guard them with their lives. You and I are going to find Emily."

"Got it."

Roberto made a call, Renaldo and Edgar joining us inside in less than a minute. After explaining the situation to the pair, we were out and in one of the SUVs.

"What the fuck, Roberto!" I shouted. "How did this happen?"

"My fault. Should've been keeping a closer eye on her. But... *goddamn*, how did they get in? We were checking everyone."

I sighed, knowing that getting pissed at Roberto wouldn't solve anything.

"I'm sure you were on top of it. Just... *fuck!*"

"Could be someone on the inside," he said. "Someone working in the gallery."

"Doesn't matter," I replied. "What does is figuring out where the hell she is. No doubt at all that Charles had something to do with this."

"My thoughts exactly. And I know just where to go."

"You do? Where?"

"The boys and I did some research on that prick. Found out that he owns a townhouse in Williamsburg."

"Then drive."

Roberto put the townhome's address into the GPS, the readout letting us know it was only twenty minutes away. Rage built in me more with each minute we drove. My mind raced with horrific images of what he might do with her. Would he beat her? Kill her? Finally sell her off to the highest bidder, as she'd been intended?

Either way, there was no doubt in my mind that if we didn't get her back quickly, I'd never see her again.

We crossed over the Brooklyn Bridge and into Williamsburg, making our way into the neighborhood. A few minutes later, we pulled to a stop.

"That one right there," Roberto said, pointing ahead. "See that run-down townhome?"

Two cars were parked in front of the building—one a black van, the other a gaudy, white sports car.

"Bet you anything those are his," I said, nodding toward the vehicles.

"I'd take that bet." Roberto reached over and opened the glove compartment. Inside were two pistols, both Glock 17s.

I took one out, checking the clip and getting a feel for it.

I passed the other to Roberto.

"Let's move."

CHAPTER 31

I was scared as hell.

But more than that, I was angry.

I wasn't sure what had come over me—maybe it was the fact that there was a child growing inside me, a little baby for whom I was responsible. I knew in an instant that I would protect my child above all.

I was ready to face down my dad. There was no question that he was the one responsible for kidnapping me. I'd spent the last thirty minutes or so blindfolded in the back of a van. I'd been worried that Dad was planning on taking me deeper into Long Island, all the way to the estate where I'd never be seen again.

When we stopped somewhere not too far from the gallery, however, I realized he had something else in store for me. What it was, I could only guess.

The car stopped, the driver-side door opening, followed by the back of the van. A hand took hold of my arm, followed by a press of the gun into my belly.

"You scream, and that's the end of it," he said. "Be smart, and you and your baby will live."

The voice was unfamiliar. Whoever it was, I wanted to claw his goddamn eyes out for threatening my baby. I went with him out into the cool evening, the blindfold coming off just enough for me to see that we were approaching some shitty, run-down townhome. The guard quickly fixed the blindfold before I could spot an address, and we travelled up a flight of stairs and inside. As we walked, the echo of our footfalls let me know the room was open and spacious.

With a shove, the guard pushed me into a seat.

Then there was silence. I sat, wondering in fear what was going to happen to my baby and me. I did my best to push the fear away, to stay strong, to hope that Logan would somehow find me.

Footsteps soon sounded, the click of expensive dress shoes on a wooden floor.

"Take off that blindfold."

Someone grabbed the blindfold from behind me and yanked it from my face. The room revealed was big and ornate, looking like something out of the nineteenth century.

And there was my father. He stood with a shit-eating grin on his face, dressed in a dark suit. He shook his head as he approached, looking me up and down.

"Emily, Emily, Emily," he said, shaking his head. "What am I going to do with you?"

"You're going to let me go if you know what's good for you," I snarled.

Anger flashed on his face and he pounced on me like a wild animal, pulling back his hand and drawing it against my cheek. A *crack* sounded out, pain exploding on my face, tears forming in my eyes. He stepped back, his chest rising and falling.

"Let's get one thing straight, you ungrateful little bitch," he said. "You're *mine*. And unless you want your teeth scattered across the floor, you'd be wise to keep your mouth shut. In fact, why don't we take care of that right now?"

He nodded over his shoulder. The guard behind me put a gag over my mouth.

"There we are," he said. "Much better. Better seen and not heard." I squirmed as the guard tied my hands and feet to the chair.

Dad swept his hand toward the room. "Nice place, huh? This was my getaway when your mother was still around. Your mother, she was a nosy one, always poking around in my personal business, always jumping down my throat when I came home too late. This is where I'd go to escape her endless nagging."

He sighed, shaking his head.

"You and this Logan prick. The plan was supposed to be simple, you know? I'd give you to him to square our debt, you'd get 'kidnapped' by some cartel, and I would hold him to blame. Little would he know, however, that you'd be back home and I'd have Stone on the hook for allowing you to be taken. But man, did you both complicate things."

Another sigh.

"But that doesn't matter now. You're here and you're still in one piece. That means you're fit to be sold. Bring 'em in!"

The guard left, returning moments later with a pair of hard-faced men in expensive suits, their look striking me as Slavic and wealthy. One seemed to be in his thirties, the other older.

"Here she is, Yuri," my father said. "The perfect bride for your son."

My gut tightened. I didn't need any more than that to

understand what my dad had in mind for me. He was going to sell me to these men, to be rid of me forever.

The older man came over, looking me up and down like I was a farm animal on auction. The younger man did the same, nodding approvingly. They spoke to one another in Russian. Lucky for me, that was one of the languages I spoke.

"What do you think?" the older man said. "Suitable?"

"Nice body, good face. Her father says no health issues, and that her virginity is intact. She'll do."

My virginity. They were buying me because they thought I was a virgin. There was no way they'd want me if they knew I was pregnant. I had to tell them, if only I could get the gag off my face.

The older man nodded at Dad, who grinned in response.

"Perfect, perfect," my father said. "Then we're still on for ten million?"

"Ten million works," the older man said in heavily accented English.

"Wait," said the younger. "I want to check her mouth, make sure she has no issues with her teeth."

He stepped over, reaching for the gag.

"No!" Dad shouted. "Don't!"

The younger man pulled the gag down, freeing my mouth.

I grinned.

"You want a virgin, huh?" I asked. "Then find another girl!" I switched over to Russian. "I'm the farthest thing from a virgin. And what's more, I'm pregnant."

The men regarded each other with wide eyes.

"Is this true, Charles?" the older man asked.

"This changes everything, if so," said the younger.

Dad shot daggers at me. For a moment, I worried he might kill me on the spot.

"You little bitch!" Dad lunged toward me, grabbing me by the throat and shoving my chair over. I fell to the ground just as the *boom* of a door being kicked in sounded out. My head slammed hard into the ground, and everything went black.

CHAPTER 32

LOGAN

"Get your fucking hands up!"

I pointed my gun at Charles, then the armed guard. Emily was on the ground, a dazed expression on her face. I'd watched her fall when I'd burst into the place, hitting her head on the ground. Fury exploded through me.

I put the thought aside as I turned my attention to the scene. Roberto was at my side, his gun drawn. Charles stood over Emily, the guard behind her, a pair of rich-looking men standing off to the side.

"What the hell is going on here?" I asked.

The younger of the two men narrowed his eyes at me.

"We were supposed to be conducting a business deal," he said, his voice heavily accented.

"What is this, Charles?" the older man asked. "Why is Logan Stone here, pointing a gun at me and my son?"

"He's not going to be around for much longer," Charles said, a tinge of worry in his voice. "Now, let's talk about this deal. I know she's not what you expected, but maybe we can work with that. How about five million? Five million and you take her right now?"

It didn't take a genius to realize what I'd walked in on. Charles was trying to sell his daughter as quickly as possible, to put this whole situation behind him. We'd made it just in time.

The older man and his son shared a look, speaking a few quick words to one another in Russian.

"The deal is off, Marone," the older man said. "Keep your damaged goods."

He nodded to his son, and without another word, the pair began to leave.

"Let them go," Roberto said in a quiet voice, as if understanding my dilemma. "We have who we came for."

Charles's guard stood with his gun pointed at us, Charles himself reaching quickly into his suit jacket and withdrawing a gun of his own. He clicked off the safety, then pointed the gun down at Emily.

"Here's what's going to happen," Charles said. "Take her, I don't give a shit. Those two will spread the word that she's damaged goods and no one's going to want her. As far as I'm concerned, she's a burden. But we're out of here. Understand? And if you take so much as a single step toward me, she's dead."

I glanced over at Roberto, his gun still aiming at the two men.

"Now, lower those pistols."

I saw movement at Charles's feet. Emily was coming back to the moment, her hand wriggling free.

Everything that happened next, happened in a blur. Emily yanked her hand out, grabbing onto Charles's ankle and pulling hard. He pointed his gun at me in a panic, the bullet going wide. I fired twice, both rounds hitting him in the chest. Roberto opened fire, dropping the guard with a triplet of rounds.

When the dust settled, Charles and his guard were down. I moved over to Emily's father, kicking the gun away from his hand and bending down to free Emily.

She was unconscious again. I turned toward Roberto, worry in my heart.

"Call an ambulance. Now."

CHAPTER 33

LOGAN

I paced back and forth in the hospital waiting room like a caged animal. Emily had been brought to the nearest hospital as quickly as possible, but the doctors hadn't told us anything.

"You get in touch with them?" I asked.

Roberto approached, slipping his phone back into his pocket. "Yeah. Pearl and Marianne are on their way, Renaldo and Edgar with them. Doesn't sound like there was any other funny business at the gallery."

"How the hell did it happen?"

"The guard I dropped snuck his way into the gallery through the back entrance, took her out the same way. You ask me, sounds like they'd been watching us for a while."

"Pieces of shit." The words came out dripping with venom.

"The good news, if we can call it that, is I managed to speak to the guard I took down."

"He's alive?"

Roberto smiled slightly. "Aimed for the knees, figured we'd want to get some info out of him. He said that this was the operation—a desperate, last-ditch effort to kidnap Emily and sell her off before she went with you forever. We acted just in time. And don't worry, cops have the guard in custody."

"Charles is dead," I said. "Checked that myself."

"Good goddamn riddance. World's a better place without him in it."

I sighed, shaking my head and running my hand through my hair.

"You're right. And after everything he's done to Emily, a quick death was a gift. All the same..."

Roberto nodded. "Yeah. All the same, you killed her dad. That's going to take time to process."

Commotion sounded out behind me, and I turned to see the guards enter with Pearl and Marianne. The four of them rushed over to me, Marianne opening her arms and pulling me into a tight hug that I eagerly returned.

"Is she OK?" Marianne asked. "Please say that she's OK."

"Don't know yet," I replied. "We're still waiting on—"

"Mr. Stone?"

I turned and was greeted with the sight of a trim, middle-aged woman in scrubs and a white lab coat.

"How is she?" I asked. The rest of the group formed up around me, all of them waiting for an answer.

The doctor smiled. "She's going to be fine, just a mild concussion from the fall. She wrenched her shoulder too, not to mention the burns to her wrist from the rope. But nothing to worry about."

The relief was intense and immediate.

"Thank God," I said.

"And don't worry," the doctor added. "The baby's fine, too. We ran some tests and didn't detect anything to be worried about. Anyway, we'll have you with her as quickly as possible."

With that, the doctor left. I stood there confused, not sure what to make of the words that she'd just spoken.

"Baby?" I asked. "What baby?"

"There's a baby?" Marianne asked.

"A *baby*?" Pearl shouted.

I was in a daze. I turned to Marianne, who stood with a big grin on her face.

"Mar," I said. "Sorry about your evening getting ruined." The words sounded like they were coming out a hundred feet away. I wasn't sure why I picked that moment to check in on her but hearing the word *baby* had done something to me, put me in a strange state of mind.

"My evening getting ruined? What're you talking about? I sold *seven* paintings! And for a lot! I told the gallery that I had a family emergency and they said that it was fine and they wanted to have another showing as soon as possible!" Her grin became even wider. "And I just found out that I'm going to be an aunt!"

Roberto put his big hand on my shoulder.

"Congrats, *papa*."

Still dazed, I turned back in the direction the doctor had come. It wasn't much longer until she returned, letting me know that I could see Emily.

"I'd recommend just one at a time for now," she said. "Her head was a little dinged up, so a whole group in there might be a bit disorienting."

I turned to Pearl and Marianne.

"Don't worry," Pearl said. "We'll head back to the penthouse and stay put." She leaned in. "And congrats, you dog." Pearl flashed me a smile before leading Marianne off.

"I'm staying here with you, *jefe*," Roberto said. "The boys will take the ladies back."

"Thanks."

With that, I broke off and went with the doctor. I felt strange as I walked, the word *baby* repeating in my head over and over again. It felt unreal, like someone was playing a trick on me.

The doctor guided me to a door and opened it.

"She just woke up not too long ago so she might still be in a little bit of a daze."

I nodded, entering the room.

Emily was laying there and it didn't matter that she was bruised and bandaged, didn't matter that she was in a hospital gown, didn't matter that her lip was swollen. She was still the most beautiful thing I'd ever seen in my life. Knowing that she was carrying my child only brought her beauty to another level.

She turned sleepily over to me, a weak, but warm smile spreading across her face.

"Wow," she said. "My head hurts."

I came over, taking her hand into mine and kissing it.

"You're safe," I said. "And you're going to be OK."

She nodded. "What about my dad?"

There was no sense in dancing around the matter. I shook my head. She turned away from me, staring off into the distance for a long moment.

Finally, she said one word.

"OK."

I knew that wasn't the end of it. Her father was a total piece of shit, a real bastard, but he was her father all the same. She'd need time to work through that.

Her eyes flashed and she turned to me with worry.

I placed my hand on her belly.

"He's fine," I said. "Or she."

Emily closed her eyes, a tear trickling down in relief.

"I'm sorry," she said.

"Sorry? For what?"

"For not telling you. But I only found out yesterday. Roberto knew too, but I swore him to secrecy. I swear I was going to tell you tonight, but—"

I didn't give her a chance to finish, leaning in and sealing her mouth with a kiss.

"It's OK," I said. "It's better than OK. I love you Emily."

It was strange. I'd been debating back and forth how I felt, whether I ought to say the words, if I truly meant them. Now that they were out in the open like that, it seemed like the easiest thing in the world.

She smiled. "I love you, too."

EPILOGUE I

EMILY

Almost six months later...

Y ou'd never know it was Logan's birthday by the way he acted. That is to say, he hadn't acknowledged it at all. Pearl and Marianne and I weren't about to let the day slip by unnoticed, of course.

"Surprise!" The three of us shouted as Logan stepped out onto the back patio of the island mansion.

Logan, looking sexy as ever in a white linen shirt and matching pants, tilted his sunglasses down a bit to get a better look at us. My eyes were on his chest, a few of the buttons of his shirt undone, enough to give me a scrumptious view of his chiseled upper body. Didn't matter that I'd seen him naked a million times—the mere sight of him was enough to turn me on.

"What the hell is going on here?"

Marianne sprang out of her seat and rushed over to Logan, throwing her willowy arms around him.

"It's your *birthday*, silly! What do you think is going on?"

Logan let out a sigh, shaking his head as he looked over the setup.

"You guys didn't have to do any of this."

"You're right, big guy," Pearl said. "We didn't. And that's what makes it special."

I stood up, waddling over to Logan and giving him a hug and a kiss.

"Happy birthday, handsome."

He allowed himself a small smile. "Thanks, gorgeous."

After one more kiss, he stepped back and looked at the display. The patio table was set up with streamers and confetti and snacks, along with a few presents, Marianne's covered in a big sheet.

"I hope this means all of you are packed and ready for the trip to New York tomorrow," he said. "We're staying there until after the baby's born."

That had been the plan we'd discussed. As fun as a natural birth on the island sounded—Logan had offered to fly in the best medical care available—I'd wanted to have the baby in a nice, safe hospital just in the event anything out of the ordinary happened. Tomorrow morning we'd all fly into New York, where we'd stay at the penthouse until it was time for our little boy or girl to come into the world.

"OK!" Marianne shouted. "Come over here and open these! But... can you open mine first? I'm really happy about it."

Logan chuckled. "As long as that's OK with everyone else."

Pearl and I gave our approval. Truth be told, I was more eager for Marianne's present than mine.

Logan stepped over and pulled off the sheet, revealing the finished painting of him that Marianne had started almost a year ago.

"It's wonderful," Logan said, stepping back to get a better look at it. He cocked his head to the side, taking off his sunglasses. "But... it's different." He moved closer. "The face is changed."

Sure enough, it was. The serious-faced glower that Marianne had painted before was gone, replaced with a sly, almost Mona Lisa smile. The mood of the painting was brighter, more inviting, not to mention truer to the man I knew and loved.

"That's right!" Marianne said. "You've been different since Emily came to live with us on the island, happier. It didn't make sense to have the painting the way it was before. I sent a picture of it to the gallery and they said they *had* to have it for my next showing. But I told them it was just for you."

"I love it, sis." Logan gave his sister a hug and kiss before the rest of the exchange began. It was right in the middle of this that Roberto came out with a cake lit with thirty-nine candles, singing, "happy birthday to *jefe*..."

We ate and drank and laughed and watched the sunset together, the five of us going over the insanity of the last year, how much our lives had changed for the better, and how much promise and potential the next year had for us.

In time, the group peeled off, leaving Logan and me alone.

"This was wonderful," he said. "I'm not much of a birthday guy, but damned if you didn't make this day special for me."

I smiled. "Get used to it, because I'm not going to let a single birthday of yours go uncelebrated. And when she's here, I'm going to enlist her in the party planning."

He raised an eyebrow. "She?"

"Just have a feeling."

He leaned over and kissed me slowly and deeply.

"I love this little life of ours," he said. "Don't know how I got so lucky."

"Whatever you did, it worked," I responded with a wink. "Now, let's go upstairs so I can give you your *real* present."

He laughed, wasting no time standing and scooping me out of the chair. Didn't matter that I was big with baby, Logan carried me upstairs like I weighed nothing at all.

We were soon in bed together, kissing slowly as we stripped one another out of our clothes. I'd been a bit self-conscious about the changes my body had gone through—the big belly and boobs, the extra weight I was carrying around. The way Logan looked at me, however, the way he touched me, you'd think he'd found me more beautiful than ever.

We made love in the slow, passionate way we so often did those days, the amber light of the sunset streaming in through the curtains as they flitted in the gentle breeze. He made me come three times, the third time absolutely exhilarating as we came together. When we were done, I lay curled up in his arms.

Logan wore a serious expression on his face as we relaxed.

"Something's on your mind," I said. "Don't try to tell me there isn't, I know that look."

He allowed himself a wry smile, shaking his head.

"Yeah, there is. Not sure if right now is the time to talk about it, though."

I sat up. "What's wrong?"

"Nothing's wrong. Just that I spoke to one of my lawyers yesterday, the one dealing with the attorney in charge of your father's estate."

I said nothing, letting him go on.

"There's a pretty good amount of money there, more than enough to work with if you want to invest it. Not to mention the house and the staff. I didn't want to bring this up now for obvious reasons. But the meeting is tomorrow, so I thought you ought to know so you can be a part of it if you want."

"I do. But I can tell you right now that I never want to see that goddamn house again."

"I figured as much. It'd be no issue to put it on the market. Long Island is hot right now; I'm sure we could have it sold within the month."

I considered the matter as we spoke, an idea taking shape in my mind.

"Let me think about it," I said.

"Of course." He wrapped his arm around me, pulling me close. "I love you, Em."

"I love you."

We kissed, and I curled up tightly next to him. Tomorrow was going to be the start of yet another adventure, and I couldn't be more grateful if I tried.

EPILOGUE II

LOGAN

Three years later...

I couldn't help but laugh softly to myself as I stepped into Emily's office.

She was the picture of beauty, seated in her rocking chair, our three-month old baby girl Anabelle cradled in her arms. The sight of her with our second child wasn't at all what I was laughing at—*that* was an image of total perfection.

Emily glanced over her shoulder, taking a break from her singing.

"Now, what's so funny?"

"That." I nodded to the painting of me that Marianne had done all those years ago. It was "on loan" to Emily, and she'd chosen to hang it in her office. It was surrounded by framed pictures of us and George, our son.

"What's so funny about that?" she asked, her voice soft as not to wake Anabelle.

"It's well done, sure, but I can't get over having a

painting of myself. Feels like I'm staring at you while you're working."

She chuckled. "Maybe that's why I put it there. If I ever find myself clicking over to Twitter or whatever, I just look up and see you there, scolding me for not being on task."

I sat down on the end of the desk. The surface was covered in papers and baby toys, and I had to move some of them over to make room.

"I mean that with love, of course," she said with a smile.

"Naturally. But you say that like you need someone to tell you to work hard. The way you've been balancing the house with taking care of the kids has been beyond impressive."

"Doesn't hurt that I have a handsome man who does his share."

"It's my pleasure." I craned my neck to take in the sight of Anabelle. She was like something out of a dream, her eyes closed, and her little mouth opened slightly as she slept. "How's the little lady, by the way?"

"Same story, this one's a night owl. Sleeps like a rock during the day, but as soon as the sun's down, she's ready to party."

"Well, last night you were on duty, so I'll take tonight. Get some rest."

She smiled. "Thanks. Got a meeting tomorrow with some investors, so I'll need to be all bright-eyed and bushy-tailed for that one."

My eyes drifted down to the papers on the desk. Years back, Emily decided to do some good with the small fortune her father had left her. After paying off the debts he'd owed to his criminal associates, and thus severing her ties with them for good, she'd taken the remaining money and invested it into turning his house into a shelter for women escaping domestic abuse—the kind of charity she'd needed when she was living with her father, she'd told me.

She'd named the shelter Marta's House, and it was a total success. The place was big enough to shelter over a dozen women and their children at a time, and Emily had managed to keep nearly all of the staff on the payroll to help take care of the place. I'd helped her a bit at first with investments to keep the place running, but Emily had shown a knack for money matters. I barely helped at all anymore.

"Want to check on the little man?" I asked.

"Let's do it."

I scooped Anabelle from her arms, the precious little girl so small against my chest. I kissed her on the forehead as we left the office, making our way to the nursery. As we walked, I found myself glancing down at Ana over and over, noting the kiss of olive to her skin, along with her chocolate-colored hair. George, with his light hair and striking blue eyes, was taking after me. Ana, on the other hand, was all Emily.

After placing Ana in her nursery, we made our way over to George's room across the way. Pearl was there, standing over George and brushing his blonde hair from his eyes.

"Sleeping well?" I asked.

Pearl turned her attention from George. "Just got him down for his nap. I swear, this kid would run around and play all day if he could."

"That kind of energy's going to serve him well."

Emily and I stepped over to George. Even at a little over three, I could tell he was going to be a handsome young man. He opened his eyes sleepily, his blues radiant.

"Daddy?" he asked. "Can we go to the beach?"

I smiled. "Go to sleep, bud. We'll talk about it when you get up. Love you, OK?"

"Love you too."

Emily leaned down and kissed him on the forehead. By the time she stood back up, George was already out.

"I'll finish up," Pearl said.

"Thanks," I whispered before the two of us took our leave.

Once we were out of the room, the task at hand, the issue that had been at the back of my mind for weeks, once again came to the forefront.

"Mind coming with me?" I asked Emily.

"Uh oh," she said. "Am I in trouble?"

"Not at all. Come on."

I took her hand, leading her into the master bedroom, and then out onto the balcony. The view was as striking as ever, the garden below us, the beach in the distance, the sun setting to the west. It was the perfect moment for what I had in mind.

Down below in the garden, Marianne was in the middle of painting a portrait of Roberto. We waved to them both, and they waved back. The two had been attached at the hip over the last week, with Marianne— the talk of the New York art world—wanting to finish her portrait of him for her next show before Roberto left in a couple of days to spend a month with his family.

"What's up, babe?" Emily asked.

I took a deep breath, ready to begin.

"I'm not one for speeches," I said. "Never have been. And more than that, I believe that the life we've shared together over the last few years has stood as more of a monument of our love than anything I could say. But there's something missing. I think you know what it is."

I reached into my back pocket, taking out the small, velvet box that I'd had in there. I popped it open, revealing the ring inside. She gasped at the sight of it, putting her hands over her mouth.

"I love you, Emily. I love you and I want you to be my wife."

Tears formed in her eyes.

"I love you, too. And you're damn right I'm going to be your wife."

She threw her arms around me, kissing me hard as I slipped the ring on her finger. Once it was on, she yelled down for Marianne and Roberto's attention, pointing to the ring on her finger.

"You better believe I'm telling Pearl!" Marianne shouted, her and Roberto rushing inside to come congratulate us.

"Looks like we're going to have some company," I said.

"Good." Emily smiled. "We've got a lot to celebrate."

"And even more to look forward to."

The End

Made in the USA
Columbia, SC
06 November 2024

45747342R00157